Angel of Solitude

Echoes

This book is for anyone who's ever been dealt a tough hand in life. I want you to know that your past doesn't define you. Once you realize that, you'll see that you have the power to shape your own future.

United States
Suicide and Crisis Lifeline

Dial 988

Contents

Angel of Solitude: Echoes
Spotify Playlist

Chapter 1

Death… It's such an uncomfortable word to hear when you're alive. I get it. But now that I'm dead, I find it amusing to talk about. Death, in and of itself, isn't that scary. It's the whole uncertainty of what happens next that messes with everyone. But honestly, after you die, it becomes much easier to accept that death is just another part of life.

I bet you're wondering… Is there a God? What's the afterlife like? Do I become one with the ancestors and continue to watch over my loved ones from the skies above?

My story will answer most of these questions. And it begins with what I thought was the end of my life.

When your body shuts down, hearing is the last sense to fade.

I remember lying on a cold hospital bed. Machines were beeping nonstop, and I could hear the muffled but urgent shouts from the medical staff and the frantic shuffling of their feet. I tried to open my eyes, but it felt like I was buried under layers of darkness, each one heavier than the last.

My mind was in a haze, but the voices of the medical staff managed to cut through the fog. "Patient's vitals are dropping! We're losing him!" Their cries echoed around the room, matching the urgency of each beat of my failing heart.

I wanted to reach out to let them know I hadn't given up and that I was still fighting to hold on. But my body wouldn't cooperate. Unresponsive and trapped in this prison of a body, all I could do was listen helplessly as the chaos continued to play out around me.

In the midst of it all, I realized something oddly comforting – CPR doesn't hurt when you're unconscious. You feel pressure, sure, but no pain.

Then, out of nowhere, there was this eerie silence. The beeping just stopped, replaced by that unsettling flatline sound. Panic started to spread through the room as the medical staff worked even harder to bring me back. I could feel their desperation as their movements got more frantic. But sadly, hope was slipping away.

In a moment of sheer frustration, the doctor's anger boiled over. I'm sure she flung a nearby bedside table to the ground with a crash that echoed through the room. I could feel her disappointment as she realized her efforts to bring me back had failed.

And then, there was this moment of stillness. I could feel the doctor's gaze, her regret hanging heavy in the air. Her hand shook as she reached for mine, whispering an apology, acknowledging the futility of her efforts.

"No... no..." The doctor's voice came through her tears. "We did everything we could. I'm sorry. I'm so, so sorry."

At that moment, a part of me wanted to reassure her that it was okay and that I understood. But the darkness was closing in on me, and I could only surrender to its embrace.

A gentle warmth washed over me just when I thought it was all over. It wasn't something I could touch, but if I had to describe it... It felt like a soothing hand cradling my soul.

I struggled to wrap my head around the sensation, as I've never felt anything like this before. It was hard to describe, but I want you to imagine stepping out of a hot shower into the chill of a winter night. Even though you're vulnerable and exposed, you still feel the residuals of that cozy warmth clinging to you, which makes you appreciate the imbalance even more. Any fear or anxiety from the chaos before this moment just melted away, and all that was left was me in a bubble of bliss and serenity.

But then, something happened. I felt this presence. It was as if someone was there with me, but not physically. Its voice wasn't something I could hear with my ears; more like it came from deep inside me. It was as if it was talking without saying a word. I know what I said doesn't make sense, but trust me. At that moment, I knew I wasn't by myself anymore.

A sensation rippled through me as a voice pierced the shroud of the void I was in. The intensity of the voice was, well, intense. "Are you serious right now!?" The words seemed to echo, each syllable heavier with disbelief than the last, making the air around me tremble.

I didn't know what was going on. The words felt like they were bouncing around every corner of my being. I don't know how, but I knew not to be afraid.

The voice grew even louder, filled with frustration. "Yes, you! I witnessed the entirety of your actions! What prompted you to do this?!" The words ricocheted around me like a pinball player going for the high score.

"Excuse me?" I responded, unsure of who or what I was talking to.

"I am fully aware that you can perceive my words!" The voice sighed heavily, making my heart sink. "I am risking my powers to save you right now."

"I'm sorry," I said, still unsure of what was happening. "I don't understand."

"Do not make me regret this..." The voice sighed again, its tone softening. "Just... hang on."

Suddenly, a sharp snap split the air, its intensity reverberating like a thunderous clap. As the echoes faded, my eyes slowly opened, and the sight of a familiar ceiling greeted me. Beige tiles that were worn down by time and neglect.

I tried to turn my attention to the voice that had accompanied the noise, but I couldn't see or sense anything. "What just happened?" I asked, curiosity bubbling up.

4

"I'll clarify momentarily," the voice replied. "For now, stand up."

Before getting up, I instinctively brought my hands into view. Relief washed over me – no cuts, no bruises, no pain. It was as if I had been given a fresh start, free from the wear and tear of aging.

As I stood up and looked around the room, I felt comfort and unease. I was in a dusty basement, its familiarity both reassuring and unsettling. Two twin beds stood against opposite walls, separated by a cheap computer desk. A half-broken television stand held a PlayStation 2 among a collection of games. The black and beige tile floor was littered with stray papers and unwashed clothes. This was undoubtedly the room I shared with my older brother during childhood.

"Why am I here?" I voiced my confusion. "And where are you?" I added, scanning the empty room for any sign of another presence.

"I reside within your mind," the voice replied, its words seeming to materialize like a second voice within my inner monologue. "And we are here because we have duties to fulfill."

Both of my eyes widened in disbelief. "Wait... You're inside my head?" I yelled while tilting my head to the side and trying to dislodge the voice with a few frantic slaps against my ear. "Nope! This isn't happening! Get out of there!"

"Why are you... Cease this immediately! I am not physically in your head," the voice interjected, confusion evident in its tone.

"No way! This is too much! Get out of my head now!" I shouted, panic rising as I continued my self-inflicted assault on my ear.

"Enough!" the voice boomed, causing me to stop my frantic slaps. "Please... calm yourself. I need you to be quiet long enough to convey the situation."

Startled by the intensity of the voice, I jumped back. "Okay, okay," I conceded, feeling the tension in my muscles ease.

"Good." The voice softened. "At this moment, we are within the spirit realm. I was able to move—"

"I'm dead, aren't I?" I blurted out, the words tumbling from my lips in a rush of panic. "Dammit... of course I am. Why did I—"

"What did I just say?!" the voice interrupted sharply, stopping my self-blame.

"Sorry!" I exclaimed. "But what's the normal response to finding out you just died? Ugh... Let me guess. You're here to judge me, right? To tell me whether or not I was a good person..."

"No one said you were dead," the voice countered.

"But you said, 'spirit realm.' What else could that mean?" I retorted, anxiety beginning to churn in my stomach.

The voice, clearly annoyed by my persistent misconceptions, let out an exaggerated sigh. "Let us try this once more. I am your guardian angel.

I wish to help you, but you must listen to me. Can you please remain silent for a moment?"

"Guardian angel?" My heart pounded in my chest as I struggled to process the information. I'd heard of them in stories but never believed they existed. "You're telling me that guardian angels are real?" I asked, my voice trembling.

"Yes," the angel responded. "I know it's a lot to take in, but we don't have much time. Please, listen to me."

"I'll try," I said, nodding and focusing on the unseen presence in my head.

"First off," the angel began. "You're not dead. You are in a link between the human realm and the spirit realm, so—"

"Limbo," I interrupted, trying to understand everything. "Why am I in limbo?"

"Oh, my Lord! You are not listening," the angel exclaimed, anger dripping from its words.

"I am listening," I said, my voice tinged with sarcasm. "I'm listening enough to know you're a guardian angel who just took the Lord's name in vain."

The angel paused, clearly taken aback. "Did you just... That's what you took from this?" it asked, its astonishment evident.

7

And it was at this point that I knew I had messed up. My weak attempt at humor had backfired.

"You know what? Fine… fine, forget this – I'm taking away your talking privileges!" The angel declared, its anger evident.

The same clap from earlier thundered through the room, but it felt closer and more forceful this time. The loud sound left a high-pitched ringing in my ears, drowning out any further protests I might have had.

The angel's patience had worn thin, irritation clear in its stern tone. "I will say this slowly. You. Are. NOT. Dead. 'Limbo,' as you call it, is a waiting room that the Lord sends souls to when their afterlife destination has not yet been decided. You can only enter Limbo upon death. And once more… You. Are. NOT. Dead. Instead, you are in something we call 'Solitude.'"

A million questions raced through my mind, but I couldn't get any words out. It felt like someone had pointed a TV remote at me and hit the mute button. Panic began to set in as I tried to cough, but again, no sound came out.

"Relax," the angel said calmly. "You can speak again once I am finished, okay?"

Unable to utter a single word, I nodded.

"Solitude. That's where we are right now," the angel said. "The concept is hard to explain to mortals, but think of it as a small tear within your soul. Now, tell me. Do you have any regrets?"

Once more, I could only offer a nod.

"Of course you do. Everyone does," the angel continued. "When you hold on to regret – whether from things you've done, things that happened to you, or opportunities you've missed – it creates a fracture in your soul. This fracture usually manifests as anger or depression and remains as long as the regret lingers."

There was a pause as if the angel was carefully considering its next words.

"I may not fully understand the intricacies of mortals," the angel continued, "but please believe me when I say that I have your best interests in mind."

I focused intently on the angel's words, my entire being hanging on every syllable. The usual distractions and wandering thoughts were nowhere to be found. It was as if the angel's voice had a magnetic pull, and it drew all my attention, leaving no room for anything else. At that moment, nothing mattered more than understanding the message being conveyed.

"When you encounter someone who seems bitter and angry towards the world, it often reflects the multiple fractures in their soul," the angel explained, its voice filled with empathy. "A life burdened with too many regrets will eventually break a mortal's spirit."

Still muted, I nodded slowly, trying to process the complexity of the information given to me.

"But there is something you can do as a mortal," the angel continued, its tone carrying a hint of hope. "See, the Lord often gives mortals opportunities to heal these fractures. Sadly, many fail to recognize these chances. They can appear in dreams, through interactions with others, or even in fleeting thoughts that, if nurtured, could lead to profound breakthroughs."

The angel's words sank in slowly as I struggled to fully grasp its words.

"As I mentioned, it's hard to explain to a mortal," the angel continued, sensing my confusion. "To you, it may feel like a bad memory that sticks with you. But that memory turns into a rift if you dwell on it long enough to have regrets. The rift can deepen into Solitude when you're on the brink of a breakthrough; I believe you mortals call it 'finding closure.' Know that success in closing these rifts depends solely on you and you alone: that's why it's called Solitude."

I stood still, blinking, trying to comprehend the angel's words. Solitude? Closing rifts? Finding closure? I couldn't help but wonder what any of this had to do with me.

"Look… when you die, we know where you're going. I know this, you know this, the Lord knows this," the angel concluded, their tone severe.

Unable to come up with an excuse, I let my eyes fall downward, consumed by the sense of shame for the choices I had made. All I could do was remain silent under the weight of the angel's truth… Well, that and the fact that I was still muted.

"Lucky for you, I am sworn to protect you at all times," the angel's voice broke the heavy silence. "I've spoken with the Lord, and He has made a promise. If you can find a way to close this rift, He will grant you a second chance. I am uncertain about the meaning of this 'second chance,' but it is undoubtedly in your best interest to follow His command."

My mind buzzed from the angel's revelation. I imagined a request from God was much like a request from your parents: framed as if you have a choice, but deep down, you know it isn't optional.

"I've restored your talking privileges," the angel said, its tone gentle. "I know I've given you a lot to process, so take a moment to gather your thoughts."

When faced with a flood of information, the best approach is often to tackle it one step at a time. But this... none of it felt real.

Even though the angel had said my speaking ability had been restored, I was still caught off guard when I heard myself make a soft "hmm." I shook off the surprise and asked, "Alright, angel. How do we start closing this... rift?"

The angel's voice, though calm, held a weight that made each word resonate with significance. "Listen closely," it began, its tone steady and deliberate. "Solitude is where mortals usually find closure, a way to mend the fractures within their minds in the human realm. But we are in the spirit realm now. Here, Solitude operates differently."

I nodded slowly, fully aware that missing even a single word could mean losing a crucial piece of the puzzle.

"Adam... The events leading to your accident began when you were sixteen," the angel said.

My eyes widened in shock. "Sixteen years old? What do you mean?"

The air around me grew warmer, and the angel's voice became more serious. "There are pivotal moments in your past that shaped your future. When you were sixteen, decisions were made, and paths were chosen that ultimately led to the accident."

"So, you're saying something I did when I was sixteen led to all this?" I asked, hoping for clarity from the angel.

"It's not so much what you did," the angel replied, "but how you dealt with the things happening in your life at that time."

I nodded slowly, feeling like I was starting to grasp the concept.

"I saw the difficulties you faced growing up," the angel continued. "You were too young to handle the hardships you endured. As a result, you have multiple rifts in your soul that have never healed."

A lump tightened in my throat as the painful memories of my childhood surged back. All the beatings, the yelling, and the never-ending sense of worthlessness. "Why are you telling me this?" I asked, my voice barely above a whisper.

"The Lord wants to give you a second chance," the angel said gently. "He wants you to become the person you needed as a child."

I scrunched my face, trying to make sense of it all. "A second chance? Become the person I needed? What does that even mean?"

"The Lord wants you to be a mentor to your younger self. You've been sent back to the year 2003 to close this rift. To heal the wounds of your past by guiding and supporting the person you once were," the angel said softly.

"Talk to my past self? What in the…" I blurted out, my mind racing to make sense of it. "Okay, so I just talk with my younger self and… what? Fix everything?"

"Not fix, Adam. Guide. Support. Be there for him in the way that very few were for you. Help him understand that he is valued. Show him that he is not alone. Prove to him that he has the strength to overcome the obstacles in his life."

I was starting to grasp what I needed to do, but one question was nagging at me. "I need to know... why did you bring me to my old room?"

The angel's voice softened as it sensed my discomfort. "Your childhood room symbolizes where it all started. It's tied to many of the memories and traumas you've carried with you. Being here makes it easier to connect with those feelings and empathize with your younger self."

"Do you have any idea how much I hate this place?" I muttered bitterly, my eyes scanning the room.

"I do," the angel replied gently.

"So, you know I left this place behind for a reason," I said, struggling to keep my voice steady. I clenched my fists, trying to control the urge to punch anything. "Why couldn't you have brought me somewhere else?"

"I did not choose this place. The Lord did," the angel explained.

I hated my old room with a passion. Every corner seemed to hold a remnant of my torment. This place embodied everything I had fought to forget. Standing in this musty basement, it felt like the walls were closing in on me. What had begun as a dream was swiftly crumbling into a nightmare.

"Being back here..." I grumbled, my voice strained with the thought of old wounds reopening.

"I know..." the angel's voice softened, infused with empathy. "But perhaps that's exactly why He brought you back here." The angel paused as if gathering its thoughts. "I've been with you since the moment you were born, following every step of your journey. This place – your old home – was the hardest part of my duty. I've lost count of how many times you've begged to be free from it. It took every ounce of my strength to keep you sane and protect you from the worst of it."

"Can we please go somewhere else?" I begged, my voice strained with desperation. "I don't know how long I can stand being in this place."

"As I mentioned, the Lord chose this place. I can't go against His will," the angel explained gently. "Clearly, you haven't truly left this place behind, and that's why you're here. He wants you to stop running from your past and confront it head-on. I believe you mortals refer to this as 'facing your fears.'"

It wasn't so much fear as it was disgust. If I had to choose between living here again or spending the rest of my life running away from Jason Vorhees, I'd take my chances with the murderous psychopath. Or, as they say in my present timeline, I would choose the bear.

"If you can't get me out of here, can we at least ask God to move me somewhere else?" I pleaded.

"First off, please know that I fully understand your disdain towards this place," the angel reassured me. "Remember, I reside within your mind. This means if you think it, I can hear it. I can also feel your emotions. So, yes, I completely understand. And secondly," the angel added with amusement, "did you just ask to speak to the manager? No, you cannot. And even if you did, He is going to tell you the same thing."

The angel's joke surprised me, a burst of humor cutting through the tension. "Wow! So, you do have a sense of humor," I said, allowing a soft smile to form on my face – a gesture I hadn't done in what felt like an eternity.

"That's how I preserved your sanity," the angel replied, its words a reminder of the bond we seem to share. "Your sense of humor: it comes from me."

I looked down while closing my eyes, a chuckle escaping me. A genuine smile spread across my face.

"Is that a smile I'm seeing?" the angel asked, a knowing tone in its voice.

I looked up, a soft smile on my face. "Yeah, I guess it is," I admitted.

"Good," the angel said, a note of satisfaction in its voice. "But now, it's time to focus. Listen closely... Your body in the human realm is being kept alive through artificial interjection. I believe you mortals refer to it as 'life support.' We only have about nine days to complete our mission. If we fail, you'll forfeit your second chance."

It quickly became clear that angels and humans spoke in completely different dialects. Its words often left me scratching my head, needing an explanation for the explanation it just gave.

"Artificial interjection?" I repeated, struggling to grasp the unfamiliar term. "I suppose it makes sense if you break the words down," I shrugged. "So, what's the plan? What are we supposed to do?"

"You are to speak with your sixteen-year-old self and guide him through the trauma you endured. Were you not listening to me?" The angel's voice echoed with concern in my mind.

"I was listening," I said, trying to clarify. "I get that I need to talk to my younger self, but you haven't explained how I'm supposed to do that."

"All of your communication with your younger self will be done through text messages," the angel said casually as if this were a normal thing to say.

"Text messages?" I repeated, raising an eyebrow. "How is that even possible? And how am I supposed to reach him that way?"

"Trust me, I'm doing you a favor," the angel added, sensing my skepticism. "I've placed a copy of your cell phone in your front pocket. You will use that to contact your past self and only your past self."

Immediately, I reached into my pocket and pulled out what looked like a replica of my phone. I glanced through the contacts, and though all of them were listed, their names were crossed out. It was a clear reminder that this device was meant solely for this task.

"Okay... so I need to 'be the person I needed' back then. Well, the person I needed back then was child protective services," I said, the words feeling more like a punchline than a solution.

"That's... accurate," the angel hesitantly agreed. "But do you truly believe that you would be entrusted with this task if there was doubt about your ability to handle it?"

I used to roll my eyes at the idea that life's trials were divine tests. Yet, as I faced this unnerving challenge, I couldn't help but wonder if this was indeed a test from God. What other explanation could there be?

"I don't know," I said, feeling uncertain. "What makes you think this is even possible? It took me twenty years to come to terms with it myself. How could I possibly help someone else unravel it in just nine days?"

"Well, it's not 'someone.' It's you. And... you haven't truly dealt with it. That's why we're in Solitude to begin with. But don't worry. You won't be alone. I'll be here to guide you every step of the way," the angel said, calm and reassuring.

"But what makes me the most qualified person to do this? I'm no therapist," I voiced my concern.

"You're right, but that's a good thing," the angel countered. "A therapist helps mortals make sense of their experiences. But you... you know exactly what will happen, when it will happen, how it will happen, and why it will happen. That makes you the perfect person for this."

The angel's words were starting to make sense, but I still wasn't entirely convinced.

"Do you think we can do this?" I asked, still hesitant.

"Yes, I do. My faith tells me we must," the angel responded calmly.

"You work for God, so I'd imagine having a strong sense of faith is a requirement, right?" I asked.

"Probably," the angel responded. "It's not a matter I've dedicated much thought to."

"Really?" I asked, feeling the question press heavily on my mind. "I'm curious... You can read my thoughts and sense my feelings. I've grappled with doubts about my faith so many times. How is it that you've never questioned it yourself?"

"Because mortals have a different understanding of faith," the angel replied, its tone filled with knowing certainty.

"Oh? And what's your take on faith?" I asked, genuinely curious.

The angel's voice took on a thoughtful tone. "Adam. For me, faith isn't about doubt or belief. It's about trusting in the purpose assigned to me by the Lord. It's difficult to explain to mortals."

"Can you at least try? I'm interested in knowing this," I replied, curiosity in my voice. "I'm all ears... or I guess 'mind' in this case?"

"Ears..." The angel paused as if searching for the right words. "Faith, for me, is absolute. It's an integral part of my existence, woven into the fabric of my being. Mortals see faith as a choice, something they can trust or doubt. But for me, it's a constant. It's like the air you breathe. You don't question its presence; you just know it's there."

I nodded slowly, trying to grasp the concept. "But I can't just... 'not breathe'... for long, on purpose. Does that mean you don't question your faith because you can't?"

"It's not that I can't," the angel corrected gently. "It's that there's no reason to. My entire existence is devoted to serving the Lord. The doubts you mortals feel are not part of my existence because my purpose is clear and unchanging. Your faith, Adam, is tested and shaped by your experiences and challenges. Mine is simply a state of being."

I slowly nodded, letting it sink in. "I guess that adds up. Your faith is a matter of fact, while ours is something we've got to keep working on."

"Correct," the angel replied, a note of approval in its tone.

As I took a moment to process everything the angel had just explained about faith, I couldn't help but feel a sense of awe. I had learned so much in such a short interaction with my guardian angel. Finally feeling more comfortable, I decided to ask the question in the back of my mind.

"Hey," I began hesitantly, "there's something I need to know."

The angel's presence seemed to shift, attentive and curious. "What is it, Adam?"

I took a deep breath, steadying myself. "What happens if we fail this mission? You mentioned putting your powers on the line. What does that mean?"

The angel paused, the air around me feeling heavier with the question's weight. "Adam, the stakes are high. Failure is not an option we can afford to entertain."

My anxiety began to creep in. "I get that, but I need to know the consequences. For you, for me... for everyone."

The angel's voice softened. "If we fail, I will lose my connection to the Lord and become a fallen angel. As for you... you will perish while forfeiting your second chance."

I sensed a faint hint of fear in the angel's voice. "Are you having doubts? I can't imagine how rough it would be to lose your connection to God. So, let me ask you again... Do you think we can pull this off?"

The angel's voice, though steady, carried a bit of unease. "Adam, I believe we can succeed, for my purpose is to guide and support you. The fear you detect is not doubt but an awareness of the seriousness of our task. I trust in our strength and determination to see this through."

I wasn't convinced. Admittedly, it felt crazy to believe that even angels can experience fear... That's when I knew this mission would take everything I had.

My mind drifted back to the term the angel had used. "You mentioned 'fallen angels.' I remember hearing about them as a child. Aren't those the angels who fell in the war against the Devil?"

The angel's reply was immediate, confusion evident. "What? No. What war are you even talking about?"

"I don't know! I was hoping you could answer," I replied.

"I don't even..." The angel's words trailed off, mirroring my confusion. "Okay. Let's shift our focus for now," it said, steering the conversation away from the unsettling topic.

I nodded, but I was unable to shake the question. "Please... What happens to a fallen angel? I need to know what exactly is at stake for you."

"They're banned from the heavens and stripped of all their powers," the angel replied, their voice heavy with the gravity of the repercussions.

"And what would have happened if you didn't... make this deal?" I pressed, feeling a sense of guilt creep in.

"I would spend eternity knowing I hadn't done everything I could to help you. Breaking my oath isn't something I could ever accept," the angel confessed.

"Kind of like a Paladin in Dungeons and Dragons?" I asked.

"...No. Nothing like a Paladin in Dungeons and—look, the point is this," the angel said, cutting itself off. "Your failures are my failures. I will do everything possible to ensure we fulfill this task," the angel insisted.

"I appreciate you saying that." I pulled out the phone, then paused when the lightbulb went off in my head. "But... I just thought of something. Wouldn't it be easier to talk to my younger self face-to-face? Or is it like *Back to the Future*, where seeing myself might cause me to go into shock?"

"Are you seriously comparing time travel to a movie from the '80s?" the angel asked, both surprised and skeptical.

"Well, maybe? Doc Brown did warn about unraveling the space cowboy continuing ...or something," I said, my voice trailing off.

23

"...Space-time continuum..." the angel said slowly, clearly trying to correct me. "And do you even know what that means?"

"No, but it sounds terrible," I said nervously.

"It means any actions done in the past could change the way things are in your present day," the angel explained.

"Is that how things work here?" I asked.

"No. It's more like Disney and Marvel, with separate universes that— Why are we even talking about this?" The angel quickly cut itself off again.

I couldn't help but laugh as I noticed the angel getting flustered.

Looking down at the phone, I pressed the issue again. "Are you sure it wouldn't be easier to just talk to my past self in person? Since we don't have to worry about the space pirates?"

"Space-time—You know what, never mind," the angel sighed, giving up on the correction. "Adam, you could technically encounter your sixteen-year-old self directly. However, considering how insufferable you were at that age, the challenge may be far greater than you expect. Do you truly possess the patience to endure that version of yourself?"

I thought back to how I was as a teenager. I remember being all over the place, full of loud opinions and a stubborn streak that could understandably annoy even the most patient person. I had this way of getting stuck in my head, jumping from one thing to another, never settling on anything. I was always so convinced that I knew everything, even when I was completely lost. Dealing with my younger self face-to-face would be a nightmare. I sighed, shaking my head.

"Sorry for doubting you," I said, shuddering at the realization."

"Apology accepted," the angel said. "I know I've given you a lot to take in. Tonight, take some time to relax and process it all. You can explore this timeline freely. You'll look the same to yourself, but to others, you'll be unrecognizable."

"Unrecognizable?" I echoed, seeking clarification.

"Yes, you won't look like yourself," the angel said, unsure where the confusion was.

"No, I get that part. What will I look like?" I pressed, my curiosity piqued.

"Does it matter?" the angel asked.

"Yes," I replied without hesitation.

The angel sighed. "...Ryan Reynolds."

I blinked, struggling to wrap my head around it. "Ryan Reynolds...? Really? Look... I know I should be excited right now, but you're telling me I'll be walking around looking like a famous actor?"

"Relax," the angel said calmly. "In this year, he isn't nearly as famous as he is now. You won't be drawing any unnecessary attention."

"But... Ryan Reynolds doesn't strike me as the kind of guy who would enjoy a bacon, egg, and cheese from the corner deli. Won't that mess with his image in the future?" I said, half-joking, but genuinely curious.

The angel replied quickly, "Disney and Marvel. It's a different universe."

"Got it," I replied, nodding.

"Get some rest. We've got a busy time ahead of us," the angel instructed, its tone turning serious once more.

"Yeah. You're right," I replied, acknowledging the gravity of the task ahead.

"Adam," the angel said softly, its voice filled with unwavering sincerity. "Your suffering hasn't gone unnoticed. But to change the future, we need to understand the past. We must face these memories together."

I nodded. The angel's words felt like a beacon of hope, cutting through the darkness of my past. Yet, as I considered the path ahead, a single thought lingered: What could go wrong?

Chapter 2

The room was thick with silence after the failed attempts to revive Adam. Dr. Patterson, who had done everything she could to save him, stood over his still form. Her face was etched with a mix of frustration and sadness.

"I'm so, so sorry." Dr. Patterson whispered, her voice trembling as tears pooled in her eyes. The crash of the bedside table still lingered in the room, a stark reminder of her desperate attempts.

Dr. Reyes entered the room, his calm and inspiring presence a welcome change from the tension in the air. He placed a reassuring hand on Dr. Patterson's shoulder. "You did your best. That's all anyone can ask," he said gently.

Dr. Patterson nodded, brushing away her tears. "We need to get him on life support," she said firmly.

Dr. Reyes gazed down at Adam with a mix of determination and sadness. "Let's get him set up and stabilized," he said. "Nurse Edwards, please go through his belongings. We need to find someone to contact."

As the medical team worked to set up the ventilator, Nurse Edwards began sifting through Adam's belongings. Among them, she discovered his phone, wallet, and a photograph of him with a woman. They were both smiling, showcasing an engagement ring. The photo, clearly an engagement shot, had "Adam & Jessica - May 19, 2015" written in elegant script on the back.

...

The sterile hiss of the ventilator filled the room as Adam lay motionless, the machine breathing for him. His chest rose and fell in sync with the mechanical rhythm. Dr. Reyes completed the task of securing the tubes and connections, ensuring everything was functioning correctly.

Nurse Edwards took a deep breath and dialed the "Jessica Grey" contact on Adam's phone. The phone rang twice before someone answered.

"Hello?" A woman's voice answered, tinged with curiosity and a hint of worry.

"Hello. My name is Maria Edwards, and I'm a nurse at Grimbley Memorial Hospital. Is this Jessica?" Nurse Edwards asked gently.

"Yes, this is she," Jessica responded, her voice steady but full of anxiety.

"Are you familiar with the name Adam Grey?" Nurse Edwards asked.

Jessica's voice wavered slightly, a mix of concern and fear seeping through. "Yes, I am. He is my husband."

"I'm afraid I have some difficult news about your husband," Nurse Edwards said gently. "He was in a car accident and is now in critical condition. We have him on life support, and we need you to come to the hospital as soon as possible."

There was a pause, followed by a gasp. "I... I'll be there right away," Jessica replied, trembling with shock and urgency.

As Nurse Edwards hung up, Dr. Reyes approached her and asked, "How did she take it?"

"As well as can be expected," Nurse Edwards replied, her voice heavy with empathy. "She's on her way."

Dr. Reyes nodded and looked back at Adam. "Let's prepare her for what she's going to see. This won't be easy."

...

As I lay in my childhood bed, the angel's words echoed in my mind: become the person I needed as a child, Solitude, guardian angels. I hadn't fully processed everything yet and was supposed to be able to help my past self figure it out in just nine days. If this was a dream, why hadn't I woken up yet?

A few hours slipped by as I lay there, staring at the faded ceiling, my mind tangled with thoughts of the task ahead. The angel, thankfully, had granted me some silence, its presence reduced to a distant echo in my thoughts.

Maybe the angel was right about doing it through text messages. I sighed, recalling how frustrating I was at that age: always seeking validation and confused about everything. I was an annoying kid, but one who needed guidance. The idea that I might be able to help him sparked a glimmer of hope.

...

With a frustrated sigh, I threw the covers off and sat at the edge of my childhood bed.

"Is everything okay?" the angel's voice broke the silence.

"No," I replied. "I can't just sit here doing nothing. I need to take action."

"Have you come up with a strategy?" the angel asked.

I sighed and replied, "Not at all. You can't exactly prepare for something like this. So, I'll just wing it and see what happens."

The angel was silent for a moment as if considering my words. "You make a fair point. You've always been someone who went with the flow. Perhaps that approach will serve you well here, too."

"I hope you're right. So, where do we start?" I asked, my nerves getting the best of me.

"Just pull out your phone and text your younger self. The contact is named 'Sixteen,'" the angel instructed.

"Sixteen? Like... the androids from Dragon Ball Z?" I asked jokingly.

"...Yes, like the Androids from Dragon Ball Z," the angel replied, unamused.

I chuckled and took a deep breath, pulling out my phone. After scrolling down to Sixteen's contact, I noticed something. "Why do Sixteen and I have the same phone number?"

The angel paused for a moment, clearly taken aback by my question. "Are you serious?" They asked.

"Well, yeah. It doesn't sound like it should work that way," I responded.

The angel paused, then replied with a hint of exasperation, "After everything that's happened – talking to your guardian angel, learning about Solitude, time travel, spirit realm – the biggest piece of the puzzle that confuses you is having the same phone number as your past self?"

"Okay, okay," I said, the situation's absurdity finally sinking in. "Point taken. Let's get this over with." I took a deep breath and tapped the contact named Sixteen.

As I was about to text Sixteen, a thought crossed my mind. "How is Sixteen going to be messaging me? I hope he isn't using those old dial pads where you press a button multiple times to get one letter."

"You won't need to worry about that. Sixteen will be using AOL Instant Messenger," the angel responded.

AOL Instant Messenger. I hadn't thought about that in years. I remembered the days of funny screen names, late-night chats, and the iconic door chime when someone came online. It had been the heart of our digital communication back then.

I couldn't help but smile at the memory. "Wow…I forgot all about that. It was such a big deal back then. It was sad when it ended. All those screen names just vanished into the ether. Although, I'm sure some of them probably turned into gamer tags."

"Focus on the task at hand, please," the angel urged, its voice pulling me back to the present moment.

"Right. Sorry. I'm just glad Sixteen won't have to spend half the day typing out one word," I said, shaking off the distraction. "So, what should we say?"

"Start with something simple. Be open and honest. Remember, you're trying to connect with your younger self and guide him," the angel said reassuringly.

I took a deep breath and nodded. "Alright… let's do this." My fingers hovered over the keyboard, the task's weight settling in. The soft glow of the phone screen illuminated my face as I prepared to bridge the gap between past and present. Then, out of nowhere, I started laughing uncontrollably.

The angel's voice pierced through my laughter, filled with concern. "Adam! Tell me, what is happening?"

Between fits of laughter, I managed to gasp, "Sorry... it's just... when I said, 'let's do this,' I couldn't help but think of someone shouting, 'Leeroy Jenkins!'"

There was a long pause, and then something unexpected happened. The angel burst into laughter. "That was kind of funny," it admitted, trying to regain composure.

"Glad I'm not the only one who thought so," I managed to say between laughs. Once the laughter subsided, I took a deep breath and looked at the screen. I knew this was going to be a wild journey.

Hey.
I need to talk to you.

Hi?
Do I know you?

I'm you from the future.

Oh word?

Yes.
And I really need to connect with you.

That's gay.

Reading his response was a shock. In my timeline, we'd immediately label this behavior as homophobic, but back in 2003, social norms were different. And even though I disapproved of his behavior, I couldn't help but think: who am I to judge when that person is literally me from the past? His words were wrong. My words were wrong. But they reflected a society still stumbling through the fog of ignorance.

Grow up.

lol

You need to listen to me.

Okay, I'm listening.

Good.
I know a lot is happening in your life, but I'm here to help you understand it all.

Cool.
Let me guess. You need my password to help me?

The angel's voice came through, unable to contain its amusement. "Your strategy is to approach a teenager with an outrageous claim. Impressive."

I sighed, frustration evident. "Can you be quiet if you're not going to help?"

"I apologize," the angel said, its tone lightening. "But it is difficult to keep quiet when you sound like an old man telling this young whippersnapper to get off your lawn."

I'm not asking for your password.

I got you.
It's ********

34

Those are just asterisks.
I don't need your password.

Are you a bot or something?

No! I am a real person.

Sure, you are.
I'm just going to block you and call it a day.

The angel's voice carried a mix of disbelief and exasperation. "So... you just told a troubled 16-year-old that you're his future self and expect him to trust you without any evidence or preparation?"

"You told me to be open and honest, remember? I'm just following your advice," I shot back.

"Open and honest, not foolish and hastily. Even in your timeline, who would place their trust in such a preposterous assertion without proof?"

I sighed, realizing the angel was right.

"It would be wise to reflect on your words before you type," the angel advised. "To Sixteen, you resemble someone unfamiliar with the internet. I believe the contemporary retort is, 'Okay, boomer.'"

"Alright, alright, I get it," I replied, acknowledging the angel's point.

The angel continued, "I'm not certain you do. What transpired two years ago?"

My mind raced to recall events from 2001, sifting through a fog of disorganized memories. Everything seemed to blend in together, but one memory stood out. "Hmm... Oh, I found a Charizard card! And Shrek came out! But I'm not sure what those have to do with anything."

The angel paused, and the silence made it clear that I had missed the point entirely. "The world, Adam. What happened in the world?"

I kept thinking, but nothing concrete came to mind. "I don't know. It's hard to think right now."

I could almost feel the angel's disbelief. "...so much for 'Never Forget.' 9/11, Adam. At this time, everyone remained on edge, including you."

The realization of 9/11 hit me like a truck. I still remember where I was when I first heard the news.

"Wow... The world was never the same after that. I know how confused and scared Sixteen must be right now, trying to make sense of a world that suddenly feels more dangerous."

"Exactly," the angel said, their tone gentler. "He's not just dealing with teenage issues. He is also wrestling with the profound existential dread that pervaded the mortal experience at that time."

"Okay, I think I'm getting it now," I said, feeling the weight of the angel's words. "So, what strategy would you recommend?"

"Approach him with empathy and understanding," the angel instructed. "Address him as you wish those around you would have addressed you during those days. This will be the most effective way to establish a connection."

"You're probably right," I said. "Back then, I would have wanted someone to prove who they were first."

"That's right," the angel said. "Just remember, you're here to guide him, not overwhelm him. We don't want him to block you."

"What happens if he blocks me?" I asked.

The angel's tone grew serious. "What happens if someone blocks you in the human realm?"

"They don't receive my messages?" I responded.

"Correct. And what happens if you cannot contact your past self?" The angel pressed.

"Game over?" I guessed.

"Game over," the angel confirmed.

I took a deep breath, knowing it was time to be serious. "All right, I'll be more careful."

Sarah Jennings and Erika Gardner.

What about them?

You have the biggest crush on those two girls.

That's not really a secret, but okay.

*Spoiler: Sarah turns you down and kind of just
disappears from your life.
Erika already turned you down. At this age, you
hope you can convince her otherwise. Trust me, you
two are better off as best friends.*

Who is this?

*I'm you.
Just keep listening, and I'll prove it.*

Okay.

*Everyone sees you as "Zack's little brother," and
you hate it.
Eventually, you want to leave your hometown and
rebuild your identity.
This has been on your mind for years, and you never
told anyone about it because you don't want people
to worry.*

*Stop messing with me.
Tell me who you are.*

*There's a sports drink you love called Nutrament.
It's a New York thing. I love them too, but you
should drink less of it.*

*No.
It says full meal replacement on the can.*

*A "full meal" shouldn't have over forty grams of
sugar. That's terrible.*

*A regular meal can have that much sugar!
What's the big deal?
It's not like I have diabetes.*

Let me be clear.
NONE of your meals should have that much sugar.
That is so bad for your health.
Also, diabetes runs in our family. In my timeline, we
are okay, but Mom and Dad have it. I urge you to be
more careful.

Whatever.
This is getting stupid.
Are you someone from school?

I'm you, twenty years in the future.
Ask me anything.

What's my favorite color?

You've got two. Black and blue.
Give me a harder question.

My favorite Pokémon?

Dude... Bulbasaur.
Are you even trying right now?
Ask me something only you would know.

You need to tell me who you are.
This isn't funny anymore.

I'm you.
Ask me something only you would know.

What is my favorite food?

Jamaican beef patties with coco bread and cheese.
Specifically from the corner deli.
Try harder. Think about something you've never told
anyone. Ask me a question that only you would have
the answer to.

Okay.
What do I want to be when I get older?

That's a tricky one.

39

You almost had me.
I knew you were full of it.

> *Just because it's tricky doesn't mean I can't answer*
> *it.*
> *You tell everyone you want to be a game designer,*
> *but honestly, you aren't sure what you want to do.*

Wrong!
I want to be a game designer.

> *No, you don't.*
> *You play a lot of video games, but honestly, you do it*
> *to escape reality. Telling people that you want to*
> *design games in the future gets them to leave you*
> *alone.*

I play video games because I enjoy them.

> *And why do you enjoy them?*

It just takes my mind off everything...
Okay, I see your point.
Are you happy now?

> *No. I'm not happy at all.*
> *But that's why I'm here.*
> *To help you.*
> *Adam... You have such a beautiful and creative*
> *mind. You may not know what you want to do yet,*
> *but you do know that you want to help people.*

Isn't every job just helping people?

> *I guess it depends on how you look at it.*
> *But I know you want to be on the front line of*
> *whatever you decide to do.*
> *You want to inspire others to be strong.*
> *You want to be an incredible leader, but you're*
> *afraid of being judged by others.*

Okay, you're freaking me out.
How do you know my name and all this stuff about
me?

I told you, Adam. I'm you.
I know it feels like whatever you do isn't good
enough.
Whether you're at home or school, people are
always coming down on you.
That's why most of your time is spent hiding in the
garage. It is the one place where you can be yourself
without anyone judging you.

I just want to stay out of trouble.
I never seem to get in trouble there.

I know.
Deep down, you're a good kid. You're kindhearted,
outgoing, and thoughtful.
I know you're used to being told the opposite. I just
wish someone would have told us that people's
opinions of us don't matter.

Even my parents?
Does their opinion not matter?

Parents… This was a touchy subject for me. Growing up, both of my parents were physically and mentally abusive. I didn't see it at that age, but I understand now. Unfortunately, I still held onto that anger, which made it difficult to stay calm.

"Breathe," the angel said calmly. "I understand your anger, but do not allow it to interfere with our purpose for being here," it advised, its voice steady and reassuring.

I took a deep breath and focused on the angel's words. It reminded me of something Sherlock Holmes would say: "This mustn't register on an

41

emotional level." After a few more breaths to compose myself, I resumed typing, determined to handle this logically and push my feelings aside.

Parents are supposed to want the best for their children. Unfortunately, our parents focus only on what is best for themselves.

What's best for me is to stop upsetting them and make them proud.

Another wave of anger hit me upon reading Sixteen's words. He hasn't been alive long enough to realize that making them proud will never happen.

The angel's voice cut through my anger, resembling a teacher reminding a student to focus. "What did I just say? You need to guide him without letting your anger take over."

I took another deep breath, struggling to keep my emotions in check. This topic was too heavy for me, so I decided it was best to shift the focus elsewhere.

Have you ever considered trying to make yourself proud? I'm sure it would start with building up your confidence.

Who says I'm not confident?

Your confidence is so low that I can see it in the words you type.
It makes sense, though. The environment you live in is terrible. You don't even have a room with a door.

What do you know about my home?

You live in a home that…
And feel free to correct me if I'm wrong.
You're blamed for everything.
Nothing you do is enough.
Even when you're right, you're wrong.
Your wants and needs come last.
You're responsible for everyone else's happiness.
Even when you do achieve something, nobody seems
to care.
Oh, and you get hit A LOT.
Most of the time, it's for no reason.

Please, stop.

Is anything I said incorrect?

No…
That's why I want you to stop.

I understand.
Adam… You don't have a journal and you'd never
post this on your MySpace. There has to be at least
some part of you that believes me.

I don't know.
This has to be a dream.

"I feel the same way, kid," I thought to myself. This whole ordeal felt like a lucid dream where I was aware and thinking clearly but couldn't control what was happening around me.

I know all of this is sudden and scary.
But please, try not to be nervous.
I'm not here to hurt you.

So why are you here then?

The angel interjected, "You might want to proceed cautiously. It's wiser not to reveal the full truth just yet."

43

I nodded in agreement, acknowledging the angel's advice.

I will be in your timeline for a while.
I figured while I was here, I might as well check up
on you and give you someone you could talk to if you
have any questions.

Are you sure you aren't trying to lure me into a van?

No.
If I wanted to do that, you would never see it
coming.

What kind of stranger danger are you proposing?

I promise I don't want to meet you.
I'm just here to talk.
And we said a lot today, so let's continue this
tomorrow, okay?

I won't be able to text you while I'm at school.

We both know you won't be going to class tomorrow
morning. You'll be in the garage, so I'll contact you
while you're there, okay?

I still don't get how you know all of this.

I'll explain more tomorrow.
Sound good?

Sounds good.
Talk to you then.

All I could do was stare at my phone, reflecting on the conversation
with my past self and how it nearly ended in disaster. My heart was
still racing from the close call of Sixteen blocking me.

The angel's voice cut through my thoughts. "Exceptional work,
Adam!" It said, offering its praise.

44

I was grateful, but unfortunately, it was overshadowed by the anger of not knowing such important information. "Any particular reason you didn't tell me that if Sixteen blocked me, the mission would end?" I asked, my anger still simmering.

"No," the angel said calmly. "Not one that you're likely to accept."

"Let me be the judge of that," I replied, still frustrated.

There was a moment of silence before the angel spoke again, its tone reluctant. "I've observed your time working in the healthcare field, Adam. You perform better under pressure."

"Wow, you're right," I responded quickly, seeing where this may be going. "Not one I'm going to accept."

"I'm not asking you to pardon my actions," the angel said firmly. "But I need you to understand: you overthink everything. What should be simple tasks turn into trials for you. Yet, under pressure, you excel. You perceive things that others overlook, all while keeping your composure. It's a rare gift, even admired among other angels."

I shook my head, frustration still bubbling. "If it's a gift, it's a very situational one."

"I've witnessed you utilizing this gift to save lives. Do you recall the instance when you had to give a patient CPR because the nurse was frozen in fear?" The angel asked.

As memories from my healthcare days flooded back, I remembered my decade as a nurse aide. One day, working under a new licensed practical nurse, a patient in a wheelchair suddenly began having a seizure. The nurse froze, but my training kicked in. Before I even had time to think, my body sprang into action, taking the necessary steps to assist the patient in their moment of need.

"I remember that day," I said, shaking my head. "I also remember being fired the next day. They claimed I should have 'grabbed a nurse from another unit.'" I shook my head in disappointment, regretting every moment I spent working at that hospital. "Honestly, I'm glad that place got shut down."

"But are you aware of why the hospital shut down?" the angel asked.

I shrugged, the memories still fresh and bitter. "I never bothered to look. I was just glad to be out of there."

"The patient you saved is connected to the Governor. Her outrage over your dismissal prompted her to share her story, which triggered an investigation into the hospital. Many died there needlessly, but you, albeit unknowingly, played a crucial role in ending it."

I was at a loss for words. Maybe everything really does happen for a reason.

The angel said, with genuine sincerity, "I apologize for the deception. Your failures are my own as well, so I must use everything within my power to ensure our success in this mission."

"Speaking of 'power,'" I asked, as a question sparked in my mind, "I'm curious... You can silence me, put me into a temporary body – which, by the way, I still don't understand why I look like Ryan Reynolds – and even clone my cell phone. Clearly, you have magical powers. So, why can't you use that guardian angel magic on my past self?'"

"It's not 'magic.' It's called 'Grace,' and it comes with its limitations," the angel explained.

"Hold on," I said, needing clarity. "What exactly is 'Grace'? I need to understand what it means in this context."

The angel paused, seemingly taken aback. "I've never had to explain it before," it admitted. "When I received my powers, I just knew what they were and how to use them. I don't think I can clarify it any better than that."

"Can you please try?" I urged, feeling the uncertainty gnaw at me. "You can't just drop something like this and leave me without explanation. It's going to nag at me until I get an answer."

"Very well, I will try," the angel acknowledged, pausing to gather its thoughts. "You mortals are given the gift of free will, the ability to make your own choices. At times, those choices may be... questionable. 'Grace' permits me to influence the outcomes of these missteps gently, but it does not give me absolute control."

"If you can influence the outcome of a bad choice, then why am I dead?" I asked, frustration and confusion evident in my voice.

The angel responded, "You are not dead. You are in Solitude."

"You know what I meant... Why didn't you protect me?" I pressed, still searching for answers.

The angel took offense, its voice tinged with anger. "Once more, 'Grace' has its limitations. You may find it difficult to believe, but I did protect you. I am protecting you even now. However, while I can influence your actions, I cannot ensure the desired outcome."

"Honestly, it doesn't seem like guardian angels are any good at protecting anyone. Every day on the news, I see innocent people suffer. Why is that?" I asked.

The angel's voice resonated with calm authority. "We do not possess the level of power you may imagine, Adam. Our purpose is to guide and protect you from your own missteps, not to command the world around you."

"That still doesn't answer my question," I replied, frustration building.

"It's not for me to answer," the angel replied, their tone acknowledging the boundaries of their role.

"What do you mean?" I asked.

The angel responded, "It means that I am aware of the answer. Even if I do not entirely agree with the methods, I must trust and believe that the Lord knows what He is doing. Thus far, He has given me no reason to think otherwise."

"Look…" I said firmly, "This is a big deal to me. If we're going to keep working together, you're going to have to give me something more to work with."

"The answer, Adam," the angel said, "is often deceptively simple. Every event, every twist of fate, is woven into the tapestry of existence for a purpose. Though the reasons may sometimes elude us, time becomes the revealer of truths. Be patient, for clarity often emerges in its own time."

I squinted, trying to make sense of the angel's words. After a moment, something clicked. It reminded me of a conversation with my best friend, Erika.

…

When Erika and I were little kids, we'd spend hours chasing birds and having fun at the local park. Well, one time while playing, I tripped and hit my head on a bench. I was bleeding pretty badly, according to Erika. She quickly grabbed some water and a paper towel from her lunch box and cleaned my cut with a gentle touch. It hurt like crazy, but I wanted to impress her with my high pain tolerance. I can admit it: even at such a young age, I liked her and wanted to show off for her.

Even as we grew older, our park visits continued. We'd walk around, enjoy the scenery, and talk about anything and everything. When graduation came around, we made a promise: no matter where life took us, we would always keep in touch. Whenever we had big news to share, we would meet at that same bench, hold each other's hands, and share whatever news we had.

I shared some news with Erika a few years after high school. It was getting late, and the sun was nearly set, but the news was too important to wait.

When I arrived at our old spot, Erika greeted me with a warm hug. Her embrace was as comforting as ever. "Hey, Adam!" she exclaimed, pulling me in close.

My body felt paralyzed even as she wrapped me in a comforting hug. I leaned into her, but my arms remained at my sides. "Erika…" I whispered, my voice shaking under the burden of the news I had to share.

She pulled back slightly to get a better look at my face, her hands gently gripping my shoulders. My expression must have mirrored a horror she had never seen before.

"Adam… what's wrong?" she asked, her concern clear as she looked into my eyes.

I tried to speak, but the words wouldn't come. Seeing my struggle, Erika gently took my hands and guided me to sit on the bench.

"You can tell me. What's wrong, Adam?" Her voice was gentle but laced with concern. It was clear to her that something was very wrong.

"Jason…" I finally managed to say, my voice still barely above a whisper. "It's about Jason. He…"

Erika's gaze remained steady, her eyes filled with quiet patience. She didn't blink; she just waited for me to continue.

Speaking slowly, with my voice cracking, I said, "His cousin found him in his room. He… he overdosed."

"Oh my god…" Erika whispered, gripping my hands tightly. Her voice was a mix of horror and sympathy.

"I knew Jason was struggling," I choked out, my voice breaking with each word. "I kept promising myself I'd visit him, but life kept pulling me away. It's my fault. He wouldn't have done this if I had been there." The guilt was too much for me. I buried my face in Erika's arms, sobbing uncontrollably. Her embrace was the only thing anchoring me as I drowned in the despair of what I believed I should have done.

Erika held me tightly, her own heart breaking from the pain I was enduring. Her voice, though steady, trembled with emotion as she whispered, "Adam, this isn't your fault. You couldn't have known. It's not on you." She remained my anchor even as she tried to hold back her own tears.

I couldn't find the words. All I could do was cling to her, my body shaking with every sob.

"Adam," she said softly, her voice trembling, "This isn't your fault and I refuse to let you blame yourself for this!"

I stayed silent, my tears soaking into Erika's shoulder. I clung to her, desperate for the comfort she offered.

"Adam, listen to me carefully," Erika said gently, her voice calm despite the moment's heaviness. "In this world, there are no accidents. Every person and every event has its place and purpose, even if we can't see it right now."

My voice became muffled and strained as my head rested on Erika's shoulder. "What purpose could this possibly serve? There's no good in any of this."

"I didn't say anything about good or bad," Erika said gently. "Just that there's a reason. You might not see why this is happening now or even years from now. But I promise, eventually, it will make sense. We both will understand."

I stayed silent in Erika's arms, the guilt over Jason's death still gnawing at me. But now, a new fear had taken hold – the fear of losing Erika, my closest female friend who knew how to make this hectic life more tolerable. Without warning, I pulled her in tighter.

Erika's arms tightened around me, her warmth a steady comfort. "You know I love you, Adam," her voice firm despite the sadness. "We're going to get through this together, just like always. I promise."

Even though it was late, we stayed wrapped in each other's arms for the next half hour, clinging to the strength of our bond. The darkness of the night mirrored the weight we both felt, and neither of us was ready to let go... of Jason or the other.

...

Her words stayed with me, even though I didn't fully understand them. Now, as I sit here in my old room with an angel in my head, I think I'm finally starting to get it.

"Erika did say that... but her words were a lot easier to understand," I murmured, mostly to myself rather than the angel.

"Erika's right on the mark," the angel said. "Not only in her message but in the manner she conveys it. She possesses a unique connection with the Lord because she has made the effort to understand Him."

"Erika's relationship with God is something I've never had," I said with a note of regret in my voice,

The angel's voice seemed to soften, a gentle warmth radiating through my thoughts. "I understand, Adam. Everyone's spiritual journey is unique. Given our current circumstances, perhaps it's time for you to… as you mortals say, 'Get right with the Lord before He gets right with you?'"

I laughed softly, agreeing with the angel. "You're right. You know what they say – the best time to start was yesterday. The second best time is today."

The angel seemed puzzled. "Who says that?"

I shrugged, acknowledging, "Not sure. I read it online somewhere."

The angel let it go, shifting focus. "Right… Adam. When was the last time you saw Erika?"

"The last time I saw her was at that same park," I replied. "It was when I told her I would marry Jessica."

The angel's tone grew warm. "Yes, I recall it now… Erika was overjoyed for you that day. You both hold a special place in each other's hearts. She always wishes for your happiness. She cherishes your friendship as much as you cherish hers."

I nodded but immediately felt a pang of guilt as I looked down. The weight of my previous grief while sobbing on Erika's shoulder felt fresh again.

The angel's voice softened. "I apologize for bringing it up. I didn't mean to upset you."

I took a deep breath, trying to steady myself. "It's not your fault… It was my decision, right?"

The angel fell silent, giving me space to process my emotions.

"Hey," I finally said, feeling curious. "I have a question. Why aren't you using your 'Grace' on my past self?"

"Because I'm your guardian angel and not his," the angel responded.

"But that's still me from the past. Wouldn't that mean you're there too?" I questioned. "Even using Disney and Marvel's logic, you should still be there."

"There's only one of me looking out for you," the angel said, its tone both relaxed and firm. "I'm not bound to the same rules as mortals, especially regarding time travel. For me, there's no 'space-time continuum.'"

I tilted my head a bit, puzzled by the angel's explanation.

"Simply put, I protect you," the angel continued. "Not the past you. Not the future you. Not you in another timeline. Wherever you go, I go."

"Does that mean you would go where I go if we fail this task?" I asked.

"Not exactly. But like I said earlier, I'll spend the rest of eternity knowing I failed my oath. That's an angel's version of 'the undesirable place,'" the angel clarified.

I nodded slowly, taking in the angel's words. Then, a thought struck me from an earlier conversation. "Random question – when you mentioned Disney and Marvel explaining time travel pretty well, were you referring to *Avengers: Endgame?*"

The angel's voice carried a hint of confusion. "Yes, what other movie could I possibly be referencing?"

I had to stop and think about that for a second. "Fair. But... does that mean you watch human movies?"

The angel's voice was steady and assured. "Why wouldn't I? Wherever you go, I go, remember?"

I laughed a little. "I guess I never really thought about what a guardian angel does. I always imagined stuff involving harps and halos."

The angel responded with a playful note, "Harps and Halos. That's the name of my rock band in the high heavens."

"Are you serious?" My eyes widened in surprise. "That is awesome!"

The angel's voice took on a teasing tone. "I was joking, Adam. But if it were true, it would be quite the gig."

"Yeah, it would be," I said while laughing at the angel's joke. Honestly, I was a bit disappointed that it wasn't real.

"Adam, you did well today. Get some rest, and please, no more messages to your younger self tonight since you've promised to talk to him tomorrow. I believe you mortals refer to this as being 'thirsty,' yes? Avoid being 'thirsty.'"

"...Never say that again," I managed to say while trying to hold in my laughter.

"Did I misuse the phrase?" The angel asked.

"I'm sure what you said is a human resource violation somewhere," I said while shaking my head. "We'll work on it later."

Chapter 3

Adam lay motionless in the hospital bed, his face pale and bruised from the car crash. His wife, Jessica, sat beside him, her eyes red and swollen from crying endlessly. She gently stroked his cold fingers, seeking solace in the touch that used to be warm and reassuring. Jessica's heart ached as she whispered words of love and encouragement, clinging to hope for a response she knew was unlikely to come.

Suddenly, footsteps echoed in the corridor. Dr. Reyes entered the room, his expression serious yet compassionate.

"Mrs. Grey," Dr. Reyes began softly, his voice full of empathy, "I need to talk to you about your husband's condition."

Jessica nodded, her heart sinking with anxiety as she braced herself for the truth she prayed wouldn't come.

"As you know, your husband was in a terrible car crash," Dr. Reyes explained gently. "Unfortunately, we found significant amounts of alcohol and drugs in his system. His injuries are severe, and his heart and liver are failing."

Jessica's breath was caught in her throat, her hand moving to clutch her chest as if trying to hold back the weight of the news.

"There's more," Dr. Reyes continued, his voice wavering. "Given the severity of his condition, if Adam doesn't show any signs of waking up within the next eight days, we would recommend taking him off life support. Even if he wakes up after those days, his quality of life will significantly diminish. Ultimately, it will be your decision whether we continue or not."

A heavy silence fell upon the room as Jessica absorbed the gravity of Dr. Reyes' words. She glanced at Adam, her eyes welling up with more tears. Through the grief and disbelief, she felt some resentment towards him for putting her into this heart-wrenching situation. She bowed her head and prayed for clarity about why he would do this and why God would allow it.

Dr. Reyes stood quietly, giving Jessica time to process the grim news. His gaze shifted to the monitors beside Adam's bed, their steady beeping a harsh reminder of the delicate balance between life and death.

"Is there any hope at all?" Jessica finally whispered, her voice cracking with desperation. "Is there anything we can do?"

Dr. Reyes sighed, the weight of his responsibility evident in his eyes. "We are doing everything we can. Sometimes, patients in Adam's condition can wake up, but it's rare. The next few days are crucial. If there's no improvement, we must consider whether or not your husband would want to stay like this."

Jessica nodded, though her mind was a storm of confusion and fear. She clung to Adam's hand, squeezing it as if sheer willpower could bring him back to her. "Thank you, Dr. Reyes," she managed to say, her voice barely above a whisper.

"I'll be back to check on him later," Dr. Reyes said softly. "If you need anything or have any questions, please don't hesitate to ask."

As Dr. Reyes left the room, Jessica leaned closer to Adam, her tears soaking into the bed sheets. She pressed her forehead against his hand, her sobs muffled by the sterile hospital air. The weight of the decision ahead felt unbearable, her love for her husband clashing with the harsh reality of his condition.

"I don't understand why this happened, Adam," she whispered through her tears. "But I need you to fight. If there's ever been a time for you to fight for me, it's now. Mi amor, please come back to me." Her voice broke as she cried out, "Please, God, I can't do this without him!"

The room was silent except for the soft beeping of the machines, a stark contrast to the turmoil in Jessica's heart. She prayed for a miracle, for any sign that Adam would return to her. All she could do now was wait, hope, and cling to the love that had once brought them together.

...

Jessica has been on my mind more than ever. I can't see or hear her, but I feel her presence like a ghost haunting my thoughts. Knowing her, she is sitting by my bedside, holding my hand and hoping I'll wake up. The idea of her suffering because of me is almost unbearable.

Her laughter, her smile, how she looks at me with such love… Oh my God. What have I done?

She is my glimmer of hope, and today, I need to hold onto that. Eight more days… I need you to be strong for eight more days. Please, sweetheart. I'm fighting for you, for us.

…

I was lying in bed staring at the ceiling when the angel's voice resonated softly in my mind, breaking through the haze of my thoughts. "You are making commendable progress, Adam. Your younger self is slowly beginning to place his trust in you."

I felt some relief, but the task still felt overwhelming. "Thanks, man. I appreciate you saying that."

The angel paused, clearly puzzled. "Man…? Adam, I am not what you mortals would refer to as male."

My eyes squinted in confusion as I positioned myself on the edge of the bed. "Wait... you're a woman?"

"No," the angel clarified, "I am a ball of divine energy. I have no gender."

"So, you're non-binary?" I asked, trying to grasp the concept.

"Non-binary?" the angel asked, confused. "What does that mean?"

I sighed, trying to explain. "It's a term for people who don't identify strictly as male or female. It's about gender fluidity."

"But..." the angel's confusion now more evident. "I'm not a liquid. I just told you I am a divine ball of energy. Are you not listening?"

I shook my head, a bit baffled. "It's not about liquids. It's about understanding that not everything fits into male or female categories. How do you not know this?"

"Because angels do not think like mortals," the angel said patiently. "We do not adhere to the same biology. We are created to serve the Lord. That is our sole purpose."

I chuckled and responded, "More like your SOUL purpose?" I nodded, chuckling at my own joke.

The angel's confusion deepened. "I... Is there a significance I am missing?"

I sighed and dropped the subject, realizing we weren't getting anywhere. "Forget it. So, it's weird calling you 'Angel' all the time. Do you have a name?"

"Yes, I do," the angel responded confidently.

There was an uncomfortable pause. I think the angel believed its response was enough to answer my question.

"So..." I asked awkwardly, "Are you going to tell me your name?"

"You wouldn't be able to comprehend it," the angel said, its tone hinting at a warning I didn't pick up on.

"Comprehend?" I responded, almost insulted. "How hard could it be to understand a sound?"

The angel sighed. "Very well..."

Suddenly, my surroundings erupted in a blinding flash of white light. It was so intense it felt like it seared into my soul, leaving me completely blinded. My ears were assaulted by a high-pitched ringing that drowned out everything else. I'd experienced flashbangs in video games, but this was much worse than they made it look.

My stomach churned violently with nausea so intense I thought I would pass out. It felt like my brain had sunk into my gut, and I was on the brink of losing consciousness. I had no control over my limbs or even my own breathing. What was happening to me?

To call it overwhelming would be an understatement. My heart pounded in my chest, and every instinct screamed for me to brace myself... but there was nothing to hold onto. Thankfully, the blinding white light slowly faded, and the ringing in my ears began to diminish.

As my senses gradually returned, my nausea subsided, and my disorientation faded, and I regained control of my body. I frantically moved my hands over my eyes, trying to brush away the residual light while processing the aftermath of what had just happened. The last thing I could remember was... No... There's no way...

"Impossible!" My voice trembled with panic and irritation. "That's not a name; that's a weapon of mass destruction! No, no, NO! A name should be short and sweet, easy to say and remember, not the verbal equivalent of the Death Note!"

Continuing my verbal onslaught to the angel, I said, "Do you have any idea how that felt!? My eyes are still burning, and my ears are ringing like I spent the day next to a speaker at a rock concert! And my stomach – oh my god – what were you thinking!?"

Still tense and shaking, "How could you just... ugh!" I yelled while stomping the ground furiously. "Listen to me! Have you ever fought Marlboro in a Final Fantasy game? You pretty much hit me with Bad Breath, an attack that inflicts every single status effect in the game!"

"Would you mind explaining that to me?" the angel asked, its tone filled with genuine confusion.

Still angry, I replied, "Poison, paralysis, slow, silence, confusion, sleep, and I'm pretty sure you reduced my max health!"

"I warned you," the angel continued, its voice steady. "You would not be able to comprehend it. I understand you believe otherwise, but I foresaw this outcome. Hence, I refrained from uttering my full name. It would have been catastrophic for you."

Still furious with disbelief, I yelled, "You didn't say your full name...to avoid catastrophe? That's your answer!? Well, I guess your influence over humans really does have its limits. Somewhere between

64

their conscience telling them right from wrong and THE FULL CONCENTRATED POWER OF THE HEAVENS!

Without warning, a warm aura started enveloping me, similar to the comforting sensation I felt on that fateful night in the hospital. While it only lasted a few seconds, it felt like an eternity. As the aura faded, the pain, disorientation, and some of my frustrations vanished, leaving me feeling better. Healthier. Somewhat happier.

"What just happened?" I asked.

"You were getting cranky, so I healed you," the angel quickly replied.

"What? You can do that!?" I asked, completely surprised.

"Yes," the angel explained. "Even though my power has limitations, I can do more in the spirit realm. Now, please, continue to calm down before we go on."

I tried to relax by taking deep breaths, attempting to regain my composure. This angel was full of surprises, each more insane than the last. As I inhaled slowly, I couldn't help but wonder what else it was capable of.

"What happened to you was intense," the angel continued. "But I'll try harder to warn you from now on if you're overstepping to the point of hurting yourself."

"Just... promise me you won't ever do that again," I said.

"Very well, I promise. By the way, you can call me Freckles."

"Freckles?" I bursted out laughing. "You want me to call you Freckles? That's such a dorky name." I kept repeating the name in a mocking tone.

Suddenly, I heard the television turn on. My attention snapped to it, and there on the screen was a familiar item from my past: a stuffed animal from my childhood – a cute golden retriever I had named Freckles. The scene shifted, showing me as a three-year-old receiving it from my preschool teacher. I hugged it tightly and ran around the room, overjoyed. That little golden retriever became my constant companion, a source of comfort and happiness I carried everywhere.

The scene changed again to me playing outside with my friends. Freckles sat on the front porch, always facing my direction, a silent guardian of my childhood adventures.

As I continued to watch these memories unfold on the television, I landed on one I never forgot. It was my cousin's third birthday, and I was seven years old. She picked up Freckles and hugged it tightly, her eyes lighting up with pure joy. At that moment, I decided it was time to let Freckles go and tell her she could have it. Her tears of happiness as she hugged and thanked me repeatedly left a permanent mark on my heart. Seeing her experience the same joy Freckles had brought me was a profound moment of connection and love I will always cherish.

The television turned off, leaving only the bittersweet smile on my face.

"Freckles..." I whispered, the name slipping out before I even realized it.

"What is it?" the angel responded quietly.

I could barely speak after reliving the happiness of those cherished memories. "Why did you show me that?" I asked, my voice choked with emotion.

"It was to show you that I have always been there with you," the angel explained gently. "And most importantly, you requested a more easily comprehended name."

A wave of warmth washed over me, mingling with the remnants of nostalgia. "You've really been with me all this time?" I asked, feeling a strange mix of comfort and awe.

"Yes," the angel replied, its tone filled with a gentle certainty. "Through every moment of joy and every trial, I've been by your side, guiding and protecting you, whether you could see me or not. And now, I am here to help you heal."

I nodded, feeling a newfound connection to the presence that had always been with me, even when I didn't realize it. "Thank you," I whispered, finally beginning to understand the depth of our bond.

Freckles gave me a moment to bask in the joy of those memories. "Shall we continue?" Freckles asked reassuringly.

"Yes," I managed to say, still feeling the warmth spread through me. Almost on cue, my phone buzzed with a new message from my younger self.

Hey. I'm here.

Good morning.
How's the garage treating you?

It always treats me well. I have a sofa, workout bench, laptop, and a Dreamcast.
What more could I ask for?

And the icing on the cake: Marvel Vs. Capcom 2's soundtrack in the background?

Marvel Vs. Capcom 2 was one of my favorite games on the SEGA Dreamcast. I was terrible at the game, but I loved the soundtrack. I can still picture myself in the garage, sitting on the worn-out sofa, the hum of the Dreamcast in the air. I'd load up the game and let my favorite songs play in sound test mode, and the catchy tunes would echo through the cluttered space. It's wild that twenty years later, I still listen to video game music while I work.

Seriously, how do you know these things?

The real question is how I know such an unnecessary detail.

Yeah? Well, if you know so much, which song is currently playing?

68

I'm not in the garage, so I don't know.
But I can tell you that the swamp stage is your
favorite song.

It's the training stage.

No. It's the swamp stage.

No, wait...
The training stage is playing now.
But yeah, you're right about the swamp stage.
Look, I believe you.

I'm happy to hear that.

You're me from the future.
This is so cool!
I have so many questions!
But...what do I even call you? Us...?

Let's make it easier on ourselves.
I'm you from twenty years in the future. You can call
me Thirty-six, and I will call you Sixteen. Or if it's
easier, just use a pronoun.

Pronouns. Okay.
So, Big Adam?

That would be a proper noun.

Sorry.
I don't know what a pronoun is.

Yes, you do, just not by name.
Pronouns are he/him/she/her/they/them/you.

Ah. Got it.

Remember this because it will become crucial in
about ten years.

Wait... what?

Don't ask. Just trust me.

69

*It's starting to sound like WE become a SHE in the
future. You opened the door, so I have to ask.
Do we?*

*No, we don't.
We'll always be male, and we have no desire to
change our gender.*

Cool. That's good to know.

*I was honestly expecting you to say something
extremely homophobic just now.*

*I don't know what that word means.
Honestly, I'm just happy we don't turn into some gay
tranny.*

At that moment, I realized I hadn't corrected Sixteen's inappropriate comment during our last conversation. To be fair, it was our first talk, and I was figuring things out. But now that I'm making progress, it's time to start teaching my past self some lessons.

It's still hard to believe that I used to talk like this when I was younger. But that's the thing about growth. It's not just about moving forward: it's about looking back, understanding different perspectives, acknowledging mistakes, and striving to improve. As long as we keep these truths in mind, change isn't just possible – it's inevitable.

And there it is...

What?

It would be best if you didn't speak like that.

It was just a joke.

Oh, I know. It may seem like a joke, but I'm telling
you that words matter.
And the ones you picked are hurtful.

But I am glad that we don't become some gay
tranny! I would never want to do that!
That's gay, and I don't want to be like that.

I get what you're saying, and I know you aren't
trying to be malicious.
But listen to me.
The world changes. People don't like being spoken
about negatively like that. The reality is that
sometimes, people are gay.

Yes, people are very gay sometimes.
Like today... I was riding my bike to the store when
this guy pulled out of his driveway without looking
and almost hit me!
I'm sure he's oozing with gay.
Horrendously gay.

Boy, if you say one more thing that is out of pocket...

Freckles interrupted my focus. "Did Sixteen just say, 'horrendously gay?'" Freckles asked, sounding thoroughly entertained. "How is this not surprising to you?"

"Because," I replied with disappointment, "I work around kids enough to know that once they learn a new word, they'll find ways to upgrade their arsenal of insults."

"'Arsenal of insults?'" Freckles repeated. "That sounds serious."

"Yeah, well, if you didn't have jokes in the lunchroom, you were done for," I sighed.

"You make it sound like the Wild West," Freckles remarked.

"It may as well have been. Only the strongest survived," I replied, shaking my head at the memory.

Okay, okay. Sorry.

We never felt the need to change our gender.
But some people do.
The part you don't seem to understand is that people who do change can be harassed or even killed for feeling that way.

Wait, wait.
Who would kill someone for being gay?

A lot of people.
Not everyone is as accepting as you think.
It's happening even now in your timeline, but you don't hear about it.

Why isn't this being talked about?

If people don't know about it, then they have nothing to be upset about.
Listen... I know your heart. I know you'd accept anyone, mainly because stuff like that doesn't affect you.
But not everyone thinks like you.
When you speak like that, you're permitting others to act the same way, and as you know, words often lead to actions.

I think I get what you're saying.
All right. I'll try to stop calling things gay.
But I still don't want to become like RuPaul in the future.

Do you mean drag?

No, a... T-word.

72

RuPaul isn't transgender.
He's a drag queen.
Not the same thing.

What's the difference?

I sighed, feeling a mix of uncertainty and responsibility. "I'm all for correcting Sixteen's behavior, but this topic is dragging on longer than I'm comfortable with," I told Freckles. "I'm not gay or transgender, and I feel like it's not my place to speak for them, especially to a kid who barely gets what's going on. It's not even that relevant right now."

Freckles paused for a moment, its tone thoughtful. "Actually, this has been prevalent for a long time, Adam. The history of LGBTQ rights extends back even before the 20th century. It was simply not as openly discussed as it is today."

I squinted my eyes, trying to process Freckles' words. "Really? I always thought it was a more recent thing."

"Yes," Freckles confirmed. "It is currently gaining a lot of traction in Sixteen's timeline."

I leaned back, reflecting on that. "That's interesting to know. I wonder why it wasn't taught to us."

Freckles' voice carried a hint of amusement. "There's much that goes untaught in your world. Different perspectives, suppressed histories, and ignored truths."

I nodded slowly. "Yeah, you might be right. But... how do you even know all of this? Earlier, you didn't even know what genderfluidity was."

"Correct. You were also unaware I could heal you earlier," Freckles stated calmly.

"I... How does that answer my question? I pressed.

"If you must know, I took the time to learn about it after our conversation," Freckles replied.

"I refuse to believe that. We were talking the entire time. There's no way you learned that much in just a few minutes," I argued, shaking my head in disbelief.

"Do you recall, there is no space-time continuum for angels," Freckles explained.

My patience wearing thin, I snapped, "Enough with the space force stuff! Just tell me how—"

"I can disorient you simply by saying my name," Freckles interrupted, his voice stern. "Do you truly find it hard to believe my powers could involve time manipulation?"

"But... ugh... fine," I conceded, realizing how ridiculous it was to doubt an angel's abilities.

"Good. Listen to me, Adam. It isn't your role to speak on behalf of the LGBT community. They're perfectly capable of speaking for themselves. You're doing your part by creating a safe space and not tolerating mistreatment in front of you," Freckles advised.

"I guess you have a point," I said, feeling more confident.

Transgender means you identify as a different gender than the one you were assigned at birth. Drag is a performance art where people dress up and often exaggerate gender roles for entertainment. Think of it like putting on a costume for a play, but it doesn't change who you are underneath.

I don't know what to do with this information.

Trivia fun fact?

Sure.
Anyway, it's just hard for me to understand why someone would kill another person for being gay. Seriously like, who cares if someone is gay?

Again, not everyone thinks the way you do.

You know what's crazy to me?

What?

We're always told that the best way to avoid trouble is to stay in our lane and mind our business. We saw nothing. We heard nothing.

Right...

But from what you're saying, people are way too interested in whether or not someone is gay: like it's contagious or something.

I agree with you.
Some people are too interested in an aspect of
someone's life that doesn't affect them.

Exactly!
It just sounds so stupid to me.
There are so many reasons to be a jerk to someone.
Why pick something they can't control?

That was oddly profound, especially coming from my younger self.

I think you're correct.
Needlessly mean but correct.

It reminds me of how the police treat us.
You know, black people.

Yes and no.
Mostly no.

Why "mostly no?"

You can hide being gay.
You can't hide being black.

Wow. That's accurate.
I never thought of it like that.

You've never had to.
But you'll learn a lot of cool stuff as you get older.

Good to know!
So, are there any other words I shouldn't use?

That is also something you'll learn as you get older.

"When you get older." Everyone keeps telling me
that. You can't just tell me now?

No.

But wouldn't a head start be nice?

I'm not having this conversation. I told you that you shouldn't say certain words and why. That should be more than enough.

Come on! Please?

I sighed, feeling a wave of frustration. I couldn't help but think back to my teenage years. I remembered similarly pestering my older brother Zack, constantly pushing for answers and never satisfied with a simple 'no.'

Freckles' voice pierced through my thoughts. "Aren't you glad we aren't dealing with this persistence face-to-face?"

I laughed, though a bit embarrassed by the thought. "Yes, I am. But there's a difference between being persistent and annoying, and this kid is flirting with the latter."

*I've already told you no.
Stepping over people's boundaries will only push them away.
I'm speaking from experience here.*

SOMEBODY is in a bad mood!

*Yes, I am.
You have the opportunity of a lifetime to talk to your future self.
Instead of asking good questions that could change the outcome of your life, you choose to waste it by acting like an idiot.*

"You're being a bit harsh right now," Freckles said, its voice resonating in my mind like a calming yet stern echo. "You might want to temper your approach before you scare him off."

"Relax. I know myself. It'll be okay. Just trust and believe," I responded, taking a deep breath and trying to ground myself in the moment.

"JuSt TrUsT aNd BeLiEvE," Freckles mocked, its voice attempting a sarcastic tone. It was funny hearing an angel attempt to imitate human frustration.

I closed my eyes, letting the memories of my younger self flood back. I remembered the constant restlessness, the needless disrespect of others' boundaries, and never taking anything seriously. It was like a film reel in my mind, scenes of me skipping classes, joking around, and ignoring advice.

Honestly, it reminded me of the younger students I help now. Their faces blur together, each one a mix of potential and recklessness. Knowing I've made a difference in their lives gave me a much-needed confidence boost.

"Alright," I said, more to myself than Freckles, "let's give him a dose of reality. He needs to hear this, even if it hurts."

Freckles' warmth enveloped me like a gentle blanket of reassurance, a reminder of its constant support. "Proceed, but tread carefully."

One word.
Just give me one, and I'll stop.

Apathy.

What does that mean?

It's the opposite of empathy.

Okay, what does empathy mean?

It means putting yourself in another person's position and trying to see and feel things from that person's perspective.

So, apathy is the lack of interest in other people. I do not see how that is a bad word.

Oh, it can be. See, I get to return to 2003, and instead of enjoying the scenery, I'm stuck entertaining a kid who almost dies in two years.

Wait, what?

I have your attention now. Good.

This joke isn't funny.

Know what else isn't funny? The fact that you don't take things seriously until it's too late.

That's not true.

It is… and I'll tell you why. Fear.

Fear?

You're a people pleaser. You're so afraid of letting people down that you can barely take action without their approval.

Nonsense.

Is it, though? People don't expect much when they ask you to do something because you can't seem to do the task unless it's done the exact way someone tells you to

79

do it.
You're so afraid of letting people down that you let
people perceive you as a kind-hearted, lovable idiot.
The truth is you know that if you don't try, you can't
fail.

The air around me felt cold as Freckles' voice cut through my focus.
"Adam! Cease this, now!"

I pretended not to hear them. I knew what I was doing and continued
to focus on the screen.

Stop!
I'm calling the cops if you don't tell me!

Do it.

Don't test me!
I mean it!

Please, I want you to.

I'm calling them now.

I can already hear the call.
"Officer! Some random guy on the internet claims to
be me from the future!
He said I almost die two years from now, but he
won't tell me how! Make him tell me how!"

Damn it!
You can't just drop a bomb on me like that and not
say anything!

Watch me.

Look...I'm sorry. I really am.
It's scary enough that you're some random guy
online who seems to know me.

You're not sorry at all.
But you will be with what I tell you next.

What?

The older you become, the more patient you are with
the things you care about and the less patient you
are with the things you don't.
I hated myself at your age. So, the next time you talk,
keep this in your mind.
If you EVER act like that again, I will walk away
from you like so many others have.

I'm sorry.

It would be best if you did much less talking and
more listening. You have a fantastic opportunity in
front of you. Use it wisely.

You're right. I'm sorry.
I truly am.

Don't be sorry. Be better.
Start by listening.

I felt the irony of my words. I told my younger self to stop talking and listen more while doing the opposite with my guardian angel. I should probably be more patient.

"Yes, you absolutely should," Freckles said, seemingly out of nowhere, interrupting my thoughts.

I squinted, trying to figure out what Freckles was referring to.

"Be more patient," Freckles said calmly. "Did you forget I can read your mind?"

"Oh yeah," I nodded slowly. "About that. I noticed that sometimes, you don't always know what is happening in my head. Why is that?"

"To simplify, I am not constantly reading your mind. It isn't automatic. I must actively connect my essence to yours," Freckles clarified.

"...I know you thought that was a good answer, but Freckles... every time you explain something, you always leave me with more questions," I said, feeling disheartened.

"Do you question how Santa Claus perceives you while you're sleeping?" Freckles responded.

"Santa isn't real!" I retorted, annoyance in my voice.

"Indeed, he is. I observe him every year on the Lord's son's birthday," Freckles said, attempting to sound serious, but I could sense they were holding back a laugh.

I let out a sigh and remained silent. The sigh was heavy enough for its weight to linger in the air.

Freckles sensed the shift, realizing I knew they were joking. "...Yes, I jest. Good observation," Freckles admitted, their tone lightening. "Adam. You did well. It sounds like Sixteen is going to try harder to listen now.

"Thanks," I said, my voice full of genuine gratitude. "Back then, all anyone ever did was yell at me. Most of the time, I wasn't even told what I did wrong..." I looked down, a bit saddened by the memories.

"I recall those days... But the past is the past. Look at how far you've come," Freckles said gently.

"You're right." I cracked a smile. "I just have to remember that it isn't about me... well, sort of. You get what I'm trying to say!"

Do you mean doing what other people tell me to do?

No.
Listening to someone and doing what they say are two completely different things.
You can listen to someone's perspective and completely disagree with it. That's okay. But at least hear them out and give them the same respect they're giving you.

What if the other person isn't listening to me?
I'm sure you know that people not caring about anything I have to say is...kind of common.

A conversation is a two-way street.
If only one person is listening, then it's probably not a conversation worth having.

I never looked at it that way.
It sounds like you have a lot to teach.
I want to learn.

I said I was here to give you someone to talk to.
What would you like to know?

Before I ask, I need to know.
If we talk, will it change you?

Like… If you were to give me a sports almanac from
your timeline, wouldn't that make you rich?

"Is *Back to the Future* really the movie that defined time travel?" I
asked Freckles, my voice containing a hint of disbelief.

"The evidence would suggest so," Freckles replied with calm certainty.
"Though it puzzles me, considering the movie is a prime example of
the bootstrap paradox."

"What's the 'bootstrap paradox?'" I asked, unfamiliar with the term.

"Do you recall when Marty played Chuck Berry's music at the
dance?" Freckles asked, their tone patient as though guiding me to a
realization.

"Yeah, of course," I replied, instantly picturing the scene where
Michael J. Fox tore it up with that wild guitar solo at his parents' prom.
"As an adult, I can now appreciate him saying, 'You aren't ready for
this, but your kids are going to love it.'"

"Too many details, Adam," Freckles said, a hint of amusement in their
voice. "Focus on this: where did Marty learn that song?"

"From MTV, I guess? Chuck Berry was already famous in his time," I
replied, trying to keep up.

"Okay, MTV works," Freckles continued thoughtfully. "So Marty
learned it by watching Chuck Berry perform it on MTV. Would you
agree with that statement?"

"Yeah, that sounds about right," I said, still trying to piece it together. "Marty learned Chuck Berry's music from MTV. Okay, and?"

"But didn't Chuck Berry just learn the music from Marty?" Freckles asked, their voice calm yet pointed.

My brain froze as I tried to untangle the knot Freckles had just tied. "Wait... so in that timeline, Marty influenced Chuck Berry's music: by playing music he learned from Chuck Berry... But then Chuck Berry learned that music from Marty... Son of a—"

"Exactly," Freckles interrupted with quiet satisfaction. "There's no clear beginning. That's the bootstrap paradox. This is precisely why I'm so surprised you mortals used this movie as your foundation for explaining time travel."

"I guess even in the afterlife, you'll learn something new every day," I admitted, feeling the complexity of the concept sink in.

Freckles' voice cut in, a hint of confusion lacing its tone. "Afterlife? Adam, you're not dead. Why do you keep saying that?"

I threw up my hands, clearly irritated. "I get it! Okay!? I get it. You know what I meant."

> *Nice reference. But, that's not how time travel works. I had the same question when I got here. I was told that Disney and Marvel had it right. The information I give you will have some influence on your timeline, but nothing you do will affect mine. You will experience most of the things that I did.*

Disney and Marvel???

It'll make sense later on.
Please, don't think about it too much.

I'll try.
So... about that sports almanac.

No.

I had to try, haha!
Hey...
Can you tell me how I almost die?
Please?

I don't know if you can handle it.

I think I can.
You said almost, right?

Correct.

I want to know.
Tell me.

Take tonight to think about it, and if you still feel the
same way, I'll tell you tomorrow.

Okay then.
Yesterday, you said you would be here for a little
while. How long is a "little while?"

Eight more days.
After that, you'll never see me ever again.

I'm sure I'll see you in the future.

No, you won't.
Disney and Marvel.

I still don't know what that means.

You'll find out later.
Let's continue this tomorrow. I gave you a lot of

information. Plus, I want to look around town and reflect on the differences in my timeline. Text me tomorrow, okay?

Will do.
But... Do you think it is a good idea to walk around town as me?
Do I look that much different in the future?

You still look like you, but older. But that's irrelevant because I'm not you in this timeline.

What?

Disney and Marvel.
Any questions about time travel, just assume the answer is Disney and Marvel.
Everything will be fine.
Just text me tomorrow.

Are you sure about this?

Yes, I am.

Okay, I trust you.

Good.
Tomorrow?

Tomorrow.
Adios, A-me-go!

...No.

Freckles' voice resonated in my mind with disbelief and admiration. "I can't believe how well you handled that. I thought Sixteen would block you for being as harsh as others."

"I know myself well enough to know that if I'm being scolded, I'll stop listening... unless you give me a good reason to," I said, yawning. "Man, I forgot how mentally exhausting it is dealing with kids. But hey, we did great today! We might even be done before the deadline!"

"You're overly confident for a man who got overwhelmed by life," Freckles said lightheartedly.

I knew Freckles was joking, but those words hit like a sucker punch. My jaw tightened, and I shot back, "You're a jerk for that one." I shook my head in disbelief.

Freckles immediately backpedaled. "Hey… that was—"

I cut them off, frustration boiling over like a simmering pot. "How do I shut you off?" I said while lightly slapping my head, hoping for an off switch.

Freckles sighed softly. "I apologize. Truly, I'm sorry. That was uncalled for," Freckles' voice softened. "In the spirit realm, guardian angels often discuss their mortals and their questionable actions. This probably doesn't help, but I've voiced far worse critiques about you. I'm still adjusting to the fact that you can hear me."

"'Questionable things?' Do you honestly think you can understand what it's like to be human?" I asked.

"You keep forgetting that I can see and feel everything you do. So, yes, more than you realize," Freckles replied, their tone steady and knowing.

"Seems like you're just confusing empathy for arrogance," I shot back.

Freckles replied, its tone unwavering, "And it seems you use your own sense of morality to dictate how angels should act. Allow me to clarify in terms you'll grasp: The way angels discuss their mortals is akin to how educators talk about their students. You may drive us to frustration at times, but ultimately, you are ours, and we desire what is best for you."

I stayed silent for a moment, trying to make sense of Freckles' words, the air in the room feeling heavier with each passing second.

"Do you want to know what I truly think of you?" Freckles asked, its voice soft like a nurturing parent.

I stayed silent, rolling my eyes.

"I regard you as a brilliant mortal with a heart of gold. You often doubt yourself, but once that doubt is lifted, you become determined to excel at whatever you set your mind to. You are a tactical genius, a jack of all trades, and you possess so much humility that you don't even know that many of your loved ones perceive you as a hero. That's why I was surprised when you decided to take your own life," Freckles said, his voice carrying a mix of admiration and sorrow.

I stayed silent, shaking my head. But I knew that Freckles was right. I honestly can't even remember why I decided to take my own life that night. But whatever the reason, I haven't stopped regretting it since I realized I might not see Jessica again.

"It was painful to watch you drink that much alcohol. A whole bottle of tequila in one sitting would have killed most mortals, but you consumed it all, along with several other drinks. You should be dead, but I pleaded with the Lord to keep you safe... at least for the time being," Freckles said firmly.

I kept thinking about Freckles' words. I wanted to stay mad, but I knew they were right.

"I'm not supposed to tell you this," Freckles said, a note of reluctance in its voice, "but you've seen me before."

"...When?" I asked, trying to let go of my anger.

"You were five years old, sleeping in an unfamiliar room, and shadowy figures kept appearing," Freckles recalled.

My mind immediately went back to that moment. I was five, sleeping in a room my young mind called "Dracula's Castle." I saw a shadowy figure moving towards me whenever I looked at the door. Straight ahead, a mirror on the wall reflected a shadowy knight on a horse flying towards me. I didn't understand it then, but it stuck with me. A core – but maybe not entirely pointless – memory.

I slowly nodded. "...Every time the figures got close, I'd close my eyes and—"

"They'd reset and start moving from their starting position," Freckles and I said simultaneously.

"Yes," Freckles said. "You were so scared... but then you looked to your right and saw a small white glowing statue of a mortal with wings. One hand held a sword proudly in the air, and the other held a sturdy shield in front of its heart. That sight completely dispelled your fear, and you went to sleep."

"That was you...?" I asked, my disbelief evident.

"Yes, that was me. We aren't supposed to show ourselves, but you were a mere child. Who would believe that you, a mere child, saw an actual angel?"

"You're right. But I have to ask... Do you still look like that? You know... less than a foot tall?" I questioned.

"I do not have a physical appearance. If I were to compare it to anything, the closest would be the air you breathe," Freckles replied.

"But... How did I see you then?" I asked.

"I can take on whatever form I want," Freckles explained. "The Lord gives us a fraction of His power, and we use it to protect our mortals."

"So... where were you the night that I... you know...?" I asked, my mind swirling with the fragments of that night.

"I was there with you," Freckles replied, its tone reassuring.

"Weren't you supposed to be protecting me?" I questioned, confusion mingling in my voice.

"I did... more than you know," Freckles responded patiently.

"How so?" I pressed, needing clarity.

"Your last memory was being in the hospital, correct?" Freckles prompted, guiding my thoughts.

My memory shifted back to the hospital staff trying to save my life. I could hear doctors and nurses yelling about how much blood I was losing. I replayed the scene in my head a few times, leaving me with a nagging question.

"Freckles... what happened that night?" I asked, confusion creeping in. "I don't remember doing anything that would have caused me to lose that much blood. At least, not enough to be a concern."

"You were in a... 'car accident,'" Freckles said, clearly emphasizing the words as if they held a deeper meaning.

"Why did you say, 'car accident' like that?" I asked, suspicion creeping into my thoughts.

"Because it wasn't an 'accident,'" Freckles revealed, the words echoing through all the corners of my mind.

I nearly froze upon hearing the news. My heart pounded out of my chest, and I struggled to keep my tears in check. The room seemed to close in around me as the weight of the revelation hit me. My breath came in shallow gasps, and a knot tightened in my throat. I tried to hold back the flood of emotions, but the shock and confusion were overwhelming.

"Adam…" Freckles said, gently. "You were trying to end your life… and I was trying to protect you. Like I said earlier, the amount of alcohol you consumed should have killed you, but I kept you alive by talking to the Lord and putting my powers on the line for you."

I slowly nodded, acknowledging that I had heard its words.

"After what you consumed didn't kill you, you decided to go to the liquor store and buy more. Unfortunately, you crashed on the way there," Freckles explained, its words painting a grim picture of that night.

My voice still barely above a whisper, I asked, "Freckles… Does Jessica know what happened?" The pain of the revelation made it hard to get the words out.

"Adam…" Freckles said softly. "The Lord's word states that I am only allowed to provide information for the realm that you are in. You have already crossed to the spirit realm."

"Please," I begged, tears threatening to spill over. "You've corrected me enough times that I know I'm not dead yet. So please, Freckles. Tell me. You don't have to give me any details about how she is doing…how she is holding up because of all this. But I'm begging you, Freckles… Please, tell me if she knows what I did."

Freckles paused, and for a moment, the silence was suffocating. "Adam," it said gently, "Jessica knows. She pieced it together. "

The tears I had been holding back finally spilled over, and I broke down, overwhelmed by the weight of it all.

I started this mission thinking Sixteen was just some foolish kid I had to teach everything to. But the further along I progressed, the more I realized that the most intelligent people are the ones who understand they don't know everything... Turns out, I'm an even bigger idiot than I thought.

Jessica... You admitted that one thing you've always loved about me is that I never turn down a challenge. When I asked you to marry me, I knew you were out of my league, but I promised to spend every day of my life trying to meet your expectations. I'm sorry that I let you down...

Chapter 4

The camera panned across the bustling newsroom, capturing the madness of journalists typing franticly, phones ringing relentlessly, and urgent conversations filling the air. Erika Gardner, a seasoned reporter committed to professionalism and integrity, stood at the center.

As the red light blinked on, signaling the start of the live broadcast, Erika's focus sharpened. Her expression steeled with determination as she prepared to relay the day's events. She detailed the latest breaking news: a tragic car accident that had shocked the community. Her voice was steady, and each word was carefully chosen to convey the severity of the situation.

"Good evening, I'm Erika Gardner with tonight's breaking news," she began. "A tragic car accident has left one man in critical condition. The victim, identified as Adam Grey, was involved in a severe collision late last night."

As she spoke Adam's name, her heart skipped a beat. Memories of their childhood flooded her mind, but she forced herself to continue. "Adam Grey, an educator and mentor in the community, is currently on life support at Grimbley Memorial Hospital."

The words felt like daggers in her throat, each cutting deeper as she struggled to maintain her composure. "Grey has been an influential figure, particularly for teenagers and young adults, helping guide them through life's many challenges. His condition is critical, and doctors are doing everything they can."

She finished the report, her professional demeanor intact, but as soon as the camera light dimmed, signaling the end of the broadcast, Erika let out a shaky breath. She turned away from the set, tears welling up in her eyes.

In the perpetual chaos of the studio, memories of Adam rushed in – his boyish grin when they first met in elementary school, the awkward but sincere way he confessed his feelings for her, and the laughter they shared when she gently let him down. She remembered his steadfast presence at her wedding, the joy on his face when he met her children, and the countless times he had been there for her over the years.

"I'm sorry, Adam. God knows I tried my best to make time to see you," she whispered to herself, regret tightening in her chest. She had known Adam was struggling. It was evident in their brief conversations. She had always meant to visit and offer her support, but her demanding career had a way of isolating her from the most important aspects of her life.

A tear slipped down her cheek as she bowed her head, hands clasped tightly. "Please, God, take care of him," she prayed, her voice barely above a whisper. "He needs your protection right now, whatever that may look like. And if I'm being honest, God… so do I."

Erika stayed there, silently praying for her best friend, her heart heavy with regret and a desperate hope that Adam would pull through.

...

I woke up to a new day but was surprised because I didn't remember falling asleep. All I could think about was Jessica. Was she angry with me? Did she hate me now? I hate these feelings because I'm powerless to change anything right now. All I can do is take solace in knowing that none of this will matter if Freckles and I can't complete this mission. Just seven more days.

...

After tossing off the covers, I sat up and glanced at the small basement window. There wasn't much of a view – just grass and a sliver of sunlight – but I could usually tell the time by the amount of natural light filtering in.

"The dawn has its own charm, does it not?" Freckles said, breaking the silence.

Startled, I blinked and replied, "Yeah, it does. I wasn't expecting to hear from you so early."

"Allow me to echo your statement from the other day," Freckles said confidently. "The optimal time to begin was yesterday, the next best opportunity is today."

All I could do was shake my head slowly, cringing at how embarrassing that sounded. Freckles wasn't incorrect in what they said, but wow. Something about the way they say it just sounds so wrong.

"Freckles..." I mumbled, still groggy. "It's too early for this."

"It is never too early for optimism," Freckles replied enthusiastically.

"That's not what I meant... Never mind." I sighed, conceding. "There's something on my mind I was hoping to talk with you about."

"Oh? What is it?" Freckles asked, its voice filled with attentive curiosity.

I took a moment to find the words. "I don't want to sound ungrateful..." I hesitated, reluctant to ask. "I understand that I drank a lot that night, and you kept me alive by talking with God. But... wouldn't it have been easier to just stop the car from starting?"

"Technically, yes. But that would involve me violating your gift of free will," Freckles regretfully stated.

"In what regard?" I questioned.

"Intervening directly to prevent your actions would undermine the free will granted to you," Freckles explained gently. "Our role is to guide and protect, not to control. Every choice, even the reckless ones, shapes who you are."

"So... if I choose to end my life, you wouldn't stop me because I made the choice?" I asked with genuine curiosity.

Freckles sighed. "It is not that I wouldn't stop you, but rather that I couldn't. I can influence your decisions and guide you away from harm, but I cannot outright prevent you from making your own choices."

"I suppose that makes sense," I said. "But I'm curious... how come—"

I was cut off by my phone buzzing with messages from Sixteen.

"It is alright, Adam. We will continue this conversation after our work today," Freckles assured.

I sighed, forcing myself to push my curiosity aside. "Okay. Let's get this over with."

I glanced at the screen, the messages from Sixteen already piling up. I couldn't help but wonder how this day was going to unfold. I couldn't help but feel guilty that I wanted today's conversation to end so I could speak more with Freckles.

I changed my mind.
I don't want to know how I will die.
Well, almost die.

Good morning to you, too.
What made you change your mind?

I asked a friend.
He told me if he had the opportunity to learn how he

would die, he wouldn't do it.
That's too much pressure.

> *It's not bad advice. I don't think I could handle that*
> *kind of pressure either.*
> *It's hard to enjoy life knowing the exact moment it*
> *will end.*
> *Or, in your case, change forever.*

Yeah! I knew I could trust Jack. It's good to know we
picked the correct answer!

I immediately thought about Jack, my best friend since seventh grade. It's funny – he once admitted that he was afraid of me before we met because I was bigger and more intimidating than most kids our age. But once we started talking, we clicked instantly and just never stopped. We first bonded over Pokémon, and over twenty-five years later, we now bond over his child and her love of Pokémon.

> *Jack usually has excellent advice. But this isn't*
> *about what Jack would do.*
> *It's about what you want to do.*

What do you mean?

> *You can't unlearn this.*
> *Knowing this will change how you approach the next*
> *two years of your life.*

Jack says no, so I probably shouldn't do it, right?

> *Again, it isn't about Jack.*
> *It's about you.*

I do...but I shouldn't... right?
What do you think I should do?

"I hate this," I muttered to Freckles. "I forgot how much I used to doubt myself."

Freckles responded gently, "I remember those days, Adam. To be fair, you're still an overthinker. But you've gained the confidence to trust your instincts more."

I let out a bitter laugh. "I'm still afraid of making certain decisions. But at least I've learned it's okay to be wrong."

"Maybe you should tell that to Sixteen instead of me," Freckles suggested.

"It's not that simple," I said, frustration creeping in. "At his age, there's so much unnecessary pressure to make the right choice. Our teachers made it sound like our decisions will define the rest of our lives. I remember it being so dramatic for no reason."

"Actions do have consequences, Adam," Freckles pointed out.

"I know," I replied. "But at his age, what action could Sixteen possibly take that would impact his life so much?"

There was a thoughtful pause before Freckles answered, "Need I remind you why we're here in Solitude, Adam?"

"...Please, don't. I get it," I conceded. "What do you recommend we do?"

"Stick to what you've been doing," Freckles advised. "Be open, honest, and vulnerable."

You're smarter than you think.

Does that mean I should pick yes?

It means that I want you to take a minute to breathe and think about the consequences.
If I tell you, this will change how you approach your life for the next two years.
If I don't tell you, you'll be wondering for the next two years and be blindsided.
There is no right or wrong answer here.

Okay.
I'll take a moment to think about it.

Freckles' voice echoed in my mind. "What do you think Sixteen will choose?"

"He wants to know the answer," I said confidently. "He's just waiting for permission to ask. It's like he's testing the waters, seeing if it's okay to voice his true thoughts."

Freckles responded with curiosity, "So, you believe he already has a choice in mind?"

I smiled, sure of my insight. "Definitely. I've always been like that – knowing what I want but needing a little push to admit it. And honestly, I'm still kind of like that."

Okay... I want to know.
Can you please tell me?

Why do you want to know?

Because you said, "almost."
I can handle "almost."

Very well.
You know how you're always complaining about a
lump in your throat? You keep trying to clear your
throat, but it never seems to work.

Yeah?
Isn't it just allergies?

No. That lump in your throat is cancerous, and it has
already started spreading.

How do I stop it?

You can't.

What do you mean I can't?
Exactly what is stopping me from going to the doctor
with this information?

I couldn't help but laugh, the sound echoing in the quiet space around
me.

Freckles' voice came through, curious. "What's so funny?"

Shaking my head and still chuckling, I said, "It's the irony of it all..."

You've been complaining about that lump in your
throat for years.
And every single time, your doctor told you it was
allergies or seasonal asthma. He never checked any
deeper than that.

You're lying!

103

I'm not lying to you.
Your doctor didn't diagnose your cancer because he
never considered it as an option. You survive
because a medical assistant remembers how you've
mentioned it several times and advised you to see a
specialist behind the doctor's back.

Cancer is NOT happening!
Give me one good reason I shouldn't block you for
this. This ISN'T FUNNY!

I'll give you two.
First, has anything I said to you been incorrect so
far?

No. But this is too much!
That's not fair!
I'm not supposed to die in two years!

But... you don't die?

Shut up!
Why would you tell me when I'm going to die!? I'm
still just a kid!

Can you calm down for one second?
I still have to give you my second reason.

This better be good.

I'm you from the future, right?

Supposedly.

You get cancer in two years.
But I'm you twenty years in the future.
The math ain't mathing here.

Get to your point.

...
I already did, but it went over your head.

104

Explain it again, then!

> *If you die in two years, that would mean you die in 2005.*

And?

> *How many years in the future am I?*

You could be using ghost magic!

> *Or... the more likely answer.*
> *YOU DON'T DIE FROM CANCER!*

Freckles' voice carried a hint of amusement. "How does it feel?" they asked while laughing. "You talk so much without listening. This is why I had to revoke your talking privileges."

I sighed, trying to stay patient. "Yeah, yeah... I get it. Just don't do that ever again."

"I'm not making that promise," Freckles responded.

Oh... That's right, you said "almost" die.
You're right. I'm sorry...
But you dropped some heavy news on me. You've
already dealt with it and put it behind you. But this
is all so new to me!

> *Cancer isn't something you just put behind you.*
> *Your body and outlook on life will be changed*
> *forever. But I need a favor.*

What is it?

> *Try to look surprised when you get the diagnosis.*

That's not funny.

Well, you survive.
So... It's a little bit funny.

It's really not.
What is it like to fight cancer?
All I remember is my grandmother getting it, and she
chose not to fight. Is it that bad?

You were seven years old when that happened. I'm
surprised you even remember.

Yeah. I do.
Aside from that and TV, I don't have any knowledge
about cancer. Is it bad, or was my grandmother a
coward?

Your grandmother wasn't being a coward. It's a
difficult battle. It's easily the most challenging thing
you've done in your life.

That doesn't really answer my question.

It's not easy to talk about.

You're the one who opened that door, Thirty-six.
You didn't leave me with much of a choice but to
walk through it.

I let out a deep sigh, staring blankly at my phone. "I don't even know
where to start," I confessed, the shadows of my cancer battle looming
in my mind.

"Choose any moment from your story and begin there," Freckles
advised calmly. Simply toss a dart, wherever it lands will be your
starting point.

I glanced around the room, half-expecting to find a dartboard. "You
mean, like, literally?"

Freckles' voice carried a note of disbelief. "No, Adam. I mean a figurative dart. Just choose any moment and start from there."

Okay then...
When you're diagnosed with cancer, it takes a bit
before it becomes real for you. Even after going
through all the surgeries and treatments, it didn't
become real until our hair started to fall out.

Wait, what!?
We lose our hair!?
And surgeries?

Yes. Your hair will fall out.
A doctor performs a biopsy on our neck, which
leaves a big scar.

What is a biopsy?

A biopsy is when a surgeon takes a big chunk of skin
from an area.
They then look at it under a microscope to see if
anything abnormal is going on.

That doesn't sound very pleasant.

Well, you're asleep.
You don't feel anything until you wake up.

Sheesh.
You said "surgeries," meaning more than
one...right?

Yes.
Another surgery was the bone marrow biopsy. That
one is painful.

Does the doctor take skin from your bones?

You don't have skin on your bones, but that's the
general idea.

They scrape off tissues from your bones and look at it to see how far the cancer has spread.

Oh my god. I'm getting chills just thinking about it, like nails on a chalkboard.

Hopefully, we never have to do that again. You also get a Mediport put into your chest.

Do I want to know what that is?

All you need to know is that a tube that goes into your chest and it makes your chemotherapy treatments a lot easier.

I'm assuming the Mediport is another surgery?

Correct.

Are there any more surgeries?

Getting the Mediport removed, I guess.

Neat...

Yeah, neat.

You said my hair falls out, too. Is it like what you see on TV?

Sort of. It doesn't just automatically vanish. Instead, it becomes weak enough that the slightest touch can remove it.

Wouldn't it be easier to just... you know... NOT touch your hair?

I mean, sure. But like... just, screw showers, right? Who needs them? Shampoo? Not important at all. Never mind the fact that you have dreadlocks that need to be twisted. Guess you could comb them out – oh wait.

OKAY. I GET IT.

Like I said, once your hair starts coming out, it becomes real to you and everyone else. Unfortunately, those around you don't know what to say or do, so they pretend it isn't happening.

That sucks.

Let's get into chemotherapy. Nurses would hook you up to a machine that would pump a bunch of "medicine" through your veins.

Why'd you put quotes around "medicine?"

Because it's basically poison going through your body, and the hope is that it does more good than bad.

Are you serious?

Yes. While going through it, certain smells will make you vomit. You also become so weak that you can barely walk thirty feet without feeling exhausted.

I can't imagine being that weak.

You're a teenager, so I'd imagine it's hard for you to picture being so weak that even going upstairs gives you nausea.

Nausea and vomiting. Those sound like the worst parts.

No. The worst part is that you go through 95% of it alone. You drive yourself to and from treatments, and nobody visits.

Not even my friends?

Not even friends, unfortunately.

Do people hate me that much?

109

What do you mean?

I try to keep to myself and stay out of trouble
because I've always felt that people don't like me.
But you're telling me that even with the possibility of
death, nobody cares enough to visit? Not even my
friends!?

A sharp pang pierced my chest as I read Sixteen's frantic messages. He was spiraling, just as I once did. The words on the screen seemed to dissolve into a haze, their meaning was lost as haunting memories of my cancer battle surged back with painful clarity. The past and present collided, with each message being an echo of my own struggles.

I know it feels that way, but it isn't true.

Really?
Because that's not what it sounds like.
Look... I'm starting to think you don't understand
how much I hate this place, so I will say it to you
bluntly.
I want to see this place and everyone in it burn to the
ground.
Everyone here treats me like I'm a big
inconvenience to them. Like I'm useless and can't do
anything right.
I thought that maybe, JUST MAYBE, my friends
could be the saving grace. But they don't even care
enough to visit?

I know you don't want to hear it... but people have
their reasons for acting the way they do.

Reasons? What possible reason could a friend who
supposedly cares about you have to not be there for
you when you really need them to be?
I've always thought this world would be better

without me. If what you're saying is true, then I want to thank you for removing all doubt.

"I remember when you felt this way," Freckles said, their tone contemplative. "I recall you sitting on the front porch, pleading with the Lord to let your cancer win because you felt like you were merely taking up space."

"Yeah... I did," I admitted, feeling the weight of those memories pressing down on me.

"Yet, despite everything, you impressed me with how you faced your battle with cancer," Freckles said.

"What do you mean?" I asked, genuinely curious.

"Even amid all your suffering, you showed up each day with a smile on your face," Freckles said, its tone filled with admiration. "No one could see the turmoil inside because you chose to mask it."

"I felt like no one cared," I confessed. "But inside, it was destroying me. I figured nobody would have to pretend to care about what was going on if I always smiled. " I sighed, the painful memories creeping back. "I understand Sixteen's feelings all too well. I also wished to see this place burn to the ground."

"I remember," Freckles said softly, "You were consumed by anger and despair. I'm glad you found a way to make peace with your past rather than holding onto a grudge."

I nodded slowly, the weight of those memories settling in. "I made peace with it," I admitted. "But it's not like I had a choice. It would be pointless to wish destruction on something that isn't going anywhere."

…

The sun was setting, casting a golden hue over the park as Jessica and I stood under the gazebo, ready to exchange our vows. Both of our families were gathered, their anticipation mingling with the soft rustling of flowers that adorned the gazebo.

An hour before the wedding ceremony, my phone rang. It was one of my groomsmen, his voice heavy with regret as he apologized and said he couldn't make it. At the same time, two of Jessica's bridesmaids were nowhere to be found. Just when we thought things couldn't get worse, a random gentleman appeared, claiming he had reserved the gazebo for a church barbecue and demanded that we move.

Jessica, overwhelmed and on the verge of tears, clutched my arm. "I don't know what to do, Adam! This isn't how we imagined today would go."

I was about to comfort her when Giselle, Jessica's best friend and maid of honor, showed up. I'd always had mixed feelings about Giselle. She had a knack for making poor decisions and always getting into trouble. I usually kept my distance and let Jessica handle her as best as she could, but today was different. Despite her usual reckless attitude, Giselle seemed determined to fix things.

"What's going on?" Giselle asked, her voice steady and urgent. "Is there a butt that I need to kick? Because I swear, I'll do it!"

Jessica quickly explained the situation. Giselle nodded and then headed straight for the man claiming the gazebo.

"Excuse me," she began, her tone firm but polite. "This is my best friend's wedding day, and I hear you want us to move. Well, we have our reservation paperwork right here. Would you mind showing me yours, please?"

The man, slightly taken aback, waved his phone in front of him and said, "I don't need it. I've got the mayor on the line, and he says I have it reserved."

"Yes, I understand that," Giselle said calmly. "But what you don't understand is that we aren't from here. Paperwork is what matters to us, not a phone call. Now, can we see your paperwork?"

The man hesitated, then argued, "Are you deaf? I said I don't need paperwork because I have the mayor's word. Here, you talk to him." He handed the phone to Giselle.

Giselle took the phone from him and calmly hung up. "Are you deaf? I said that paperwork is the only thing that counts," Giselle said, standing her ground. "I'll make this easy for you. We aren't moving until you show us your paperwork."

113

After a few tense moments, the man stepped away. When he returned, he begrudgingly conceded. "So, I've decided to be nice and let you keep the gazebo." Clearly, the words of a man who didn't have his paperwork.

Jessica and I watched in disbelief as Giselle came back to us. "Don't worry about the gazebo. It is all yours," she said confidently as she hugged Jessica. "And I know you're worried about the missing people," Giselle's gaze was primarily directed at me. "Listen… Everyone who is meant to be here today is here. Their absence won't stop this from being an incredible day. Honestly, it's their loss."

I nodded, realizing that Giselle's actions spoke volumes. I had often been critical of her, but today, she showed a side of herself that I hadn't seen before.

For years, I'd harbored a quiet resentment toward Giselle, believing her questionable decisions were a bad influence on Jessica. I wished she'd disappear from our lives, hoping things might be simpler without her. But in that moment, as Giselle stood up and took charge, I was struck by a profound realization. She is my wife's best friend; regardless of my feelings, she isn't going anywhere. She was a constant in Jessica's life, a presence I'd have to accept as part of our shared future. It was an emotional awakening that this woman, despite my reservations, was now an inseparable part of our journey together. And I could either choose peace or continue to hold a grudge. I prefer the former. After all, peace doesn't mean I have to like her. She still makes horrible decisions. But it's much easier than spending the rest of my life holding a grudge against someone who isn't going anywhere.

...

"Yeah... peace is always easier. You know... Giselle still makes foolish decisions," I said with a hint of frustration.

Freckles' tone grew playful. "Indeed. But you're not immune to foolish decisions yourself. After all, who made the decision that brought us on this mission together... as ordained by the Lord."

I couldn't help but chuckle at Freckles' lighthearted jab. "You love reminding me of this, don't you?"

"I may joke about the mistakes mortals make, but your fight with cancer? I've bragged about that to other angels," Freckles said reassuringly.

"Really? You mean that?" I asked, my surprise evident.

"Yes," Freckles said with sincere conviction. "You were dealt a terrible hand, but you made it through something that breaks most mortals. I'm proud of you."

"I appreciate you saying that," I murmured, feeling warmth spread through me.

Freckles replied, their tone both sincere and comforting, "You do make my job challenging at times, but it's truly an honor to be your guardian angel. Our situation is tough, but if I have to guide someone through this mess, I am glad it is you."

"Thank you," I said, genuinely touched. "So, what do we do next?"

Freckles' voice carried a note of wisdom. "We continue this mission. Remember: you weren't looking for someone to tell you what you wanted to hear, but rather, what you needed to hear."

> *I don't blame you for feeling that way.*
> *It's crazy… you're talking with someone*
> *who knows your thoughts, goals, dreams, fears,*
> *insecurities, strengths, weaknesses, and even your*
> *worst nightmares: The one person in the world who*
> *knows exactly how you feel right now.*

Yeah, yeah, I know.
You're me. I understand that.
But how do you justify all of this?
Are you going to tell me that this was a good thing?
That we needed this to happen?

> *I can't justify it at all. There is no reason we should*
> *have gone through that alone. It should never have*
> *happened, and it is unforgivable.*

So, you agree.
How are you not angry about it?

> *I was angry about it.*
> *I was furious. And just like you, I wanted to see this*
> *place burn to the ground.*
> *You weren't even an adult yet, and you proved just*
> *how strong you really are.*

It doesn't sound like I had much of a choice.

You always have a choice.
Like you said earlier, your grandmother made the
decision not to fight her cancer.

Freckles' voice interrupted my thoughts. "This is how free will works."

"Seriously, Freckles? I'm kind of busy here," I shot back. "We'll talk about that later."

From what I heard, she wasn't going to win that
battle.

Probably not...
But that doesn't change the fact that you battled a
disease that kills millions of people every year.
Nobody can take that from you.
In the future, people will try to downplay it by telling
you it couldn't have been that bad.

Why would someone downplay someone fighting
cancer? That's horrible.

Sometimes, people suck.
I wish I had a better answer than that.

As I read the words I had just typed, a memory of my father, Remy, crashed into my thoughts. I recalled the day I was asked to speak at a high school. I was excited to do it because I'd be talking with troubled teenagers who weren't aware of their options after high school. It was a chance to share my story with those willing to listen.

Remy had been furious. His face twisted with anger as he spat, "You think you're some kind of big shot because you had cancer?" His voice dripped with venom. "How smart can the school be if they asked you

117

to go? I'd tell these kids right from wrong and straighten them out quickly."

He grabbed me by the face, his grip squishing my cheeks together, and mocked me with his words. "Oh, look at me, I get to parade around as a victim who beat my itty bitty case of the sniffles!" He let go and spat on the ground. "You're a joke, kid. That's why I'm glad I never came to any of your treatments. I'm so thankful I didn't have to witness your pitiful display of weakness."

Looking back, I could see it was jealousy. But in that moment, it felt like pure hatred. Anger welled up inside me, my hands trembling as I gripped the phone.

Freckles' voice cut through the haze. "Adam! I swear, everything reminds you of that man. My Lord... Just once, I wish you would just let it go!"

I get that...

Okay, maybe I have a better answer for you. Every day, you'd go to chemotherapy by yourself. I believe the reason that nobody worried about you is that nobody would have guessed that you would be going through something like this alone. But you did. You put on a display of strength so powerful that even the medical staff felt inspired just being around you. Even though you went in every day with a smile, it was a dark time you'd rather forget. Sadly, our father uses it against us.

Dad uses cancer against us?
How?

> *He basically says if you can get through it, anyone*
> *can get through it.*
> *You know... because you're weak, according to him.*

That's so messed up.
Why would he say something like that?

> *Because he is jealous of us.*
> *Dad needs to be the center of attention at all times.*
> *Hearing how you went through cancer on your own*
> *messes with him in two ways. The first is that you*
> *look powerful for doing it alone. The second is that*
> *he looks weak for letting you do it alone.*

Even with cancer, he doesn't want to be around me.

> *Correct.*
> *Haven't you noticed that he always attacks your*
> *accomplishments?*

I think so.
I haven't been able to put it into words, but you're
right. He does.

> *You are stronger than he will ever be.*
> *He knows this, and he fears it.*
> *He breaks you down often, but seeing you get back*
> *up is more than he can handle.*

I was still fuming, my anger simmering just beneath the surface. Then, Freckles' voice came through. "That went better than I thought it would."

I took a deep breath, trying to rein in my emotions. "Thanks. You know how much I've been dealing with hatred towards him. I know we say peace over destruction, but I don't ever see it happening with

119

that man. He has crossed the line too many times, and I can only try harder not to let him affect my judgment. It's still a work in progress."

I see...
But can you answer this for me?
How come even my friends don't visit me?
That's so messed up.

        I'll answer it after you answer this for me.
        Why are you getting so worked up about something
        that hasn't even happened yet?

I don't know.
Things are already bad, and it's painful to listen to
how they'll only get worse.

        That's a fair and unfortunate point.
        Okay. I'll answer.
        Yes, it was messed up that our friends did not visit
        us. Even after beating cancer, I never forgot how
        lonely and let down I felt. Not a single person kept
        me company in the hospital. I hated it.

I don't want that to happen to me.

        And it won't.
        As long as you learn from my mistakes.
        I urge you to go easy on your friends when this
        happens.

Learn from your mistakes?
I'll be the one fighting for my life in the hospital
while life goes on for my friends, and I'm supposed
to "go easy on them?" Why? Give me one good
reason!

        Because they never forgot either.
        They know they let you down and have never
        forgiven themselves.

What do you mean?

> *Bad things will happen in this life and people will*
> *not rally behind you the way you think they will.*
> *People are going to let you down.*
> *But if you can take a moment to see things from their*
> *perspective, it gets easier to deal with.*

What was their perspective?

> *You and your friends were only seventeen and*
> *eighteen years old. At that age, stuff like that doesn't*
> *feel real.*
> *They didn't visit you because they were trying to be*
> *malicious.*
> *Instead, it was because they had trouble dealing*
> *with the thought of losing you. Thankfully, people*
> *grow up, get wiser, and become more aware of their*
> *actions.*

How do you know this?

> *Because one day, you and your friends will sit down*
> *and discuss it. They tell you how awful they feel for*
> *letting you face that alone and that they don't have*
> *any excuse for not being there for you when they*
> *should have.*

Are you serious?

> *Jack and Garrus could barely look at you without*
> *tearing up because they felt guilty. They knew they*
> *messed up at a time when they shouldn't have.*

That...
I don't know what to say.

> *There's really nothing for you to say.*
> *People have their reasons.*
> *You may not know them at the moment, but you'll*
> *eventually find out.*

Wow!
Alright, I promise I'll try from now on.
As you said, it hasn't happened yet, so hopefully, I'll
be more prepared.

> *Honestly, I don't think anything will prepare you for*
> *that. It will be one of the worst moments of your life,*
> *and going through it sucks. But thankfully, you*
> *survive and come out of it a lot stronger.*

So... it needed to happen?

> *Hell no! I wouldn't wish this on anybody. It didn't*
> *need to happen, but some good did come from it.*

That's okay then, I guess.
You know, you're not a bad guy. It seems like I
turned out okay. I guess I always thought I'd be a
huge disappointment.

> *What do you mean by that?*

Well, you know what I'm going through. You know
that I'm... not happy.

> *Yeah... we've established that.*
> *But let me remind you that you can be open and*
> *honest with me. You can't lie to yourself: literally*
> *and figuratively.*

I needed to hear that.
Thanks.

> *We've been texting for a while today.*
> *Let's continue this tomorrow.*

Tomorrow won't work for me.

> *What do you mean tomorrow won't work?*
> *What day is it today?*

Today is Friday. Tomorrow, I'll be doing dungeon
raids all day in Ragnarök Online. Pantharo, Ariana,

Doc, Vida, and I are going for Baphomet and Doppelganger.

Ragnarök Online... It was the first massively multiplayer online role-playing game I ever played. It was one of the few things I looked forward to at the end of each day. I can still remember the incredible people I met during my time there. An unforgettable friend group from Spain welcomed me into their gaming family.

Pantharo was like the father of the guild, always guiding us with a mix of authority and care: a true leader. Ariana, his girlfriend at the time, was the heart of the guild. She had this incredible ability to keep everyone motivated, especially when we went into some of the most challenging battles in the game.

Then there was Doc. He was incredibly laid-back, which made him easy to talk to. Whether he was talking about the game or things in real life, I always appreciated the advice he gave me. Lastly, his girlfriend, Vida, brought a lot of energy to the group. I didn't talk to her much, but she balanced Doc's calm demeanor.

We'd spend hours leveling up, strategizing, and, most importantly, enjoying each other's company. Those friendships meant so much to me. They still do. They're memories in gaming that I'll cherish forever.

I remember those days. If you have time today, you should try to level up your assassin. Can't have you falling after getting hit once.

But I'm level 75.
I'll be fine.

Spoiler: no, you won't.

Whatever!

Take some time to reflect on what we spoke about
today. We'll continue on Sunday.

Yes, sir.
Guess you can say that it's time to…
bid myself, adieu!

Stop it.
Get some help.

"You know, I'm impressed with how much he opened up to you today," Freckles said, their voice filled with admiration. "I remember you going through a lot of what he mentioned. It was hard to watch back then."

I nodded, feeling the old pain resurface. "I used to pray a lot during those times. Sure, I wanted the cancer to go away, but my biggest prayer was to get out of that home."

Freckles' tone turned curious. "Tell me. Why don't you pray as often now?"

I shrugged, feeling a pang of guilt. "I don't know. I guess I feel like other people need it more than I do."

"That's not quite how it works," Freckles replied gently. "You should always pray. Believe it or not, I hear them."

I blinked in surprise. "Wait… YOU hear the prayers? I thought they go directly to God."

Freckles' tone was both amused and patient. "The Lord does hear them, but there are billions of mortals and only one of Him."

"Isn't God capable of everything?" I asked, genuinely curious.

"Absolutely," Freckles confirmed. "But I'm sure you've heard the saying that 'God's work can be done through others?'"

"Yeah?" I replied slowly.

Freckles chuckled warmly. "Hi, I'm 'others.' Nice to meet you."

"I thought that meant other people…" I said, slowly understanding.

Freckles laughed softly, though with a hint of disbelief. "You mortals really think you have the power to help the Lord? That's…adorable. Quite an inflated sense of self-importance."

"You know…" I said, starting to see Freckles' point, "When you put it like that, it actually makes sense."

"While we are focused on the topic of prayers, there is something you should know," Freckles began, their voice steady but with a hint of frustration, "You mortals have a way of making the Lord's job harder than it needs to be."

"How so?" I asked, genuinely curious.

"Do you know what the most common prayer is?" Freckles inquired.

I thought for a moment and then joked, "Winning the lottery? Like in Bruce Almighty?"

There was a pause in Freckles' response, almost like a mental sigh. "Are you seriously getting your spiritual knowledge from a Jim Carrey movie?" Freckles asked, disbelief evident.

I chuckled. "Well, yeah. It was a good movie."

Freckles fell silent. If angels have eyes, Freckles definitely rolled theirs.

"It was," I insisted. "You know it was."

Freckles sighed. "Alright, I'll give you that one. To be fair, lottery prayers are in the top ten. But the most common one is what you mortals call 'The Serenity Prayer.' You know, the one that starts with 'Grant me the serenity to accept the things I cannot change' and so on." Freckles' tone carried a hint of mockery.

I nodded, recognizing it. "Yeah, I'm familiar with it. But honestly, it doesn't sound like a real prayer."

"Exactly," Freckles agreed. "It's self-righteous nonsense that mortals say to make themselves feel better about doing nothing."

I was taken aback. "Whoa. Really?"

"Indeed," Freckles continued. "The most common prayers are from mortals asking for things they can change on their own. Those rarely ever capture the Lord's attention. The prayers that do resonate are the ones where divine intervention is necessary."

I pondered this, realizing the depth of Freckles's message: "So, it's about asking for help when we truly need it, not when we can fix it ourselves."

"Precisely," Freckles said. "You mortals often ask for the easy way out instead of the willpower to do what needs to be done."

"So, if I pray to cure someone's cancer, would God hear it?" I asked, hoping for clarity.

Freckles' response was immediate and reassuring. "The Lord will hear every prayer. But that one would get the Lord's attention."

But then, a troubling thought crossed my mind. "If these prayers are being heard, then why do innocent people die every single day?"

Freckles' tone remained calm but firm. "Just because the Lord hears a prayer doesn't mean it will be answered as you expect. Mortals might not understand in the moment, but the Lord always does what is best."

I felt a surge of frustration. "I disagree. What about all the tragedies in the world? War, racism, murder... Is that what God thinks is best?"

Freckles responded gently, "No, of course not."

"Then how can you say that?" I challenged.

Freckles' voice grew solemn. "Because the actions you speak of have nothing to do with the Lord. Those are situations created by mortals."

I shook my head, still not entirely convinced. "But why doesn't God get involved, especially if He knows it will happen?"

Freckles answered, "Free will."

"Free will makes no sense if God already knows what will happen," I countered.

Freckles responded with a tone of patience. "Mortals have a hard time seeing the big picture. The Earth is billions of years old – a timespan you can barely begin to comprehend. There are things you won't understand, even in your lifetime."

Freckles continued, "Free will is a gift. One that the Lord doesn't have to give but chooses to. And it's astonishing to see how mortals use this gift for their own benefit."

I listened, feeling overwhelmed by the enormity of what Freckles was saying. The magnitude left me momentarily speechless.

I sensed Freckles' frustration as it went on. "There's an entire book of things you shouldn't do, which can be summed up into one sentence: Thou shall not be a jerk. Yet, mortals use it to shame others into doing what they want for their selfish gain."

Freckles' words hit hard. It wasn't just a matter of right and wrong but of the deeper implications of our choices. I nodded slowly, processing its words.

"My sincerest apologies for ranting. I shall get back to the topic of prayer." Freckles added. "A prayer without action is merely wishful thinking. The Lord hears your prayers, but you must also take steps toward your request. Prayer should be coupled with effort. That would be akin to asking for weight loss but refusing to adopt proper eating habits and exercise; it is nothing more than an empty wish."

I sighed, realizing the truth in what Freckles was saying. "I guess we really do make things harder than they need to be."

"The Lord does not expect mortals to be perfect, Adam," Freckles said, its tone softening. "It's about striving to be better, understanding that your actions have consequences, and using your free will wisely."

I looked down, deep in thought. "I'll try to keep that in mind. Thanks for the perspective."

All the things we blame God for – God has nothing to do with them. He doesn't tell us to go out and sin. All He wants for us is to care for ourselves and be good to one another.

I wouldn't be surprised if God was fed up with us. We've got this knack for avoiding responsibility for our actions. We somehow convinced ourselves that God is to blame for the messes we make.

Sure, bad things happen to good people, but that doesn't mean God is causing it. Most of the time, it's just people making foolish decisions.

You know that quote, "The greatest trick the Devil ever pulled was convincing the world he didn't exist"? Want me to blow your mind? The Devil exists, but he's not responsible for most of the terrible things that happen. Nope, that's on us. It's all because we don't understand how much of a gift free will is.

Chapter 5

The hospital room was dim and quiet, with only the soft beeping of the machines breaking the silence. Reina, Adam's little sister, approached his bedside with unsteady steps. She had always admired him for his strength and resilience, especially after their difficult childhood. Seeing him so frail and vulnerable now was almost unbearable for her. Her heart felt heavy with a mix of gratitude and sadness. Each beep of the machine seemed to echo her fears and the depth of her emotional pain.

Reina's eyes stayed on her brother's still form. She reached out and gently held his hand, feeling the slightest bit of warmth even though he lay motionless. It had been a few days with no signs of improvement, and the doctors had prepared her for the worst. She took a deep breath and gathered her strength for what she needed to say.

"Adam," Reina began, her voice trembling, "It took everything I had to come here. Seeing you like this is... it's too much for me to handle right now." Her voice cracked as tears streamed down her face. "But... I promised myself I'd do this." She took a shaky breath, trying to steady herself. "I hate seeing you like this. I'm so used to seeing you get back up every time you get knocked down, so why aren't you doing that now?" Her tears flowed freely, her chest heaving with emotion. "I need you to be here because I don't know how to handle this!"

Reina sat in the chair next to Adam's bed, her hands gripping his with a desperate need for connection. As she sat there, memories of their time together flooded her mind – days filled with laughter, playful teasing, and deep conversations. Adam had always been her rock, protector, and guiding light in the madness of their lives. Now, with him lying so still, she felt the weight of those memories pressing heavily on her heart. Each recollection was a reminder of the strength and love he had always given her, making his current state all the more heart-wrenching.

She recalled the countless advice her brother had given her over the years. His words of wisdom had shaped her into the person she was today. Adam had always been her biggest supporter – cheering her on from the sidelines, encouraging her dreams, and catching her when she stumbled. Each memory of his guidance and support only deepened her sense of loss, making it even harder to see him lying there so still.

"You've always been there for me," Reina said, her voice cracking as tears streamed down her face. "You knew how to make me laugh. You'd always encourage me to go for the things I want. I don't even mind that you were a pain sometimes." She tried to smile through her tears. "But it was okay because you always made me feel loved. You always made me feel like I mattered."

She took a shaky breath, her voice breaking as she continued. "I'm so grateful for everything you've done for me, Adam. Through every hard time, you were always there. You taught me what it means to be strong and to keep pushing forward, no matter how tough things got."

132

She took a deep breath, trying to steady her voice. "I want to be angry with you… I'm supposed to, right?" Her tears flowed freely. "Damn it! I don't get it!" Her voice broke, and she struggled to keep control. "I don't understand why you felt you had to do this… and I don't think I ever will." She choked on her sobs, her words coming in broken gasps. "But I wish—" Her voice staggered. "I wish you could see just how much we need you here with us."

She let go of Adam's hand and placed her own hands on her face, struggling to control her tears. Her sobs continued, each one a reminder of the pain she felt. "I don't know if you realize this," she cried, "but you were my hero. No matter how scary things got, I knew everything would be okay as long as you were around. I always felt like I could do anything because you'd be there to catch me if I fell." The tears streamed down her face uncontrollably. "And now you're just gone."

She placed her hands in her lap and leaned back in the chair, her body slumping with exhaustion and sorrow. "I'm sorry, Adam," she said, her voice quivering as she fought to keep it steady. "This is really hard for me. It's just so difficult to picture life without you. I…"

Suddenly, the door creaked open, and Reina's head snapped toward it. A young girl stood hesitantly in the doorway. She had long, dark hair and wore a school uniform, her wide eyes reflecting uncertainty and concern.

"Hi," the girl said softly as she stepped into the room, her voice barely above a whisper. "I hope I'm not intruding... My name is Kristine. I'm one of Mr. Adam's students."

Reina looked up, her eyes red and swollen from crying. She wiped her tears away, trying to compose herself. Despite the sadness etched on her face, she managed a faint, welcoming smile. "You're not intruding at all. Please, come in."

Kristine walked towards Adam's bed, her eyes shifting from him to Reina and back again. "You two look very similar," she said softly, taking in the resemblance. "Are you Mr. Adam's sister?"

"Yes, I'm Reina," she replied, a gentle smile forming despite the sadness. "It's nice to meet you, Kristine."

Kristine managed a small smile, her eyes still glistening with tears. "Ms. Reina, is it okay if I talk to Mr. Adam?"

Reina laughed softly, her first in what felt like ages. "You don't have to be so formal with me. Reina will be just fine. And yes, of course, you can speak with him. Would you like me to leave the room?"

Kristine shook her head quickly. "No, please stay with me. This... this is kind of scary. Your brother always made me feel safe."

Reina nodded slowly, her heart aching for both Kristine and her brother. "That was one of his best traits," she said softly. She stood up from her chair, stepping back a bit. "Okay, Kristine. I'll be right here if you need me."

"Thank you, Reina," Kristine said, her voice quivering. She then turned her full attention to Adam, her eyes brimming with tears. "We did it. The University of Pennsylvania accepted me," she said, her voice breaking with emotion. " Just like you said they would."

Reina moved closer to Kristine, placing a comforting hand on her shoulder.

Kristine continued, gathering her composure. "One day, you had asked us about our goals and…well, I wanted to go to UPenn. It was just a silly dream I had, but you helped me turn it into a reality. You told me…" She mimicked Adam's voice with a touch of fondness, "'Grades are good, but personality is better; and it helps that you're the personification of a troll. Now, get out from under your bridge and show the world who you are, you little troll." She laughed softly through her tears, and Reina joined in, sharing a bittersweet smile. Kristine continued. "Mr. Adam… You believed in me at a time when I didn't believe in myself… and I want you to know that I love you for that."

Reina's arm wrapped around Kristine's shoulders, offering a comforting embrace.

"I can't say goodbye to you, Mr. Adam," Kristine's voice cracked. "I don't… I don't want this to be the end." She turned to Reina, her eyes red and full of sorrow. Reina pulled her into a tight hug, whispering reassurances.

"It's going to be okay, Kristine," Reina said softly. "Keep going…"

Kristine nodded and looked back at Adam, tears streaming down her face. "I'll see you again one day. This isn't goodbye." Her voice trembled as she spoke. "This is just a 'see you later,' right? You… you'll be in front of the class tomorrow, right?"

Reina hugged Kristine even tighter, her heart breaking for the young girl.

Reina held Kristine close, tears welling up in both their eyes. "You'll see him again," Reina whispered, her hands gently resting on the back of Kristine's head to comfort her as the girl continued to cry. "He wouldn't have it any other way."

They stayed like that momentarily, sharing a profound, quiet bond that connected them through Adam's memory. Their silent embrace was a testament to his impact on both their lives.

Kristine slowly lifted her head to look at Reina, her eyes red and swollen from crying. "Thank you for being here with me, Reina."

Reina gazed down, her eyes meeting Kristine's with a gentle, reassuring look. "I'll be here as long as you need me," Reina said.

Kristine gave a slight nod, her voice trembling with gratitude. "You're just as kind as your brother. Can I ask you something?"

"Of course," Reina said, gesturing for Kristine to sit beside her. "What is it?"

Kristine sat beside Reina, taking a deep breath before speaking. "How did Mr. Adam become... well, who he is? He always seemed so strong and confident and would always see the potential of others. I want to be just like that, but I don't know where to start."

Reina looked at Kristine, her eyes glistening with sadness and admiration. "Adam certainly had his struggles, just like all of us. But somehow, he could always see the best in others, even when he didn't see it in himself. He believed in people with his entire heart and wanted them to recognize their worth." Reina's voice faltered, tears forming as she smiled through her sorrow. "My brother... He'd always tell me that he wished that I could see myself the way he sees me. It took me years to understand what he meant."

Kristine listened intently, her own eyes brimming with tears. "He also said that to me, but I never quite understood what he meant."

Reina nodded, her expression softening. "I believe Adam was trying to remind us to be kind to ourselves. We're often our own harshest critics."

"Yeah, that makes sense," Kristine said, her voice gaining strength. "Mr. Adam spent so much time making sure we were confident. I appreciate it even more now."

Reina smiled, her eyes reflecting the warmth of her brother's wisdom. "When you focus on lifting others, you end up finding strength within yourself."

Kristine chuckled softly. "That sounds like one of Mr. Adam's cheesy lines."

Reina laughed, a hint of her brother's humor lighting up her face. "It is! He had so many cheesy one-liners. He was like one of those walking inspirational posters."

Kristine grinned. "He really was! Wow. Mr. Adam was always so positive."

Reina nodded, her gaze turning reflective. "He wasn't always like that. We had a rough upbringing, but thankfully, he never let that define him."

Kristine's eyes widened with empathy. "Mr. Adam shared a bit about his childhood. It sounded really tough."

"It was," Reina confirmed. "But Adam always tried to see the silver lining. He found comfort in helping others because he knew what it was like to feel alone and unsupported. He made it his mission to become the support he never had."

"I hope you know that he succeeded," Kristine said, her voice shaking. "He was always there for me. Even when I doubted myself... he never did. I want to be like him when I get older."

Reina gently lifted Kristine's chin, her eyes filled with understanding. "Kristine, you're more like him than you realize. Just by being here and caring so deeply, you're showing the same courage and compassion he did. My brother may see the best in people, but he's selective about who he believes in. Adam believed in you for a reason. Remember that."

Kristine's lip quivered, but she managed a smile. "Thank you, Reina. I really needed to hear that."

Reina took Kristine's hands in hers. "You're going to do amazing things. So, instead of trying to be like Adam, you should try to be more like yourself. That's probably what he would say."

Kristine nodded, her eyes filled with determination. "You're right. I promise to at least try." She glanced at Adam, her voice breaking. "Reina... I'm going to miss him."

Reina nodded slowly, her own heart aching. "I'm going to miss him, too. I may not be Adam, but I'll be there for you if you need anything."

Kristine's eyes lit up with hope. "Do you mean that?"

Reina nodded firmly. "Yes, I do. So you better get out there and make everyone proud, 'you little troll.'"

Kristine laughed through her tears, throwing her arms around Reina in a heartfelt embrace. "Thank you!"

Caught off guard by the hug, Reina pulled her in closer, her voice gentle. "I have to ask... what did Adam mean by calling you a troll?"

Kristine laughed softly. "During class, we tease each other a lot. Neither of us would back down, and we'd have these stalemates. Well, I guess not really a stalemate since he'd tell me to sit down, and we'd move on with the next lesson."

Reina laughed, too, her face reflecting Adam's playful spirit. "That sounds just like him. He's not easy to beat in a battle of wits."

As they finally parted from the hug, Kristine looked at Adam, tears streaming down her face. "He's so amazing... I'm still not ready to say goodbye to him."

Reina nodded with empathy. "So, don't."

"But what if I miss my chance to?" Kristine asked, her voice trembling.

Reina shook her head gently. "As long as you carry him in your heart, you'll never truly say goodbye."

Kristine smiled through her tears. "Another one of his cheesy lines?"

Reina smiled softly. "No, that one's mine. Honestly, I'm not ready to say goodbye either, and I'm not going to. He'll always be right here," she said, pointing to her heart.

Kristine nodded as a hopeful smile spread across her face. "I like that. I'm glad I met you, Reina."

Reina returned the smile. "Same here, Kristine."

"I should get going. My parents are waiting for me downstairs," Kristine said quietly, giving Reina a tight hug. "Thank you again, Reina. For everything."

Reina pulled Kristine in close. "Of course. And remember, I'm here if you need me."

Kristine pulled away and smiled as she gave one last look at Adam, then exited the room.

As the door closed behind Kristine, Reina took a deep breath, her emotions still raw. The room was quiet again, except for the soft beeping of the machines. She sat beside her brother, staring at him, reflecting on her interaction with the young girl.

Reina gently took her brother's hands, her fingers trembling slightly. She leaned in closer, her voice a whisper.

"I hope you saw that, Adam," she said softly, her eyes brimming with tears. "This is the impact you have on people."

She brought Adam's hands closer to her chest, clutching them tightly. "I love you so much," she continued, her voice breaking as tears streamed down her cheeks. "Thank you for being so amazing to me."

Her tears fell freely now, mingling with her heartfelt words. She squeezed her brother's hands tighter, hoping her love and hope could somehow reach him through the silence.

Chapter 6

The hospital room was eerily silent except for the rhythmic beeping of the machines keeping Adam alive. With five days remaining until Jessica had to make a decision, the situation's weight felt heavier than ever. As he lay there, trapped in a body that couldn't move, a familiar figure stepped into the room.

As the door creaked open, Joshua Molina, Adam's favorite high school teacher, walked in. Joshua had always been a pillar of strength and support for Adam – his stoic demeanor was balanced by a playful sense of humor that made learning effective and enjoyable. His presence in the room now, however, was a stark contrast to the vibrant teacher Adam had once known. His face, usually welcoming and encouraging, was now etched with a deep sadness as he took in the sight of his former student.

Joshua approached Adam's bedside and looked down at the still form of Adam, his eyes brimming with unshed tears. "Hey there, Adam," he said softly, his voice cracking with emotion. "It has been a while..." Joshua's hands trembled slightly as he reached out to touch the edge of the bed, his usually steady demeanor giving way to the grief of seeing someone who had once been so full of life now lying so still.

"I brought something with me," Joshua said, reaching into his pocket and pulling out a neatly folded newspaper clipping. "I don't know if you remember this, but you were featured in an article a few years back. I read the interview… and wanted to share some highlights with you."

He unfolded the newspaper clipping, the headline: Minorities Striving in the Education Field. His fingers traced the ink as he found the section where Adam had been interviewed. With a gentle sigh, he began to read aloud, hoping the sound of his voice might somehow reach Adam.

"They asked what inspired you to get into education," he said, a warm smile touching his lips despite the somber setting. "I loved your response…"

He read aloud from the article, his eyes softening as he continued. "'It kind of just fell into my lap. While in college, I was lost and changed my major about six times. Then, I met Dr. Quentin, an educator who became a mentor to me. He put me in a student ambassador role, which involved interacting with current and prospective students. Through that experience, I realized I had a knack for it. Dr. Quentin saw potential in me and offered me a job as a counselor after graduation, and I fell in love with it."

Joshua took a deep breath, his gaze fixed on Adam as he spoke softly, "I've never met Dr. Quentin… but anyone who can have that kind of impact on you must be wonderful. It sounds like he helped you find your path, and I'm grateful for that."

Joshua continued, moving his finger to the next section with a faint smile, though his eyes still held a trace of sadness. "They asked you about the challenges you faced as a minority educator."

He cleared his throat and began to read, "Far too often, it feels like my logic and credibility are taken into question despite my achievements and accolades. It's as if I'm somehow seen as less than some of my colleagues, no matter what I do. Despite being in the education field for several years, it feels like much of what I say is put under a microscope. Some of my colleagues take my constructive criticism as insults or a simple disagreement as wanting to start an argument. I don't know if it is the unfamiliarity of working with minorities or racism rearing its head."

Joshua looked up from the newspaper, his eyes reflecting sadness. He turned to Adam's motionless body and spoke softly, "Adam, you know, there aren't a lot of minorities in the education field... I wish I could say that was just a coincidence, but it's not. The challenges you faced were not just about being a minority but about breaking through barriers that shouldn't have existed in the first place."

Joshua continued reading the article, "It's frustrating at times... but I love being able to help teenagers and young adults find their way and help guide them to discover their own paths. It's a calling, a passion. If I could do this without working in education, I would."

Joshua's voice softened as he read the next part of the interview. "The interviewer then asked why you said you wouldn't be opposed to leaving the education field. And wow, you were blunt with your response." Joshua couldn't help but let out a small chuckle, his eyes misting as he continued.

Joshua's voice grew heavier as he read the next part. "You would think that education is the one place where hard work guarantees success, where the American Dream is alive and well. But that's not how it is at all. Moving up often depends on who you know or whether you fit the image that the institution wants to project. It's a system where hard work isn't always rewarded, so many lose their drive. It can make you really jaded."

Joshua paused and looked towards Adam, his expression a blend of pride and deep respect. "Adam, your honesty has always been your strength. You've never shied away from the tough truths, and that's what made you stand out." He took a deep breath. "If things were different – if… this… didn't happen. Then I do not doubt that you'd be the one leading the charge for change. You'd be the one pushing for a better system."

Joshua took a deep breath, his voice trembling with grief. "Adam… I still remember having you in my class. You were always so kind and curious," he said as a proud smile formed across his face. "I've kept up with your journey through your social media posts, and honestly, I wasn't surprised by all you've accomplished. You've always shown so much potential, and I'm happy you've finally realized it." He wiped a tear from his cheek. "I'm proud of the man you've become."

Joshua glanced down at the newspaper, then back at Adam with a thoughtful look. "There was a question about your teaching style. You said you based it on me, but I've seen videos of you in action and witnessed firsthand how you interact with your students." His smile grew full of pride. "You didn't get that gift from me."

He folded the newspaper with care, tucking it back into his pocket. "Still, I'm honored to have been part of your life. To have seen all the good you've done in your community." Joshua wiped his eyes, his voice softening. "But what impressed me the most is how far you've gone in your academic career. You've shared your personal hardships with me when you were a kid. Hearing about them always broke my heart... but you didn't let it stop you. You turned those struggles into lessons." He paused, thinking of his next words. "It's funny... you admired me without realizing how much I admire you. To go through so much and still find a reason to smile every day." He paused, pride evident in his voice. "You are truly something special, Adam."

Joshua placed a hand on top of Adam's head, his voice barely above a whisper. "I cherished every moment we spent together. I'm so thankful to have learned so much from your example," he nodded, gratitude in his voice. "I'm so thankful that our paths crossed. Adam... Thank you, for being you."

...

Yesterday was a good day. Sixteen took the day to participate in his video game raids and couldn't talk, so I had some downtime... which,

147

naturally, I spent thinking about Jessica. I'm pretty sure Freckles got tired of me being in my thoughts because they suggested I go out and explore the timeline. At first, I wasn't going to, but then Freckles told me I could eat whatever I wanted in the spirit realm without getting full or sick.

Their exact words were, "Adam, your appetite will not be bound to mortal limitations in this plane of existence." Understanding Freckles feels like having to translate another language. One that I'm slowly becoming fluent in.

I was curious to see if Freckles was right, so I went to my favorite corner deli. And uh… let's just say there is a picture of Ryan Reynolds grinning at a camera while holding a beef patty in each hand and surrounded by dozens of food wrappers. Honestly, I wish I could tell you this was the weirdest part of the journey.

…

"Freckles, are you there?" I asked, unsure if they could hear me.

"Yes," Freckles replied softly. "I'm always watching."

"Um… It's kind of creepy when you say it like that," I said with a nervous laugh.

Freckles, sounding puzzled, replied, "What do you mean?"

"You said you're 'always watching.' Does that mean you see... everything?" I asked, my mind racing with the implications.

"Everything?" Freckles paused as if weighing the question's meaning carefully. Sensing my unease, it added, "You know what... just forget it. I'd prefer not to delve into that."

"Well, you aren't saying no..." I said, raising an eyebrow.

Freckles's voice resonated with a calm certainty. "I'll put it this way: Angels aren't mortal, and we do not deal in shame or judgment. Our purpose is to protect and guide you. We don't waste energy on trivial matters."

"There was nothing trivial about my wedding night," I said jokingly, trying to lighten the mood.

Freckles responded with genuine confusion, "What does that mean?"

"Never mind. It was just a joke," I said, disappointed that Freckles didn't get it. "So... how long have we been in Solitude? I feel like I'm losing my mind."

Freckles's voice echoed gently in my head. "This is the start of day five. Time moves differently here."

"How so?" I asked.

"It's difficult to explain," Freckles replied, "but it's similar to how time moves when you mortals dream."

149

I thought for a moment. "Is it like how we can have a dream that feels like it lasts forever, but when we wake up, only a few minutes have passed?"

"Hmmm," Freckles mused. "Okay, I guess that wasn't so difficult to explain."

I laughed and said, "Has the student finally become the teacher?"

Freckles sounded genuinely puzzled. "Who are the student and teacher you're speaking of?"

I was stunned at Freckles' lack of understanding. "How do you know so much and so little— okay. Freckles. You're the teacher. I'm always learning from you, but no—"

Freckles interrupted. "I'm not your teacher. I'm your guardian angel."

I sighed, feeling a bit defeated. "Never mind, Freckles. Never mind, forever."

My phone buzzed, interrupting us. I picked it up and saw it was Sixteen. "Saved by the bell! It's time to go to work, Freckles." I said, relieved to change the topic.

Freckles responded, "But we aren't going anywhere?"

Frustrated, I shouted, "It's a figure of speech, Freckles!"

Hey, me!

Hi, me.
How did your raids go yesterday?

Pantharo saved the day!

He usually does.
How many times did Ariana have to revive you?

That's not important.

Twice?
Three times?

Seven.

Seven isn't too bad.

Seven on the first boss.

...Seven is bad.
Just gain some levels and get some gear.

Easier said than done!
Anyway, there is something I've been meaning to ask
you.

Sure, what is it?

I did some thinking while playing, and I realized... I
hate going to school.

That's not news to me.
At all.

No, listen. The only time I care about school is when
I'm around my friends.
I just... I always feel like my classmates and
teachers hate me.

As I read Sixteen's message, memories came flooding back to me. I could still see the inexcusable reality of my high school experience: bullying that happened right in front of teachers who just looked the other way, the voices of classmates and teachers telling me I wouldn't amount to anything, and some teachers outright refusing to help when I asked, calling me a lost cause. I didn't think about high school much after leaving; I was just happy to finally be out of there. But after taking a moment to look back at the experience, it shouldn't be surprising that I never wanted to go there.

I remember those days...
What's your question?

Oh... Haha!
I guess I didn't ask you anything. Umm.
Well, I want to know why it was like that.

Sure, I'll give you some insight.

Okay.
But please don't give me the whole "he's so smart
but doesn't apply himself," nonsense. I'm sick of
hearing that.

Listen...
Regarding classmates not liking you, there is
admittedly some truth in that.

What?

Every day, you give your classmates reasons not to
like you. You skip class and brag about it like it is
some badge of honor.
And when you do show up, you cause a disruption.

...I'm sorry, but exactly how is this supposed to
make me feel better?

I never said I was trying to make you feel better. I
said I wanted to give you some insight.
Now, shut up and listen.

Freckles interjected, its voice calm. "Remember what I said about being too hard on Sixteen."

"You can shut up, too," I snapped at them.

Freckles sighed, the sound reverberating through my thoughts.

Okay. I'm listening.

> *Kids can be cruel, and they often don't realize the impact of their actions.*
> *Right now, you don't realize the impact of yours.*

What do you mean?

> *Your classmates are trying to keep their grades up in hopes of being accepted to the colleges they want to attend.*
> *Furthermore, higher grades make them eligible for scholarships. Your actions are interrupting them, and they understandably don't like it.*

Wow… I never thought about it like that.

> *How did you think your actions affected others?*

I don't know. I never thought about how my actions affect others.

> *Exactly. That's why I'm here to help you. I want to be a temporary support system that holds you accountable for your actions and puts you on the right track.*

This is…
I don't even know what to say right now.
I deserve everything I get.

> *Stop that.*
> *There are things you deserve, but you also*

experienced a lot of nonsense that should have never happened in the first place.

Like what?

In two years, someone is going to tell you to kill yourself right in front of a teacher. And the teacher is going to ignore it.

Sometimes, we joke like that. We probably shouldn't, but I'm sure it was a joke.

No, it wasn't. Not in this context...

...

It was the last week of senior year in high school, and the halls buzzed with the excitement of seniors signing yearbooks and talking about the future. I moved quietly through the crowd, feeling like an outsider in the place I was once forced to go to. My presence that day wasn't to celebrate with former classmates; I was there to say goodbye to my friends.

As I turned a corner, I saw Erika. Her familiar smile lit up when she spotted me, and she rushed over, pulling me into a warm hug. For a brief moment, the world felt okay.

"Adam!" she exclaimed, holding onto me tightly. "I've missed you. What's going on? You said you had some news for me."

I looked down hesitantly, trying my best to hide the nervousness in my expression. But Erika knows me too well and noticed it quickly. Her gaze then fell upon the faint scar peeking out from my neck.

"Adam, what's that scar? And why do you look... different? What's wrong?" she asked, concern replacing her earlier joy.

I gave her a half-hearted smile that didn't reach my eyes. "We're supposed to share our news at the park, remember?" I said, trying to deflect.

Erika wasn't letting go. She gripped my shoulders tightly, her eyes filled with worry. "Adam, please... just tell me now. What's going on?"

I let out a heavy sigh. This wasn't how I wanted to do this, but I couldn't avoid it any longer. I gestured for Erika to sit with me on the floor in the hallway. She hesitated for a moment, then slowly sat down beside me, her eyes never leaving mine.

I took her hands in mine, staring at the ground as my voice barely rose above a whisper. "I was diagnosed with lymphoma. It's... it's a blood cancer. And they found it late."

Erika's mouth fell open, her breath catching in her throat as the words sank in. She tried to form a response, her voice trembling as she began to ask, "W-what's going to happen to you, Adam? Are they going to—"

Before she could finish, a sharp voice interrupted her. I didn't even need to look to know who it was. Henry, a spoiled rich kid who had made my life hell for the past four years, stood nearby with that familiar grin on his face.

"Why don't you do everyone a favor and skip the treatment?" Henry sneered, venom lacing his every word. "You're just wasting space, and when you're gone, no one will care. The world would be better off without you."

My jaw clenched as I glared at him, fury boiling beneath the surface. But my body was too weak, drained from the early stages of chemotherapy to do anything more than stare.

Erika's gaze darted to Ms. Ferringo, a teacher who had overheard the exchange. For a fleeting moment, Erika hoped she would step in, that someone would say something to stop this cruelty. But instead, Ms. Ferringo smirked as if Henry's words were a clever insult rather than a twisted form of malice. She turned and walked away, leaving us to deal with the aftermath.

Erika's eyes filled with tears as she looked back at me, unsure of what I'd do. But I just shook my head, too worn down to respond with anything but silence. The weight of it all: my diagnosis, the cruelty of people like Henry, and the apathy of those who should care settled over us like a dark cloud.

For a moment, neither of us spoke. The world around us kept moving, but it felt like we were frozen in place, trapped in a moment too heavy to escape.

...

I don't know what to say about that.

156

Every field has people who shouldn't be there.
Education is no different.

How do you know all this?

Because you eventually become a teacher yourself.

Are you serious?

As serious as the cancer you get in two years.

THAT IS NOT FUNNY!

Before I could reply, Freckles' voice echoed softly in my mind. "Actually, that's pretty funny."

I paused, a bit shocked by Freckles' laugh. "I'm surprised you understand this kind of humor."

"Of course," Freckles replied with a touch of smugness. "I've helped shape your sense of humor over the years. I'm sure you're familiar with gallows humor."

I nodded, a faint smile forming. "Of course. It's about laughing in the face of hopelessness."

You know who would have thought it was funny? Mr. Molina.

He probably would!
How is he in the future?
You know… in the future?

He's Dr. Molina now and is still the most amazing person ever. I promise he has not forgotten about you in my timeline.

157

That's good to know...
I always felt like he was the only teacher that doesn't
hate me.

I get that feeling.
But I promise, your teachers didn't hate you. They
hate that they have no idea what to do with you.

What do you mean?

You skip class all the time.
And somehow get better grades than many students
who have been there all year.

That's impossible.

Those aren't my words.
Those were your principal's words.

Principal Armstrong?
Are you sure?
I seriously doubt he took the time to talk to anyone.
He's always busy with meetings.
Still... if he did, that's much better than Assistant
Principal Garland. He goes out of his way to torture
me. I wish he'd go away.

Reading Sixteen's text, I realized I'd made a mistake. I hated Mr. Garland so much that I forgot he was still the assistant principal in Sixteen's timeline.

Every time I hear that man's name, it drags me back to the memories of how he constantly tore me down. He seemed to make it his mission to make me feel worthless. I can still hear him telling me to drop out of school, get a job at McDonald's, and pray that I could be helpful to society.

It took me years to let go of that anger. Every accomplishment I achieved, I did it while cursing Mr. Garland's name. Even after becoming an educator myself, I questioned his methods. I understand that some students need tough love, but it's supposed to be love, not cruelty for the sake of it.

"Are you going to correct Sixteen?" Freckles asked, its voice calm and steady in my mind.

I sighed, momentarily forgetting that Freckles was even there. "I don't know. Should I?"

"Given the circumstances, it's probably best not to burden him with that knowledge," Freckles advised. "It might only add to his anxiety."

I nodded, still unsure but trusting Freckles' judgment. "You're probably right."

"I hope so," Freckles agreed reluctantly. "Let's focus on what Sixteen needs to know now."

I'm confident that those were the principal's words.

If you say so.
I don't understand why anyone would be upset at good grades.

They aren't upset with the grades. They're upset because they see how capable you are. You don't want to hear it, but they see your potential and how you're wasting it.

You're right, I don't want to hear it.

Then maybe hear it like this... Educators aren't mirrors. It infuriates them that you can't see yourself the way they see you.

They have a weird way of showing it. Whenever I try to talk to my teachers, they make me feel like I'm wasting their time.

Dismissing you isn't the right option. But in all fairness, you do waste their time by giving them a bunch of unnecessary paperwork to fill out.

What paperwork do they have to do if I'm not there?

Teachers are state employees, and you're still a child. This means that the state is responsible for you while you're there. When you aren't there, teachers must fill out paperwork noting that you were not in class.

So, they just put an 'X' on my name on the attendance sheet. So what?

If only it were that simple. The state is essentially babysitting you while you're at school, and they're responsible if something happens to you while you're in their care. But it's not on them if they fill out paperwork proving you weren't in class. It's more than simply putting an 'X' by your name. There's more going on in the background that you know nothing about.

I...never knew that.

It's not something you'd need to know. Look... I know you have a lot of distrust towards your teachers, but not everything is their fault. They have to work within the confines of an unfair and outdated system.

Outdated system? Like... Windows 95?

More like the ENIAC.

The what?

> *The first computer. Came out in 1945? We're getting*
> *off-topic here.*
> *Your teachers don't know what's going on in your*
> *life at home. I know you think it's because they don't*
> *care enough to learn, but there's only one of them*
> *and dozens of students. While they do have some*
> *blame, it isn't entirely on them.*

How is it not all their fault?
I try to tell them all the time, but they dismiss me.

> *Simple.*
> *You're not special.*
> *They have other kids to take care of.*

Wow... I don't think you're allowed to say stuff like
that to your students.

> *You aren't one of my students.*

Fair point.

> *The part that is their fault is that they knew*
> *something wasn't working. They had multiple*
> *opportunities to put you in contact with a counselor,*
> *but they didn't.*

What would be the point? Wouldn't it just result in
another person telling me to call me a screw-up?

> *Not necessarily.*
> *I'm technically counseling you right now.*
> *And if your teachers took the opportunity to talk to*
> *you one-on-one, they'd realize that you aren't being*
> *challenged in their class. You should have been in*
> *advanced courses.*

Advanced courses!?
You must be joking right now.

Not at all.

You know damn well that we'd fail out of advanced courses in a heartbeat!

Do you want to hear a fun fact?

No, not really.

Too bad.
Your regents exams are the same whether you're in advanced or general courses. You've surprisingly scored higher than many advanced students.

You're lying.

By omission, yes. Let me fix that.
You're scoring as high as you are because you're going to many of the after-school review sessions. Those review sessions are meant for advanced students.
Somehow, you do great there.
Many advanced students mess with you, but did you ever wonder why they only mess with you outside of those review sessions?

I've literally never wondered why they only mess with me outside of those review sessions.

A simple 'no' would have worked, but okay.
You're supposed to be this idiot who isn't doing anything with his life, yet you're keeping up with them. You fit nearly a week of school into three hours of review sessions.
On top of all the nonsense you endure at home, you can still keep up with the best of the best. I'm not saying you're a genius, but you are no dummy by any means.

I appreciate you saying that... But I'm only good enough to get by. That's it.

162

*That's funny. You said the same thing about college
and you graduated at the top of your class.*

I go to college?

*Yes.
All of your teachers have at least four years of
college under them.
Do you want me to blow your mind?*

*...go for it.
How much crazier can it get?*

*During your time as a teacher, you end up dealing
with a student who believes in herself just as much...
or rather, as little as you believe in yourself right
now.
Because of everything you've gone through, you
were able to help her – To take someone who saw
themselves as worthless and inspire them to live
their dream.
Her name is Yessenia Costa Ramirez, and I have no
doubt you will meet her in the future.*

*There's just no way any of this is true. I hate school
so much, and you're telling me I make it my career?*

*Kind of, yes. It was meant to be temporary, but we
were good at it. So, we decided to stay and see
where it took us.*

And where did it take us?

"It took you straight to the spirit realm," Freckles quipped, then
followed up with a drawn-out, theatrical "Ooooohhh," as if it had just
delivered the perfect burn.

My jaw dropped, leaving me feeling confused, but admittedly, a little
bit impressed. "Did you seriously just say that?"

163

"What? It's gallows humor," Freckles replied, sounding entirely too pleased with itself.

I shook my head, fighting a smirk. "Yeah, well, you're doing it wrong."

Career-wise... not very far.
But you get to have a direct impact on people's lives.
That sounds...lame.

Freckles interjected, sounding unimpressed. "That does sound pretty lame."

"How so?" I asked, raising an eyebrow.

"Well, why don't you talk about your favorite parts?" Freckles suggested, its tone softening, encouraging me to open up more.

We started as a GED instructor. We were put in
charge of a classroom full of misunderstood students
who have rarely felt success in their lives... similar
to you.

Oh? How did we do?

We were terrible at first. We treated it like a high
school and used the same methods our teachers used
on us.

Us being terrible at things sounds about right.

It's okay to be bad at stuff. More importantly, it's
okay to make mistakes. We may have been terrible
when we started, but we asked one of our college

mentors for advice – Ms. Miranda Van Etten: one of the most influential educators in the country.

That name sounds so... old-school.

Yeah, well, she could kick your butt if she wanted to. She's a sweetheart, but she has way more power and influence than you'd expect, kind of like a mafia boss.
Anyway, she reminded us about our troubled upbringing and suggested that we give our current students what we needed back then. It completely changed our perspective. That simple shift turned us into the instructor with the highest graduation and retention rates throughout the county.

That's impressive. But you said we have the highest detention* rate?
Do we seriously become THAT teacher?

What are you talking about?
I never gave anyone detention.

You said "retention," but that was a typo.

Retention.
It's a real word, and I spelled it correctly.
It means that your students keep coming back.
Honestly, it's one of those buzzwords that they use in higher education that isn't as glamorous as it sounds.

But wouldn't you want your students to keep returning to class?

Technically, yes. You want students to keep returning until they finish. But you taught GED classes. The goal is to get them to graduate, not to keep returning and spending years obtaining their high school equivalency.

I guess that makes sense.
Why spend six years completing high school when
you can complete it in less?

Correct!
Our students started trusting us more when we
showed them our GED scores. They realized we
were in a similar position and saw that we could
relate to what they were going through.

Hold on! Wait one second.
Are you saying I don't graduate high school and get
a GED instead?

Yes. That's exactly what I'm saying.

How does this even happen?

You're diagnosed with cancer one month before
graduation and drop out of high school because of
it.

That's so messed up!

The messed up part is Dad being excited about us
following in his footsteps of not graduating high
school.

Wow…
Are you serious right now?

Yeah, I am.
The only way to make him proud is by reminding
him that he's better than you.

That's… sadly, not surprising.
But I just thought of something.
You said anything I do doesn't affect your timeline,
which is cool.
But with all the information you gave me…
Won't that allow me to take steps to prevent
dropping out of high school?
Won't that change the outcome of my life?

I'm hopeful that some stuff will change. But this won't. According to Disney and Marvel, this is an absolute point in time.

You told me not to worry about Disney and Marvel stuff, but you keep bringing it up!
Now you're talking about 'absolute points' in time?
What even is this?

Before I could type my response to Sixteen, Freckles chimed in with a teasing tone. "You're really leaning into this whole Disney and Marvel thing, aren't you?"

I sighed, trying to justify myself. "Well, you didn't give me much else to go off of other than saying Disney and Marvel explained time travel well. Considering this is a big moment, it felt like the right thing to say."

Freckles paused, then reluctantly conceded, "Alright, fair enough. But do you really think Sixteen is going to buy this?"

I shrugged. "He doesn't have much of a choice. But tell me... Are absolute points in time real?"

Freckles hesitated before finally admitting, "Yes, they're real. We call them 'sanctified epochs,' but the concept is the same."

A wave of relief washed over me. "Thank God."

Freckles' voice dripped with passive aggression as it replied, "Indeed, by the grace of the Lord, you are spared. I extend my powers to save you, yet it is He who receives your thanks. Not even a slight nod or a moment of recognition for my efforts."

I couldn't help but chuckle. "You know I appreciate what you're doing. Really, I do."

"That's not a thank you," Freckles quipped, clearly waiting for more.

I sighed again. "Alright, alright... Thank you."

"Was that so hard?" Freckles asked, feigning innocence.

"Yes, it was," I shot back with a smirk, shaking my head.

> *I know. And you're right. I'm sorry about that. I honestly don't know how else to explain it. But all you need to know is that some things will happen to you regardless of what we talk about.*

Okay then.
I'm guessing cancer is one of those moments.

I blinked, then focused my thoughts on Freckles. "Hey, is cancer one of those absolute points in time?"

Freckles responded with a hint of impatience. "Yes, it is. You both seem to have forgotten that you told Sixteen it was spreading and nothing could be done to stop it."

"In my defense, I only said it because he was getting on my nerves," I muttered. "I figured it was probably true, but I just wanted to know for sure."

Correct. It has already started.
All you can do at this point is wait for the diagnosis.
Again, please act surprised.

I'm so excited to almost die in two years!
I wish you could see the big smile on my face.
It's going to be incredible!

That's the spirit!

Hey. I hate to end this chat early, but I have to get
ready for a track meet today.
I hope you aren't mad.

Why would I be mad?

I figured you had more to say, and I'm cutting you
off without warning.

That's completely fine.
You have an obligation to your team.
Where are you competing?

I don't know. I just get on the bus and do whatever
the coach says.

Alright, we'll continue this tomorrow.

Yes, sir!
I appreciate you taking the time to talk to me today.

Sure thing. I'm glad I could help.

Smell ya later!

Why are you like this?

After putting my phone away, I leaned back on my bed and stretched
out. I felt this nagging doubt creeping in like I hadn't accomplished
anything today.

Freckles chimed in, picking up on my thoughts. "You're doubting yourself again. Do you really think you didn't do enough today?"

I let out a long sigh, staring up at the ceiling. "Honestly? Yeah. It feels like today's conversation didn't cover anything important. Just... empty words."

Freckles took a moment before responding. "I get it, Adam. But whether you believe it or not, you did good today."

I shook my head, still feeling that doubt. "I don't know... it didn't seem like Sixteen even wanted to talk. I couldn't connect with him like I needed to. I feel today was a waste."

Freckles, trying to be the voice of reason, replied, "Adam, you know better than anyone else that not every student is receptive to learning daily. But that doesn't mean you give up or stop trying."

I nodded slowly. Freckles wasn't wrong, but this wasn't just a normal teaching situation. "I get that, but there's a lot more on the line right now. This isn't just any student – it's me, my younger self. If I can't get through to him, then who will?"

Freckles agreed. "You're right, Adam. But you have to be patient. We both knew this wasn't going to be easy."

Even though I knew Freckles was trying to reassure me, the frustration still lingered. "It just feels like we didn't make any progress today."

Freckles reminded me of the small victories. "You did. You talked about something important to Sixteen – his classmates and his distrust of teachers. You even told him you'd become an educator in the future. That's no small feat."

I knew Freckles had a point, but it didn't change how I felt. "Yeah, I know... but it still doesn't feel like enough."

Freckles picked up on my underlying frustration and asked, "Adam. What's really bothering you? I know this isn't it."

I closed my eyes, letting those old wounds surface. "I just wish things had been different when I was growing up. I wish I had someone to tell me there are consequences for my actions. A support system... I never had that."

Freckles stayed silent, just listening.

"I wish things had been different with my classmates, too," I continued, the regret creeping into my voice. "Whenever I think about high school, the bad memories always drown out the good ones. I feel like I ruined everything back then. I kept telling myself that I didn't care... and now, I care so little that I have zero interest in even reaching out to them."

Freckles finally spoke up, softly but open. "So, what are you going to do about it?"

I furrowed my brow. "What do you mean?"

"You can either sit with the pain of wishing things had been different, or you can take that pain and do something positive," Freckles explained. "You've always used pain to help others avoid feeling like you did. What's wrong with continuing with what you know is working?"

I let Freckles' words sink in. Even though I knew Freckles was right, I just wasn't ready to let go of that sadness yet. "Yeah, maybe..."

Freckles didn't let up. "You know what it's like to feel worthless, like a burden. That's why you're the one who can make a difference – not just for Sixteen, but for others too."

"Freckles," I finally said, my voice barely a whisper. "I don't mean to change the subject, but I need to know. How's Jessica holding up?"

Freckles was silent momentarily as if weighing the gravity of the answer. "You know," it began slowly, "that's not something you should focus on right now."

"I need to know," I insisted, my heart aching with the need for connection. "Please, tell me."

Freckles sighed. "Jessica is struggling. She's worried and heartbroken but also trying to be strong. She's showing incredible resilience, Adam."

I nodded, feeling a mix of relief and sorrow. "I figured as much," I said quietly. "That woman has always been strong."

"Indeed," Freckles agreed. "That's why you married her. But it would be best to shift your focus to the task at hand. Jessica needs you to succeed here."

"I know," I replied, pushing the emotions aside. "It's just... hard."

Freckles' tone softened. "I understand. But you're doing this for her, too. Keep that in mind. We'll get there: one step at a time."

Chapter 7

The hospital room was painfully quiet, except for the soft, steady beeps of the machines keeping Adam alive. Erika stood in the doorway, her heart hammering in her chest as she took in the sight of her best friend lying so still. She could barely recognize him like this, surrounded by tubes and wires, his skin pale under the harsh fluorescent lights. Her breath quickened, the moment's weight pressing down on her shoulders like a boulder.

Erika's husband, Warren, lingered behind her, staying near the door. He was close enough to offer support but far enough to give her space. He knew this was something she had to do on her own.

Erika hesitated, her feet refusing to move, but she forced herself forward, one shaky step at a time. When she finally reached Adam's bedside, she just stood there, staring at him, unsure of what to say. She opened her mouth, but the words caught in her throat, and all she could manage was a sharp breath.

Her tears blurred her vision, and she quickly wiped them away, struggling to regain her composure. She couldn't fall apart now – not in front of him. With a deep breath, she lowered herself into the chair beside his bed, her hands trembling in her lap.

"I want to tell you..." she began, her voice faltering. She looked over at Warren, searching for strength in his eyes. He gave her a subtle but encouraging nod, his gaze filled with empathy. Erika swallowed hard, wiped her tears again, and turned back to Adam.

"Adam... I'm sorry," she whispered. "I... I know what I want to say, but..."

Her voice cracked as she bit down on her lip to keep from sobbing. She remembered all the times they'd shared news – how they'd always held hands on that park bench, whether good or bad, grounding themselves in each other's presence.

She reached for Adam's hand with trembling fingers but stopped just inches away, afraid her touch would hurt him. As her heart raced, she hovered there for a moment before finally letting her hands rest on his. His skin was cold, only adding to her uncertainty.

"Adam," she whispered, "we always share news hand in hand, right?"

She closed her eyes, took a deep breath, and squeezed his hand gently, wishing for him to respond. "Jessica told me that doctors have been... preparing her for the worst." Tears streamed down her face, but she refused to let go of his hands. Her grip tightened as if she was trying to pull him back from wherever he had gone. "But I don't care. You've always overcome the worst odds, and I need you to do it one more time. Please, Adam... do this for me."

Her voice broke, and she couldn't hold back the sobs any longer. They came in waves, and she started to hyperventilate, the grief overwhelming her. Warren, who had been standing near the door, took

175

a step forward, instinctively wanting to comfort his wife, but before he could move any closer, Jessica, who had been waiting just behind him, gently placed a hand on his arm.

"Let her do this," Jessica whispered, her voice thick with emotion. "Trust me, I want nothing more than to go to her right now, but Erika must do this alone."

Warren looked at Jessica, his face showing his helplessness. He sighed deeply, his shoulders sagging in defeat, but he nodded and stayed put.

Erika, meanwhile, had sunk to the floor beside Adam's bed, her hands still clinging to his as she cried into his chest. She didn't care about the machines or the wires. All she wanted was for him to wake up, to laugh with her, and tell her that everything would be okay. But she knew it wasn't going to happen – possibly ever again.

Warren watched helplessly, every fiber of his being wanting to comfort his wife, but Jessica's words echoed in his mind. He had to let her have this moment.

After what felt like an eternity, Erika slowly lifted her head, her face streaked with tears. She looked at Adam, a faint, broken laugh escaping her lips through the sobs. "I'm always getting snot on you," she said, shaking her head. "You've been such an amazing friend. You always knew what to say to make me laugh and smile..." Her voice caught as more tears fell, but she giggled through them. "And cry... But you knew how to make me feel loved – like I was the most important girl in the world... You were the benchmark for how any partner should treat me, and I love you so much for that..."

She leaned forward and wrapped her arms around him in a gentle hug, resting her head on his chest. "You'll always be my best friend," she whispered, her voice barely audible now. "I love you so much."

Jessica stood quietly by the door, her heart breaking as she watched the scene unfold. She could feel every ounce of Erika's pain, and it made her own grief almost unbearable.

Warren sighed, knowing he could do nothing except let his wife have this time with Adam. The helplessness gnawed at him, but he understood.

Erika slowly pulled herself up from the floor, her movements shaky and slow. She pressed a soft kiss to Adam's forehead and lingered there momentarily, her tears falling onto his skin.

"When I see you again," she whispered, "I promise I will have so many stories to tell you."

She turned around, her legs feeling like lead, and took a few steps toward Jessica and Warren. The tears streamed down her face more intensely now, her body trembling with the weight of her emotions. Jessica couldn't hold back any longer – she rushed over to Erika and wrapped her in a tight embrace. They held each other, both crying, sharing in the unspoken bond of their shared grief.

Warren stood a few steps away, his heart aching as he watched the two women he cared about lean on each other. He understood that sometimes, all you could do was let people hurt, even if it broke you to watch.

...

I looked around my room, reflecting on the progress so far. Each day had been a whirlwind of emotions and memories. I had talked to Sixteen about so many things, trying to guide him away from my mistakes. Even now, I wasn't certain if I was making a difference. Sure, there were moments of understanding, hints that maybe he was starting to get it. But other times, it felt like talking to a brick wall. It was frustrating.

I thought about our conversations, the ones that seemed to click and those that didn't. Freckles had reminded me that these small moments were still significant to Sixteen. The child didn't have my knowledge and experience. He is a kid trying to find his way, and I was his guide. It was easy to forget how monumental these insights could be for someone still figuring things out.

Despite my doubts, I took a deep breath and promised myself to keep going, to give it everything I had. Sixteen deserved that much. No matter how hard it got, I'd keep pushing forward, be the person I needed back then, and tell him what he needed to hear. Because, in the end, that's all I could do. And hopefully, it will be enough.

…

"Freckles, assemble!" I shouted, channeling my inner superhero with a grin.

Freckles' laughter filled my mind, a warm, familiar sound. "Really, Adam? Is that how we're starting the day?" it asked, fully amused.

"Yup! Exactly like that," I replied without any regret.

Freckles' laughter continued, but then it shifted, becoming more thoughtful. "You seem happier than usual today."

"Yeah, I am!" I admitted, glancing around my room. The soft morning light filtered through the curtains, casting a golden glow. "We've only got four more days to finish this mission! But…" I hesitated as a question popped into my head. "How will we even know if we've completed it?"

Freckles was quiet for a moment, considering the question. "I'm not entirely sure. The Lord said you'd know when the time comes."

"God said I'd know?" I repeated, letting it sink in. "Alright, I'll trust in that." Another thought surfaced. "Hey, Freckles, I've got another question."

"What's on your mind?" Freckles asked, concern in its tone.

"How has my mind been so sharp lately?" I asked.

Freckles responded quickly. "What do you mean?"

"Well," I started to explain, "I've got ADHD, and normally, I take medicine to help me focus. But since we started this, it feels like I've been on them the whole time – my mind has been laser-focused."

Freckles paused as if considering my words. "That's a good observation... but I don't have the answer to that one either."

I let out a light laugh. "Wow. I'm surprised by how much you don't know."

"This mission is new for me too, Adam," Freckles admitted, their voice almost reflective. "I'm learning right along with you. I won't always have the answers."

My phone buzzed, snapping me back to reality. I pulled it from my pocket and the screen lit up with more notifications than usual. It was a clear reminder of why we were handling this mission through text instead of face-to-face.

Hey!
Are you there?
I have an important question for you!
Heyyyyyyyyyyyyyyyyyyyyyyyyyyyyyy!!!!
Please don't make me spam you.
Please.
Respond.
Right.
Now.
Please.

Thirty-six!
Respond.

                                                    STOP IT!

Now.
Hey!
I have a question for you.

                    Do not ever spam me or anyone else like that ever
                              again. That is so annoying.

Well, yeah.
That's the point.
I needed your attention.

                    How would you feel if someone sent you a bunch of
                              messages while you were busy?

Are you busy?

                                                    Irrelevant.
                    Look... if you need to get someone's attention, there
                    are ways to do it. Sending a bunch of messages is
                                                    not it.

Okay.

                    I'm being serious. You don't get it now, but
                    spamming someone with messages does the opposite
                    of getting their attention. It shows a complete lack of
                                        respect for them.

How so?

                    You're telling someone to stop what they're doing
                    and pay attention to you. It's like a five-year-old
                    constantly nagging their parent for attention.

But what if it's an emergency?

If it were that much of an emergency, you wouldn't be spamming them with messages. You'd be calling them.

I would, but I don't have your phone number!

A realization hit me shortly after reading Sixteen's message.

"Freckles. Sixteen is using AOL Instant Messenger, right?" I asked, needing confirmation.

"Correct," Freckles replied. "We've gone over this already."

"I know we did," I responded. "But if Sixteen doesn't have my phone number, how is he messaging me?"

Freckles didn't miss a beat. "Just like anyone else, Adam – through your AOL screen name."

"Screen name," I thought to myself while being hit with a wave of nostalgia. Your screen name was the original gamer tag for chatting with people online. Back then, your screen name was everything: It was how people knew you and how you presented yourself to the world. It wasn't just a username: it was your digital identity. You'd spend way too much time coming up with something cool or funny: something that felt like you.

"I'm almost afraid to ask... but what's my screen name?" I asked, my voice tinged with hesitation.

"Does it matter?" Freckles reluctantly asked.

"Yeah, it does," I insisted, feeling the dread building. "What is it?"

There was a brief pause before Freckles answered, "RyReynolds76."

I froze. My eyes widened in shock, and the phone slipped from my hand, hitting the floor with a dull thud. I just stared into space, struggling to process what I'd just heard.

Freckles' voice broke the silence. "Adam, is something wrong?"

I picked up the phone, still reeling from the shock. Without thinking, I blurted out, "Freckles… What is your obsession with Ryan Reynolds? Seriously, what is it? I'm not typing another word to Sixteen until you answer this."

"I don't know what you're talking about," Freckles responded, sounding almost innocent.

"Freckles," I said, my tone firm. "I don't care if we forfeit our second chance and spend the rest of eternity in the 'undesirable place,' as you call it. Nor do I care if you become an infamous oathbreaker. I will personally doom us both if you don't answer this question."

Freckles remained calm, almost amused. "Ryan Reynolds appears to be a popular and well-loved figure in your timeline. It seemed fitting to align you with something familiar and admired. Plus, his charm and humor resonate with you, Adam. It made sense to use him as a point of connection."

I blinked, slowly shaking my head. "No, Freckles. That's not the answer. Tell me the truth."

There was a brief pause before Freckles admitted, "… fine. It is because even angels can't resist his charm. Are you happy now?"

"I…" The words caught in my throat, completely blindsided by Freckles' bluntness. I swallowed hard, trying to gather my thoughts. Finally, I let out a sigh, shaking off the surprise. I turned back to my phone and started typing again, determined to repress everything Freckles just said.

Fine.
What is your question?

Something isn't adding up.
You're here in my timeline, which is already bizarre.
But you're spending a lot of time talking to me. You don't seem like the creepy stalker type.

I already told you I'm here to help.

Listen to me.
You also admitted that you hated the way you were at my age. So… why are you spending so much time with me? You're giving me all these life lessons and being more patient with me than anyone else.
You said anything we talk about does not affect your timeline, so there's nothing in it for you.
There has to be a reason that you're here.
So, tell me. Why?
There must be a reason you're here doing this because there is nothing in it for you.
So…
Tell me, why?

Ain't nothing but a heartache!

What???

Ain't nothing but a mistake!
I never want to hear you say!

Oh my God! Will you stop singing Backstreet Boys
and answer my question!?!?

I stared at the question on my screen, my fingers hovering over the keyboard. "Was I really that much of a detective when I was a kid?" I asked Freckles. "The way Sixteen pieced things together... it felt almost too sharp for someone his age."

Freckles' voice broke into my thoughts, a hint of laughter in their tone. "Yes, you were. What you're seeing right now is one of the joys of untreated ADHD."

I tilted my head, not quite getting it. "What do you mean?"

Freckles' tone shifted to something more explanatory. "Do you remember what hyperfocus is?"

I thought about it for a second, and then it hit me. "Hyperfocus... it's when your mind locks onto something so intensely that everything else fades away. The only thing stopping it from being amazing is that you can't control what your mind decides to obsess over. Honestly, it's like having a superpower you can't control." I shook my head, letting out a sigh. "What are you getting at?"

185

Freckles' voice came through, calm and patient. "Adam, Sixteen must have been reflecting on your conversations. He was probably hyperfocusing on a part that didn't make sense to him."

I frowned, trying to understand. "I don't think that's Sixteen hyperfocusing. I know they call it attention deficit, but it's not really a lack of attention. It's more about having trouble controlling what you pay attention to."

Freckles paused, then asked, "What do you think is happening?"

I thought for a moment, trying to piece it together. "I think you're right that Sixteen has been reflecting on our conversations. But I think his anxiety is working to his advantage right now. When I was his age, I always felt like people had hidden motives when interacting with me. From his perspective, I hate my younger self, yet I'm spending a lot of time with him. That's stupid. There must be something in it for me or I wouldn't be doing it."

Freckles sounded impressed. "That's an insightful observation, Adam. The psychology of mortals is fascinating."

I couldn't help but laugh. "Well, you better hop on your 'angel internet' or whatever you call it and do some research."

Freckles responded with a calm and amused tone. "I'll be sure to use my AOL later on."

I blinked in disbelief. "America Online? Angels use America Online?"

"No," Freckles replied, "Angelic Online."

The disbelief was too much for me. I sighed, shaking my head. "I shouldn't be surprised... and yet, everything about you could be turned into a meme."

Freckles seemed confused. "What is a meme?"

"Know what. Just... forget it," I said, waving it off. "So, how do you think we should respond to Sixteen?"

Freckles' voice took on a more serious tone. "It might be time for you to tell him the truth."

I nodded, realizing they were right. "Yeah? Okay. Honesty it is."

> *You're not wrong.*
> *Can't lie to yourself, right? So here goes.*
> *In my timeline, we try to kill ourselves.*
> *I'm trying to prevent you from doing the same in*
> *your timeline.*

Freckles' panic was almost palpable. "Adam, what on earth are you doing? You can't just rip the bandage off with news like that!"

"But you said, it MiGhT Be TiMe To TeLL HiM tHe TrUtH!" I shot back in a mocking tone.

Freckles signed, then reminded me, "Did you forget our conversation about easing into it?"

I shrugged. "That was days ago. We're more than eased in. We're in pretty deep now."

Freckles responded, confused. "What does that even mean?"

I thought for a second, "You know what... That sounded a lot cleaner in my head. Just trust me. We'll be okay."

Oh. Well, I guess that makes sense.

You don't seem surprised by this at all.

I mean... I am a little bit.
But after talking with you for so long, it makes sense
that I would do this.
Can you tell me when this happens?

Freckles immediately interjected, "Don't you dare..."

I nodded to myself, already knowing better. "I won't," I reassured Freckles.

That's not something you need to know right now.
What matters is that we're here to change things.

It matters to me.

No. You can't unlearn this one.

You said the same thing about cancer, and I think I
took that well enough.

First off, you didn't take that well.
Like, at all.
Second, this is different than cancer.
Cancer almost kills you. This one... Even I'm not
sure if you will survive.

But I'm going to survive!
With everything you're telling me, I'm not just going
to take my own life like that.
Things eventually improve, so why would I throw it
all away when things will get better?
Or... is this one of those absolute moments?

I paused, then asked Freckles, "Is it an absolute moment?"

Freckles hesitated. "I'm not certain. I don't know what the Lord has planned in Sixteen's timeline."

A thought occurred to me. "But if Sixteen knows where he ends up, wouldn't it deter him from taking that path?"

Freckles's voice was calm but firm. "You knew exactly what you were doing, and it didn't stop you."

I sighed, conceding, "That's a fair point."

I'm not sure if it's an absolute point in time.

Good! So you have nothing to lose by telling me
when it happens.

That is not going to happen.

Fine.
But there is something I'm confused about. If you're
from the future and are currently trying to stop me
from killing myself, does that mean you're a ghost?

It's a complicated answer. In my timeline, we are
still alive, but not for much longer.

That... What?
What does that even mean?

As Sixteen's question lingered, a wave of anxiety surged through me. "Freckles, I need help answering this. Sixteen is asking good questions."

With a hint of amusement, Freckles replied, "Well, you're on a roll with the honesty. Just tell him you're 'closing a solitude.'"

I groaned, clearly unimpressed. "Seriously? You want me to tell a depressed sixteen-year-old that we're 'closing a solitude' and that he might end up dead if we fail? Are you really going to say that to me with a straight face?"

Freckles replied dryly, "...but you can't see me."

I could almost hear the smirk in Freckle's voice. "Damn it, Freckles! I don't need to see you to hear your confidence!"

With a sigh, Freckles softened. "I am simply suggesting that you find a way to make it make sense."

I nodded, preparing to text Sixteen back, fully aware of the delicate balance I needed to strike in my response.

> *Okay... Do you remember that part in that Super Nintendo game, Chrono Trigger, where you had to let the moonstone rest for billions of years?*

Yes. That quest still annoys me to this day.
It sounded so simple: just travel back to basically the beginning of time and leave the moonstone in the sun shrine.
The sun shines on it for billions of years, and it

190

evolves like a Pokémon into the sunstone.
But at some point in time, some losers come through
and steal the moonstone!
So, I had to play time detective to find the moonstone
again and set things right.
I love that game so much! But what does that have to
do with me?

"I see what you mean about the untreated ADHD," I said, shaking my head. "He's right about everything, but a simple 'yes' would've worked."

Freckles laughed, adding with a hint of humor, "Why use one word when you can use fifty, right?"

Correct!
In this scenario, you're the moonstone.
You were on a path with a specific purpose until
something knocked you off course. We're playing
time detective to right that wrong because your
timeline will be completely ruined if we don't

I think I get it now...
But... how ruined is "ruined."

Guaranteed death.

That...sucks.
So, how do we fix this?

We correct it by talking things out.

Forget conversation.
Let's take action!

And what do you think action looks like?

I don't know.
You're the adult here.

191

The "action" looks like what we've been doing for
the past few days.
And I believe we're making good progress.

But talking is boring!

I get that. But the events that led to your suicide
attempt were caused by the things happening in your
timeline right now.

But I feel perfectly fine, though.
I keep to myself in the garage, play video games, and
work at the department store for extra money. What
more can I ask for?

The things that actually matter.

Like what?

A stable support system.
People who genuinely care about you.
A partner who is there for you at the worst moments
of your life.

You're making this sound like a cult.

Freckles chimed in, its tone laced with amusement, "Honestly, you are making this sound like a cult."

I rolled my eyes as I retorted, "Religion sounds like a cult, too. Shush."

After a brief pause, Freckles responded with a chuckle, "Touché."

It's not a cult but rather a reminder that there is only
one life... and in my timeline, life gets cut short due
to the inability to deal with what is currently
happening.

I hate school, and I want to move out of this house.
You keep telling me things get better, so won't I just
put it all behind me?

> *Not at all. If you were able to, we wouldn't be in this*
> *situation.*
> *All those negative feelings you have... honestly, they*
> *never go away.*

I get what you're saying, Thirty-six.
But I'm having trouble believing it. There's no way
my friends would ever let me do something like that.
The thought of leaving behind Jack, Garrus, Erika,
and Sam... Even now, I don't know where I would be
without them.
Everyone else seems to just tolerate me. But them... I
love them all so much. Those four are the most
important people in my life right now. Well, they and
my sister are, of course!

Freckles' voice interrupted my thoughts. "You know... meeting those

four were absolute moments in time."

My eyes widened in surprise. "Really?"

"Absolutely," Freckles affirmed. "Let's start with Jack. If you—"

I chuckled and interrupted Freckles. "Heh, you said 'absolutely' after

saying 'absolute moment.' I see what you did there."

There was an uncomfortably long pause. "...Nevertheless," Freckles

continued. "had you not met him, you would never have understood

what a stable support system truly was. Jack anchored you when life

grew turbulent, and his parents embraced you as their own. Without

Jack, it's uncertain where your path might have led."

I nodded, acknowledging the truth. "Yeah... Jack has always been my rock. And no, it's not just because he's bald, black, and kind of a big deal. Ha ha! Yahtzee!" I added with a smirk.

Freckles groaned – it actually groaned. "...If you're not going to be serious, I will take away your talking privileges again," Freckles warned, a note of exasperation in its voice.

"You said you wouldn't!" I protested, trying to sound outraged.

"I made no such promise. I believe you mortals say, engage in folly, and you shall uncover the consequences," Freckles replied sternly.

I squinted, trying to decipher what Freckles had just said. The words didn't quite add up. "Were you...Freckles. Were you trying to say, 'mess around and find out?' Because the way you said it doesn't sound threatening at all."

Freckles' voice carried a hint of a smirk. "I wager that the sound of thunder, coupled with your sudden inability to speak, would indeed be quite menacing." Freckles said, the warning clear in their tone.

I knew better than to push my luck.

"Alright, alright, sorry..." I raised my hands in mock surrender. "I get it, okay? You're right... I did drift a lot. But Jack and his family – they were always there to pull me back when I was headed down the wrong path," I admitted, my voice softening. "Honestly, I can't even imagine where I'd be without their kindness."

"They saved your life, Adam. And truthfully, so did Erika," Freckles said calmly.

"Erika?" I asked, genuinely puzzled. "What did she do?"

Freckles' voice resonated softly in my mind. "Erika taught you what it means to connect with someone – to see them for who they really are and not what you wish them to be," it said gently. "Your strengths balance her weaknesses, and through her, you've been able to recognize and understand your own flaws."

"What does that mean in plain English?" I asked, a bit confused.

Freckles sighed, the sound almost carrying a weight of patience. "Erika revealed to you that true strength doesn't lie in concealing your pain, but in embracing it. She showed you that it's alright to be vulnerable. Most importantly, she helped you see that you are capable of love, worthy of being loved, and deserving of happiness."

"Yeah, you're probably right," I admitted with a sigh. "I thought I'd messed up our friendship when I asked her out. But Erika... she's something special."

"I remember that day, Adam," Freckles replied, a touch of warmth in its voice. "You should be proud of yourself. The line you used was very smooth."

"You think so?" I asked, a little surprised.

"I know so. You told Erika that you had met a girl who was so special and perfect for you. She encouraged you to ask her out, but you told her that you were afraid to. When she asked why, you took her hands and told her, 'Because I'm not sure if you would say yes.'"

I laughed, the memory bringing a smile to my face. "When you say it like that, it does sound pretty smooth. Even Erika thought so, too. She complimented me on the cleverness of that line."

"Do you remember what happened afterward, Adam?" Freckles asked, its tone shifting to something more thoughtful.

"I'll never forget," I said, the memory crystal clear. "She told me that I wasn't actually romantically interested in her, but rather, just comfortable with her. I had no idea what she meant until she decided to prove it to me." I smiled, the moment still vivid. "She kissed me... and then asked what I felt afterward. I wasn't sure what I was supposed to feel... but I can tell you that there wasn't some romantic spark."

"That was your first real kiss, Adam," Freckles noted, almost as if marking a milestone.

"I guess she was, yeah," I replied, my voice softening. "You're right... She showed me how to see people for who they are instead of what I think they are. I love her, I always have, and I always will. But I was never in love with her... And I'm glad it worked out that way because her friendship helped me see what love truly is."

"She feels the same way, Adam," Freckles said gently. "Now, let's talk about Garrus. Without him, I can almost guarantee you would have ended up in prison."

"Prison!?" I yelled, surprised. "That's a bit of a stretch, don't you think?"

"Not at all. Remember, you would openly skip class, lie to people, and disrespect others for no reason. You've done it for years, but have you ever wondered how you got away with it all the time?"

"Of course. I was a lost cause, and nobody cared about me at all. But why would they? I didn't even care about myself!"

"That's not true… Garrus cared. A lot more than you think. As a matter of fact, he was the first person to hold you accountable for your actions."

My mind flashed back to how I met Garrus. We met in elementary and became best friends during recess. We were inseparable until his family moved unexpectedly. Several years later, we met again in summer school and picked up our friendship right where we left off. It was as if the years we spent apart never happened.

"Look… I know you're right," I said. "If I'm being honest, Garrus knew I could do better and always pushed me to do so. I would half-ass something and celebrate as if I gave it all I could, but he saw right through it and made me do it again. He always demanded better from me because he knew I could always do better. Slacking in front of him was not an option. Whenever I did something wrong, he was never afraid to call me out on it. It... made me a better person. It's a trait I've tried to emulate in my own way. We're best friends, so we need to call each other out because that's how we improve. Wow... I'm starting to think prison isn't such a stretch now," I said, running my hands through my hair, finally seeing the realization.

"I'm glad you see it that way. That's one of your strongest bonds. You make each other better through accountability."

I nodded, fully taking in Freckles' words.

"Let's move on to Sam," Freckles continued. "Without him, you would never have learned to see things from different perspectives. You always thought the world was black and white, but Sam showed you that there are countless shades of grey. He's the reason you have the empathy you do."

I thought about Sam. We met in elementary school but never really spent time together until he started coming to Jack's house to play video games. We clicked, our friendship blossoming amidst the glow of TV screens and the sounds of digital adventures.

"Yeah," I acknowledged. "I thought he was a bit of a 'know-it-all' when we first met. But after many years of conversation, I realized we had way more in common than I could have ever imagined."

"And what would you say is the most important thing you have in common?" Freckles asked.

"We both enjoy discussions, especially when we have different opinions. Our views may conflict, but through discourse, we end up teaching each other unexpected lessons. It's sobering."

"That's a great way to be," Freckles said, encouragingly.

"It really is. Through his influence, I learned that if you take the time to learn another person's perspective, you see that you have way more in common than you think," I said confidently.

"Precisely," Freckles agreed.

"I think I'm starting to see a pattern. All of my closest friendships happened because we just started talking to each other and never stopped. It was the same way with Jessica, too," I said while reminiscing.

I smiled as I remembered the night I met Jessica. A mutual friend wanted to have his birthday party at a pub. The night's theme was salsa dancing, and they gave everyone lessons. I asked Jessica to dance, and while she moved gracefully, I embarrassed myself. Despite my clumsiness, she smiled and laughed, and we kept dancing.

We ended up talking the entire night. It was funny: Jack interrupted us, saying it was time to go. I tried to ignore it since we just started talking; at least, that's what I thought. It felt like a few minutes, but in reality, seven hours had passed. It was now three o'clock in the morning in the middle of the city that never sleeps. We exchanged phone numbers. We talked and just never stopped... until all of this.

Freckles responded, its voice full of empathy. "I understand. And I'm thrilled that your friendships fell into place so smoothly. But I must say, you mortals love to complicate things. Life really could be that simple."

I nodded, feeling a mix of nostalgia and sadness. "Yeah, I guess it could."

Freckles urged gently, "You should probably get back to typing. This was a well-inclined break but remember... Jessica is waiting for you."

> *I can promise that you wouldn't be who you are today without them.*
> *I'm glad you used the word 'tolerate' because there is something I want to teach*

Oh? What is it?

> *I have an extra copy of God of War.*

God of War?
Yahoo search says Ares is the God of War.

Freckles' voice interrupted my thoughts. "That game doesn't exist for Sixteen yet. God of War was released in 2005."

I grumbled. "Okay... swing and a miss. Let's try again."

> *Never mind. It's a video game that doesn't exist for you yet.*
> *I have an extra copy of Def Jam: Fight for New York.*

You know I don't care about music like that.
No... Wait a second. That's not music.

Are you telling me there will be a follow-up to Def Jam Vendetta!?

Freckles interjected again. "You're getting warmer. That game was released in 2004."

"Oh, come on!" I yelled, throwing my hands up in frustration.

...yes

Oh my god!

It's one of the greatest games ever made. When you buy it, please do not sell it. You will regret it.

Noted! So, you have an extra copy. Can I have it?

No. I don't actually have an extra copy.

But you just said you did.

I'm trying to tell you a story! And even if I did have an extra copy, I just told you not to sell it. Why would I give it to you?

Because you love me?

Nope. Guess again.

Wow. Ouch.

Moving on. I have an extra copy of Halo.

Ah, on Xbox.

Correct.

201

Okay, I'm following.

I could give the game to you.

Eh. Why?

Because I have an extra one.

Um... I'm not going to do anything with it.
I already have it. Well, Zack has it.

Alright then.
What if I were to bring it to Gamestop?

I mean... you could.
They would only give you five dollars, maybe.

That's kind of low, considering it just came out this
year. But it isn't doing anything for me. It's just
collecting dust.

I'm guessing that there are like, fifteen Halo games
in your timeline now.

Currently, there are six and a bunch of spin-offs.
Stay in character, please.

Okay, sorry.

What if I were to give the game to Garrus?
Didn't he just get an Xbox?

Yeah!
He did! He would love it!

Perfect.
I'll see if there's a way I can send Garrus a copy of
the game while I'm still here.

Freckles sighed, interrupting my thoughts. "Fine... I'll try to get Garrus a copy of Halo. I'll speak with his angel and see what can be done."

"Please and thank you," I said, smiling.

But do you see how the value of the game seems to change depending on who gets it?

I suppose, yeah.

Think of yourself as Halo and think of other people as the places you'd bring it to.
The people you need to be around are the ones who see your value.
I'm going to request that you stop spending time with people who don't see it.

Alright. I think I get it now.

You have a small group of friends who genuinely love and cherish you.
Spoiler: They're the ones you spend the most time with, so make sure you keep them close.

Do you really think so?

Yes. I'm speaking from experience here.
You don't realize it now, but they genuinely care about you and your well-being.

Do you really think so?

Stop saying that.
I know what I'm talking about here.

It's just hard to believe, is all.

Well, start believing!

Um... I don't think it works like that.
It's not like I can just flip a switch and believe.

Fair.
I bet you see the amazing things they accomplish and sometimes feel like you're falling behind.

I do feel that way sometimes. Things just seem to click for them. They always tell me I should take risks, but I'm too afraid to.

                    Can I tell you a secret?

Sure!

                    You're comparing yourselves to them.

...That's not exactly a secret.

                    No, listen.
        You're comparing yourself to people who have support systems.

A support system?

                    They have people taking an interest in their lives.
        They're consistently told to take risks because they have people to catch them when they fall.
                    That's a luxury we didn't have growing up.

But... I'm sure my friends will be able to catch me if I were to fall. Right?

                    Yes and no.
        See, they're your peers. Think of life as a path you're supposed to walk down. Currently, they are walking on the same road as you.
                    But they have a huge advantage.
        They have the guidance of someone who has already walked down that path.
        They have someone to teach them — to let them learn from their mistakes.

Oh. Doesn't Dad always say we're supposed to support ourselves?

I felt a surge of frustration rising within me. I took a deep breath, trying to keep my cool.

"Good. Now, remember to exhale," Freckles said, half-jokingly.

I slowly let out the breath, feeling the tension ease just a bit.

> *Yeah, he does.*
> *But he also never stood on his own.*

What do you mean?

> *He always says the reason he got this far in life is*
> *because of... what word does he use?*

Luck.

> *Yep.*
> *But honestly, it's not luck.*
> *He has had help the entire time.*
> *He is good at making people believe he is a loving*
> *father who is just down on his luck. People feel sorry*
> *for him, so they help him.*

I mean... maybe, yeah.
But he still does what he can, doesn't he?

> *He does less than the bare minimum.*
> *If these same people knew how he spends money on*
> *alcohol or gambling...*
> *Or worse: how he takes his frustrations out on you.*
> *If people knew that, they would never talk with him*
> *again.*

He's not perfect, but he's still Dad.

> *That is not an excuse!*

I know, but what am I supposed to do?
I spend my days walking on eggshells.
I try to just do what he says, which helps me avoid
getting into trouble with him. This is why I must
learn how to stand on my own. To be strong like
him.

I understand exactly how you feel... I did the same thing at your age. Later on, you learn that he does absolutely nothing to teach you how to stand on your own.

Instead, all he did was teach you how to survive being around him.

That's not true! I'm learning... He wants me to be tough, but I suck at it. I'm always struggling... I'm not strong enough yet, but eventually, I will be!

Sixteen... Dad is supposed to protect us. To teach us how to be men. To help us discover ourselves. Instead, he constantly calls us worthless and blames us for everything bad in his life.

He probably wouldn't get so mad if I didn't mess up all the time. I struggle to meet his expectations. I'm sorry I'm not as strong as you, Thirty-six. I'm sorry that I'm a failure right now. But I promise, I will get stronger!

Stop it, right now. Listen to me. Being an adult male makes you a man, sure. But it doesn't automatically make you a good man. A good man doesn't throw a tantrum whenever things don't go his way. A good man doesn't turn to alcohol to numb his pain. A good man doesn't use his youngest boy as a scapegoat to take his frustrations out on. Notice how he always gets physical with you but has left Zack alone once he turned eighteen.

I don't know if I can agree with that. I don't know what "an escape goat" is.

A scapegoat is someone put in place to take all the blame when something goes wrong.

I don't know.
What if I just try harder?

> *No matter how hard you try with him, it won't be*
> *enough. But thankfully, one day, you'll see that*
> *despite everything Dad did, you never let his words*
> *break you.*

I don't know if I can believe that.

> *It's okay if you don't right now. Just keep it in the*
> *back of your mind.*
> *I can't wait for the day you get to look back and see*
> *how far you've come.*

You keep saying how far we've come. Do we become
like... millionaires in the future?

> *No, we don't.*

What about Garrus and Sam?
They seem like the type who would make it happen.

> *No, they don't, either.*
> *Financially, we all did pretty good for ourselves.*
> *Just not millionaires.*

Oh wow.

> *Yeah, I know. If anyone was going to do it, it would*
> *be those two. But life doesn't always turn out the*
> *way you want it to.*

So... Do we at least make the most money in our
friend group?

> *There's more to life than just money and titles. It's*
> *about being happy with who you are, the difference*
> *you're able to make in other people's lives, keeping*
> *amazing people around you, and finding what you*
> *love doing and devoting as much time to it as*
> *possible.*

207

Those sound like the words of the person who makes the least.

Freckles interrupted my thoughts. "Sixteen isn't mistaken. Among your friends, you do earn the least."

I rolled my eyes, trying not to let the comment get to me. "Whatever. Unlike you, I actually have money."

Freckles quickly responded. "And unlike you, I have no need for money."

I shook my head, "Mmmhmm. Those sound like the words of a broke angel."

Anyway...
You're a huge inspiration to your friends.
I may have said you're lucky to have them but know
that they're just as lucky to have you.

I appreciate you telling me that. That's amazing to know that I have a good set of friends.

They're the best.

Oh, crap!
I have to go to work!

Go.
We'll continue tomorrow.

Alright.
Chow!

It's "Ciao."

No. It's "Sixteen."

The conversation with Sixteen had taken a lot out of me, but it also left me with a sense of accomplishment. We still had much to do, but for the first time in a while, it felt like we had made some real progress.

"Well done, Adam," Freckles' voice echoed in my head. "You did a good job!"

I smiled while shaking my head. "No, Freckles. We did a good job," I corrected.

Freckles' voice sounded genuinely confused. "Adam, what did I contribute exactly?"

I laughed, shaking my head. "You helped me through that entire conversation. And we all know there's no 'I' in 'team.'"

There was a pause before Freckles responded, sounding unsure. "Correct. There is no letter 'I' in the word 'team.' But I fail to understand what that has to do with our situation."

I looked up, letting out a small groan. "Don't worry about it, Freckles. Just know that I couldn't have done it without you and your input."

"Ah, I see. I am happy to be of assistance, Adam." Freckles responded, pleased with themselves.

"Freckles," I started, hesitating, "I have a question that has been bugging me for a while, but I didn't know how to ask. So, here goes... Does the Devil exist?"

Freckles answered immediately. "Yes, Adam. The Devil does exist. But where is this question coming from?"

"Well... we've been in Solitude for a while now. With everything I've been learning about angels, I figured I should know about the Devil as well." I said, voice full of curiosity.

"Your curiosity makes sense, Adam. You've been exploring deeper truths and trying to understand your place in all this." Freckles said softly.

I nodded slowly. "Thanks. So, tell me about him. What is he like?"

Freckles paused before speaking, knowing this wouldn't be easy to explain. "The Devil is the opposite of a guardian angel. My purpose is to guide and protect you while the Devil seeks to cause doubt, fear, and temptation. I work to maintain order while he thrives on creating chaos."

I nodded, trying to take it all in, but another question was bugging me. "So, there are multiple angels and only one Devil. Is the Devil that much stronger than angels?"

Freckles'continued. "The Devil was once an angel: one with immense power. He led a rebellion against the heavens, but he ultimately lost.

As a result, he was banished from the heavens. To answer your question: Regarding raw strength, yes, the Devil is stronger."

My eyes widened, and a knot formed in my stomach when I heard those words. "That's... that's terrifying. To know that he exists and is stronger than you."

Freckles sensed my anxiety and was quick to reassure me. "There is no need to be concerned, Adam. The Devil does not engage in combat, nor would he ever directly confront you. His true strength is not in physical force but in temptation and offering choices that lead you mortals astray. He is a master manipulator, and as powerful as he may be, even he cannot go against free will."

I nodded, slowly processing that. "That's a relief. But why does God even allow him to exist? What's the point of having someone around just to mess things up? It kind of feels like God is intentionally setting traps for us."

Freckles' tone softened. "I know it can feel that way. But good can only exist if there is also the potential for evil. The universe, heavens included, relies on balance. Light has no meaning without darkness. Without the Devil, there would be no contrast, no choice. And choice is the foundation of free will – the ability to choose between right and wrong, light and dark, good and evil."

I took a deep breath, still trying to piece everything together. "I get that, but does he really need to exist if all he's going to do is cause chaos?"

"Yes," Freckles answered. "His existence challenges mortals to exercise their free will. Virtue would be meaningless without him, as there would be no vice to overcome."

"Does that mean…" I asked hesitantly, "The Devil is responsible for all the bad things people do?"

Freckles' voice grew more serious. "Not completely. The Devil may create opportunities, but he is not solely to blame. He may tempt, whisper, and even provide options, but mortals are the ones who decide whether or not to follow those paths. Remember, Adam. He is not stronger than free will. Even he cannot force you to do anything you do not want to do.

I let out a long breath, feeling the weight of that truth. "Wow… I never thought of it like that. We blame a lot of our bad choices on the Devil and the outcome on God… but in reality, it's just humans being stupid."

Freckles' response was gentle but firm. "Yes. Mortals and their questionable decisions. Most of what happens are the results of your own choices."

I nodded, the conversation leaving me with much to think about. It was strange learning that the Devil does indeed exist. I hope he and I never cross paths.

Chapter 8

The room was quiet except for the heart monitor's soft, rhythmic beeping. Adam lay motionless in the hospital bed, his face pale and peaceful, as if he were merely sleeping. Only three days remain until Jessica would have to make the most difficult decision of her life.

The door creaked open, and Xander and Chrysanthia stepped inside. Two of Adam's coworkers were now faced with the surreal sight of their friend lying so still. It was strange to them to see someone usually so full of energy now completely motionless.

Xander, a man who had seen the ups and downs of working in education, stood firm. He had always been a mentor to Adam, guiding him through the often frustrating world of academia. Yet, as he looked at Adam now, he couldn't help but feel a mix of sadness and deep respect for him. Adam had become more than just a colleague, he was a friend, an equal, and someone Xander was genuinely proud of.

Chrysanthia, on the other hand, was visibly shaken. Her breaths came in shallow gasps, and her hands trembled as she clutched her bag to her chest. Adam had been her safety net: the person she turned to whenever she felt overwhelmed, whether it was with work, or the challenges life threw her way. He had been her mentor, her guide, and her friend. The thought of him lying there was more than she could bear at the moment.

Xander was the first to move toward Adam. His steps were slow as he was trying to take in the entirety of the situation. He placed a hand on the foot of the bed, gripping it lightly. His eyes lingered on Adam's still form, and after a long pause, he cleared his throat.

"Adam... I hope you can hear me," he began, his voice low but steady. "The school's just not the same without you. The students keep asking about you, wondering when you're coming back." He forced a slight chuckle. "I'm running out of things to tell them, so, you know... you have to get up."

Chrysanthia stepped closer to the bedside, her movements hesitant. She sat in the chair next to Adam's bed, her face was pale, and the fear in her eyes was clear as day. Seeing her mentor lying motionless shook her as she was struggling to find the right words.

Xander glanced at her and noticed the fear gripping her. "Chrysanthia," he asked gently, "are you sure you are okay to do this?"

She shook her head slightly, her voice barely above a whisper. "I... don't know. Where would I even start with something like this?"

"It's hard. But don't overthink it," Xander encouraged softly. "Treat him like you would any other day and say the first thing that comes to mind."

Chrysanthia nodded, her eyes still locked on Adam. She sat there momentarily, just breathing, her hands clenched in her lap as she fought to collect herself. Xander rested a hand on her shoulder, giving her a reassuring squeeze.

Finally, she spoke, her voice trembling. "Adam… I was going to tell you this the next time you stopped by my office. I accepted a new job." She paused, her breath catching as she tried to push through the tears. "I should be starting in two months."

Xander's eyes widened. Chrysanthia worked under him, and this was the first time he'd heard of her leaving.

She grabbed Adam's hands gently as she continued, tears slipping down her cheeks. "Remember Faithful Conversations, that talk show I kept telling you about? Because of you, I applied for the coordinator of public relations position, and they accepted me!" Her voice broke as the tears came faster. She squeezed Adam's hands even tighter. "Want to know the best part, Adam? I get to sing the outro live, on every episode. You know how much singing means to me."

She continued to choke on her sobs, her words now coming in broken pieces. "You always believed in me. You kept telling me I could do it, and now… I'm finally doing it. I just… I wish you could hear this."

Xander, still processing the news, smiled gently. "He can hear you… and he is so proud of you, Chrysanthia. We're all proud of you."

Chrysanthia gave him a small, grateful nod, then looked back at Adam, wiping her eyes. Her voice was thick with sorrow. "I just wish you were here to see me perform. You'd love it." She leaned forward and hugged Adam, her tears soaking into his hospital gown.

...

As the first rays of sunlight filtered through the small basement window, I sat quietly at the edge of my bed, reflecting on the journey with Freckles. The lessons, struggles, and moments of connection feel like puzzle pieces slowly coming together. I'm starting to feel more confident in my ability to help this kid, believing that every small breakthrough is progress. Yet, there's a nagging sense that something deeper is waiting to be uncovered.

But with the growing light comes the creeping doubts. Thoughts of Jessica – her smile, her laugh, and the fear of never seeing her again – continue to press heavily on me. The idea of losing her forever is unbearable. I know I need to stay focused, no matter what, but it's so hard to push these fears aside. I need to see this mission through.

...

I sat on the edge of my bed while staring down at the floor. The stress of the mission was finally catching up with me. I sighed, trying to shake off the anxiety that had settled in my stomach.

"Adam, are you okay?" Freckles' voice broke through the silence, gentle but laced with concern.

I nodded slowly, even though I wasn't entirely sure I believed it myself. "I'm okay as I can be," I said, my voice sounding more tired than I intended. "I've just been thinking… There are only three days left, and I guess I'm a bit worried about what is going to happen."

Freckles responded, its voice full of empathy. "It's understandable to feel that way, Adam. These are difficult circumstances, and the uncertainty is hard to bear."

I hesitated for a moment, then asked the question that had been gnawing at me. "How much progress do you think we made?"

Freckles paused, considering its words carefully. "I believe we are making fine progress, Adam. But there isn't a way to confirm that right now. We just have to trust in what the Lord said: that we'll know when we've completed the mission."

I nodded, but it didn't make me feel any less uneasy. "Yeah, I know, but it's so hard! I want to tell you that I'm putting every ounce of faith into God, but I'm starting to have my doubts." I sighed, feeling defeated. "I don't know what is going to happen, but I told myself I'd see this through to the end. It's not like I have any other choice, right?"

Freckles' voice softened. "Adam, the fact that you're moving forward, even with doubts, is still an act of faith. Mortals often think faith means having complete trust without hesitation, but that's not entirely true. Faith isn't just about believing everything will work out perfectly. It's about taking the next step even when you're unsure of the outcome. It's continuing to do the work, even when you don't see immediate results."

I let those words sink in, feeling a little of the weight lift from my shoulders. "Wait. So, you're telling me that I'm showing faith even when I don't think I'm showing faith?"

"Kind of, yes," Freckles replied. "Faith is not the absence of doubt but the willingness to keep going despite it. You're still here, still trying, and that's what matters."

I continued to let Freckles' words sink in and felt a bit relieved. "That is surprisingly deep," I admitted, "Thank you for that. I really think it was something I needed to hear right now."

Freckles responded, its voice full of satisfaction. "I'm glad to hear that, Adam. It's good to see you finding some peace in this. But I have to say, your lives would be easier if you mortals would stop overcomplicating things."

I chuckled, shaking my head. "You keep saying that! But you have to admit that life would be easier if we all had our guardian angels to solve the puzzles for us." I pondered, half-jokingly. "Maybe you could talk with God and suggest some kind of like, 'heavenly reform.' You know, where all guardian angels can be in direct contact with their humans. Get rid of all that guesswork."

Freckles laughed, "As entertaining as that thought may be, Adam, it would undermine the very essence of faith. Your time on Earth is meant to be a journey – one where the path is often unclear. If angels were to intervene directly, mortals wouldn't be acting out of true belief or goodness. They'd be motivated by fear of consequence rather than from a place of conviction and love."

I nodded, understanding the truth in what Freckles was saying. "Faith means nothing if you already know the outcome. That makes sense."

"Precisely," Freckles replied. "But Adam. Now, I have a question for you. It's about Y2K."

"Y2K?" I repeated, my mind flashing back to the chaos and confusion surrounding the turn of the millennium. "You mean the whole panic about computers failing when the year 2000 hit?" I stumbled on my words, completely in shock at what Freckles was saying."
Like…What? This is so random. I'm afraid to ask… but what could you possibly want to know about it."

Freckles responded with no hesitation. "I was wondering, Adam, do you think—"

Before Freckles could finish, my phone buzzed loudly, the screen lighting up with a few notifications.

I glanced at the phone, but my curiosity about Freckles' question was stronger. "Sixteen can wait. I have to hear this question, Freckles."

Freckles' voice softened, almost as if it was smiling. "No, no. Let's begin with Sixteen. My question can wait."

I sighed, picking up my phone and glancing at the messages. "Alright, but this isn't over. I want... no. I NEED to know what an angel could possibly find interesting about Y2K."

Hey. Are you awake?
It's not an emergency. But something happened at
school, and I want your take on it.

Yes, I'm up.
What happened?

I got yelled at by a teacher.

What did you do?

Well, they were asking about the Civil War and why
the North went to war with the South.

A vivid memory from my high school days surfaced as I read Sixteen's message. It was a social studies class, and the teacher, Mr. Stevenson, asked the class why the North went to war with the South, starting the Civil War. The room was silent as nobody wanted to volunteer an answer. I tried to shrink into my seat, but unfortunately, Mr. Stevenson's gaze landed on me.

"Adam, why did the North go to war with the South?" he asked, his tone stern.

I cleared my throat, feeling the eyes of my classmates on me. "Because of slavery?" I answered, my voice unsure but hopeful.

Mr. Stevenson's face contorted with frustration. "NO!" he shouted, the word echoing off the classroom walls. My heart sank as he proceeded to lecture me in front of everyone. He went on about economic differences, keeping the states together, and political power as if my answer was the most ignorant thing he had ever heard.

The memory stung, and I could feel the embarrassment and anger bubbling up, even after all these years. It was one of those moments that made me question everything I thought I knew and instilled a fear of being wrong in a group setting.

Freckles' voice interrupted my thoughts. "You remember this well," it said, their tone softer than usual.

"Yeah, I do. I probably shouldn't but I do," I replied. "Sixteen has such a distrust towards teachers and moments like this... Ugh, it's hard to blame him," I sighed, frustrated by the memory.

I kept thinking about how Mr. Stevenson's harsh reaction did nothing to encourage critical thinking or a deeper understanding of history. Instead, it just made me more hesitant to participate in class.

"I want to tell Sixteen that the system isn't always right," I continued. "Teachers are human, and sometimes, the way they do things can cause more harm than good."

Freckles finally spoke, its voice thoughtful. "Maybe that's a conversation worth having. Helping Sixteen see that one teacher's opinion isn't the end-all-be-all could be valuable."

I nodded, agreeing with them. "I think you're right. Moments like this suck, but I think if he understands why it happened, it'll be easier to let it go."

With that, I turned my attention back to my phone, ready to share these thoughts with Sixteen and help him navigate the complexities of his education with a bit more clarity.

You gave the wrong answer.

Yeah, I think I did.

I wasn't asking.
I'm telling you that you gave the wrong answer.
*But I do remember that day. Mr. Stevenson didn't
have to be a jerk about it.*

Yeah, he really didn't.

Mr. Stevenson meant well.

He certainly has a weird way of showing it.

Let's look at it from his perspective.
*He's a white male teaching in a predominately black
school about a very sensitive topic.*

What makes the Civil War so sensitive?

Seriously?
The answer you gave. Slavery.
*Do I really need to go into detail why this is a
sensitive topic for black people?*

No...
But you're going to do it anyway, aren't you?

Damn right, I am.
*Slavery isn't just history. It's something that shapes
and directly affects our lives today. Our ancestors*

223

fought to be free, and a lot of the harsh realities they
endured were often silenced.

Okay... I get it.

Did you know that Abraham Lincoln admitted that if
he could stop the South without freeing slaves, he
would do so?

Wait, really?
Are you serious?

Yes, I am.
This is known, even in your timeline.
It just isn't taught.

Wow...
So why are we celebrating this racist?

He was the USA's 16th President, got us through the
Civil War, and signed the Emancipation
Proclamation.
He did a lot of great things.
I agree that his legacy should be taught, but we need
to include the bad as well. That's what Mr.
Stevenson was trying to do.

Emancipation Proclamation?
That sounds like an awesome name for a band.

No, it doesn't. It sounds like the bill that freed the
slaves within the Confederacy.

Okay... So why is my answer wrong?
He ended the war and freed slaves.

The question was, WHY did the North go to war with
the South? It wasn't because of slavery. It was about
the South seceding from the North and President
Lincoln wanting to keep the country together.

Oh, okay, I see now.

*It would be a disservice if Mr. Stevenson didn't
teach you and your classmates this.*

*I guess I can appreciate that.
Still, he didn't have to be so mean about it.*

*I agree with you.
There are ways to correct someone without being
mean. It's called having tact.*

What is a "tact?"

*Tact is the art of making a point without making an
enemy.*

That sounds...profound.

Isaac Newton said it.

The dude with the apples?

*Yes.
The dude with the apples.*

Didn't he die a virgin?

He did.

This might be TMI but...

I sighed, shaking my head. "I just know Sixteen's going to ask if we die as virgins."

Freckles chuckled, its laughter echoing in my mind. "You mortals and your rites of passage." "Why does that even matter?"

"To a sixteen-year-old? It's like the pinnacle of existence," I replied, rolling my eyes.

Freckles tried to hold back more laughter but couldn't. "And how exactly do you plan to answer this... pinnacle question?"

I smirked. "Expeditiously."

> *No.*
> *We eventually marry a beautiful woman named Jessica.*

From band class!?
Wow... you're right.
She is stunningly beautiful.

> *Even twenty years later, she is still beautiful, both inside and out.*
> *But no, I'm not talking about her.*
> *Her name is Jessica Klammer.*
> *You meet her in seven years.*

Klammer...I love that last name.
Sucks that she loses that gem.

> *What?*
> *"Loses that gem?"*
> *What do you mean?*

When we marry her.
Instead of Klammer, won't her last name change to Grey?

> *You would think so, but no.*
> *She is Latina, so she keeps her last name.*

What!?
Doesn't the wife take the husband's last name?

> *Women don't have to, but they usually do.*
> *In American culture, it's kind of a tradition.*

So...
What does her being Latina have to do with her

keeping her last name?
I wouldn't switch if I was her.
Grey is kind of...bland.

> *It is bland...*
> *In many Latin cultures, both men and women have*
> *two last names.*
> *One from each parent.*
> *Her full name is Jessica Klammer Herpin, but she*
> *changed it to Jessica Klammer Grey.*

That's cool then. So, tell me about her. Is she an
absolute point in time?

As I read Sixteen's question, I felt a bit of apprehension. "Is she an absolute point in time? I know she's important... but is it set in stone?"

Before I could even finish the thought, Freckles' voice exploded in my head, louder and more intense than ever. "Yes, Adam! She is THE absolute point in time! The singular moment around which all things turn! She is the axis of your very existence, the cornerstone of everything you are and will become!"

The sudden burst of energy made me cringe. "Whoa, Freckles, you need to calm down! It's really not that serious."

But Freckles wasn't having any of it. Its voice was brimming with conviction, almost vibrating with urgency. "No, Adam, you must understand – Jessica is the anchor, the constant that holds everything together. She's not just important: she's the absolute core of your journey, the reason you fight, the reason you're here. Do not forget that!"

I blinked, stunned by the force of Freckles' words. The realization hit me like a ton of bricks. Jessica wasn't just significant – she was everything. But I guess deep down, I already knew that.

> *She is an absolute point in time...*
> *And if we complete this mission, you'll learn all*
> *about her, one day at a time.*

I can't wait to meet her.
Does she play video games?

> *She does, but very casually.*

Cool! I can deal with that.
So... Can you tell me about your time working as an educator?
You seem to know so much about the field.

> *This feels sudden, but sure. I'll tell you all about my experience. We started at a community college and eventually started working at a university.*

Oh wow. What's the difference between community college and university?

> *Community colleges are usually smaller and allow you to obtain your associate's degree and some certifications.*

What is an associate degree?

> *Think of it as the first half of your bachelor's degree.*

What is a bachelor's degree?

Freckles could sense my patience slowly draining, and its voice gently urged me. "Adam, don't lose your temper with Sixteen. Remember, no one's ever shown him this stuff. He's figuring this out just like you did."

I sighed, feeling the tension ease a bit. "That's fair," I admitted. "You don't know what you don't know. At least he's admitting it."

An associate degree is your two-year degree and a bachelor's is your four-year degree. Certifications are mostly for trade skills like plumbers, electricians, and cosmetologists.

Cosmetologists?
Like...working with the stars?

No. Working with hair. Like cosmetics. You're thinking of Astronomy.

Oh! I see now.
What about University?
What makes those so special?

Universities are typically what you see on TV. They're usually bigger and have a lot more resources for students. They offer bachelor's, master's, and doctoral degrees.

Guessing the master's is a six-year degree and the doctoral is an eight-year degree?

Not exactly, but it's correct enough.

Okay, I think I get it now.
I'm not sure why some of our teachers keep making jokes about going to community college.

Because some of your teachers are stupid.

Whoa!
You're allowed to say that?

Why wouldn't I be?

Wow.
I'm just so used to teachers being quick to defend each other.

With any field you go into, you learn to see things from the customer's side, as well as the worker's side.
Knowledge truly is power, so, if an educator is making fun of where someone goes to further their education, then that educator is a fool, and you shouldn't listen to them.

You sound like a fair educator. I love that you're taking the time to talk to me about it. Usually, teachers just ignore our arguments.

It's mainly because you're still a kid. Honestly, I don't waste my time arguing with kids either.

Ugh... So, you're no different than them.

There's a difference between arguing with a kid and listening to what they have to say.
If you present well-thought-out points, are respectful, and are open to feedback, then I will make it my duty to give you all the time you need to talk with me.

I can respect that.
But Thirty-six. I need your advice on something you just reminded me of.

Sure.
What is it?

I got in trouble today for something that wasn't my fault.

What happened?

I went to orchestra class, and someone messed up the bridges on all of the basses.

Ah, the instrument: the bass.
I read that as a bass fish.

What is a bass fish?

Don't worry about it.
Continue your story.

Okay, weirdo.
I told the chairperson that the instruments were
messed up, and she wasn't listening to me.

I remember that day!

You do!?

Yes!
You were trying to set an example for the younger
members of the orchestra and reported the problem
to the chairperson because it kept happening.

Yeah!!! That's right!
I tried explaining what was happening, but she kept
talking over me.

You even told her, "Please listen."
She responded, "No, you listen," and then
proceeded to kick you out of her office.

Yes!
Oh my goodness, yes!
How do you still remember that?

I had a similar situation with one of my students. I
thought back to that moment and remembered how
Ms. Conroy made me feel, and I promised never to
do that to a student.

Ms. Conroy sucks.
I tried to do the right thing, but she ended up giving
me detention for it.

As I read through Sixteen's message, my eyes widened when I saw the
word "detention."

I sat there for a moment, trying to wrap my head around it. The memory was clear as day. Ms. Conroy had been angry, sure, but detention? That never happened, not to me. What the hell was going on?

"Freckles," I said, confusion evident. "I remember that entire incident with Ms. Conroy. I guarantee you that I did not receive detention that day. Why is Sixteen saying I did?"

Freckles took a moment before responding. "Adam, keep in mind, this is a different timeline. We've been at this for almost a week now, and there's a good chance your presence is already shifting things for Sixteen. Your influence may be making waves, even if you can't see them yet."

I wasn't sure how to feel at that moment. "I'm glad we're having an influence, but it resulted in detention – that's not exactly a win."

Freckles remained calm, its tone reassuring. "Adam, just because something seems negative to you doesn't mean it isn't happening for a reason. This could be leading to something bigger and maybe something necessary for Sixteen's growth."

I couldn't help but smile. "Erika could probably word this better."

Freckles didn't miss a beat, adopting a tone that was softer, more like Erika's. "Sometimes, a small setback is what we need to push us in the right direction. It might not feel good now, but it could be exactly what's needed to help Sixteen grow into who he's meant to be."

232

I laughed, feeling lighter. "That was pretty good."

That sucks…
I'm sorry you got detention.

It's okay.
Mr. Molina was there. We ended up talking about
Pokémon the whole time. He even let us out earlier
because I told him about MissingNo and he wanted
to go home and try and catch it.

I stopped in my tracks again, my mind spinning as I read Sixteen's message. "Wait, hold on," I muttered, more to myself than anyone else. "I taught Mr. Molina about MissingNo, but that was after class one day, not during detention."

Freckles' voice chimed in, sounding puzzled. "Adam, what exactly is a 'MissingNo?'"

I couldn't help but chuckle. "MissingNo is a glitch in the old Pokémon games. It was this weird, broken piece of code that showed up as a messed-up sprite if you did certain things in the game. It wasn't supposed to be there, but people found out about it and spread the word. I taught Mr. Molina about it, and he got a kick out of it. But again, this did not happen during detention."

Freckles sighed, and I could practically hear the regret of asking in its voice.

I shook my head, trying to piece together what was going on. "Okay, Freckles, seriously – what's happening here? Why is Sixteen's life happening differently than mine?"

Freckles paused for a moment, then responded thoughtfully. "Learning about MissingNo might have been an absolute moment. An absolute moment guarantees that something will happen, but not necessarily in the exact way it originally did."

I sighed, thinking it over. "This isn't exactly how Disney and Marvel explain it, you know."

Freckles' voice took on a slightly amused tone. "I said they did a good job explaining it, Adam, not that it was completely accurate."

I laughed, despite the situation. "Fair enough, Freckles.

"Probably better to not tell Sixteen about this," Freckles advised, its tone cautious.

"Yeah, yeah, I know. His anxiety, blah blah blah," I replied, waving it off with a sigh.

That's awesome!
I forgot that Mr. Molina is a gamer.

He plays here and there.
But back to Ms. Conroy. Do you remember what she gave me detention for?

I don't remember.
What for?

*For not telling her about the destruction of school
property.
Lady, I tried!*

> *You shouldn't have gotten detention for that. It
> should have been brought to someone higher up.*

*I thought about that, but the higher-ups don't exactly
like us, remember?*

> *That's depressingly fair.*

*Situations like this made me realize just how many
problems there are in the education system. It
sounds like we get to make a difference, so that's
cool. But still... I hate it.*

> *What problems do you think the education system
> has?*

Everything.

> *Okay.
> Pick a starting point.*

I don't know... the whole thing just sucks.

> *Can you try to name something specific?*

*Alright then...
We learn a lot of stuff that we are never going to use
in real life. Seriously, have you ever used A squared
plus B squared equals C squared?*

> *No, I've never used it outside of a classroom.*

*Exactly! So why put so much emphasis on having us
learn it?*

> *Because most of what you learn isn't about the
> material itself.
> It's about teaching you how to think critically.*

How so?
I'll never be in a situation where I need to use
Pathagorim's Serum or anything close to it.

I stared at the screen, my eyes narrowing in disbelief. "Did Sixteen just say 'Pathagorim's Serum?'" I asked, half expecting the words to change before my eyes. "And why does that sound like a third-party cough syrup?"

Freckles chuckled. "This, coming from the guy who still can't properly say, 'Space-time Continuum.'"

...It's Pythagorean's Theorem.
Construction, carpenters, architects, and some
engineers will use this. But again, it isn't about the
material itself. It's about training your brain to think
about things differently.

Oh really?
Can you give me an example?

The Pokémon weakness chart.

What about it?

In what world is flying weak against rock, ice, and
electricity?

If I throw a rock at a cardinal, that bird is going
down.

A cardinal is small enough to likely go down if you
throw anything solid at it.

Okay... but what if I were to freeze the cardinal's
wings?

That's just cruel.
But I suppose it wouldn't be able to fly. It would be

236

the same result if we did anything to damage its
wings using any element.

FINE! But at least flying being weak against
electricity makes sense. I wouldn't want to be in an
airplane and get hit by lightning.

Airplanes get struck by lightning about twice a year.
But planes today are so big that they'll likely just
shrug it off.
Unless they get hit directly in the fuel tank, which
rarely happens. I wouldn't necessarily call that a
weakness.

Well, flying is strong against bugs.
That makes perfect sense.

Freckles suddenly interrupted. "Adam, how is this debate helpful?"

I paused, my fingers hovering over the screen. "I just want to prove him wrong," I insisted. "I'm going to tell him about Zombie Snails and what happens after a bird eats an infected caterpillar."

Freckles sighed, struggling to keep a gentle tone. "You've already proved your point by showing him how to think differently."

Reluctantly, I had to admit Freckles was right. "I understand, but Zombie Snails is gonna be the final blow to this argument."

"Adam, don't," Freckles warned. "That will just cause more anxiety."

I couldn't help but push a little further. "Alright, alright. But, can I at least talk about Murder Hornets?"

Freckles' voice took on an uncharacteristic sharpness. "Stop. Please."

I let out a defeated sigh. "Fine... Back to the boring stuff."

Okay. I concede.
But you did just prove my point.

What do you mean?

You're thinking about Pokémon and elemental
weaknesses differently because of your exposure to
it. That's essentially what educators are trying to
teach students when they know it's material they
likely won't use.

Hmm...
I guess I kind of see it now.

You will see it even more in the future.
What else is wrong with the education system?
What else have you got for me?

It fails to encourage creativity! All of us have to do
the same assignment instead of the stuff we are
interested in.

In high school, I agree with you.
But in college, that changes.
You get to pick the majority of the classes.
When you first start college, you'll learn a little bit
from several different subjects. But the further you
go, the more you specialize in one area.
Once, I got to pick my own research topic.
My data was published in local newspapers.

That sounds so cool!
What did you research?

Happiness.
Jessica was going for her PhD.
This means that she became friends with other
students going for their PhD.
Most of her friends told me not to go for that degree
unless it was required for my line of work.

I can imagine how awesome it would be for people to call us Dr. Grey.

It would be awesome. But that is a lot of work for a title that we won't even care about.
Anyway, I asked my professors if they were any happier with their PhD., and all of them said yes. I told them what Jessica's friends told me and then proposed the question, "Does your level of education increase your overall happiness?"

Does it?

Kind of. It's like this.
Statistically, the more education you have, the more money you will make. But money isn't the biggest factor in happiness. Rather, it is about having a meaningful job and a healthy work-life balance.

I don't know what that means.

Happiness is getting a decent-paying job with flexible hours that allows you the freedom to do the things you're passionate about.
After all, money means nothing if you don't have time to spend it

That makes so much sense... but if you know the secret to happiness, why did you... Why did we do what we did? Why are you here in my timeline trying to prevent my doom?

I read Sixteen's words and felt a familiar knot tighten in my stomach. His question was fair. It was more than fair. And while I know he didn't mean any harm by it, the question struck a nerve.

Before I sunk too deep into my thoughts, Freckles' voice cut in, breaking my focus. "Adam, what are you going to tell Sixteen?"

The shift in my mood was instant. "I'm not ready to talk about it," I said, my tone flat, almost cold.

Freckles pushed a little further. "Adam, maybe it's time—"

"I said I'm not ready to talk about it, so drop it." I snapped, the words coming out sharper than I intended. The silence that followed was deafening. I could feel Freckles' concern, but I wasn't in the mood.

I turned my attention back to the screen, trying to bury the thoughts that had started to surface.

I'll answer that later.

It's just weird to me. It's like having the answers to a test and somehow still failing.

What part of "I'll answer that later" do you not understand?

Okay, okay.
I'm sorry.
Do you want to pick this up again tomorrow? I feel bad about asking you that question.

I sighed, feeling the guilt settle in, realizing I'd just let my emotions get the best of me. I hadn't just snapped at Freckles, but I'd also shut down on Sixteen. The shame started kicking in, and I knew I needed to make it right.

"Look, Freckles... I'm sorry," I said, my voice softening as I tried to push past the frustration.

240

Freckles was quiet for a moment before speaking, its tone gentle but firm. "You should take Sixteen's advice. End today's conversation and pick it up again tomorrow."

"But I can control—"

I started to make an excuse, trying to justify why I should keep going, but Freckles cut me off. "Adam. There is nothing wrong with coming back to this when you are calm. Continuing might do more harm than good."

I sighed again, feeling the internal struggle. And after a short pause, I responded, "No."

Freckles paused, clearly surprised. "No?"

I doubled down, straightening up as I made my decision. "No. You said this mission is about facing fears, right? Well, time is running out for us, and I'm not going to back down just because I'm afraid of the truth. I have to do this. I owe it to Sixteen, to Jessica, and yes, even you. I must push through this."

There was a moment of silence, and I could feel Freckles processing what I'd said. Finally, it responded, its tone softer, but with a hint of respect. "If that's your choice, Adam, I will support you."

> *Sixteen. You have nothing to apologize for.*
> *You asked a fair question… but it's a sensitive*
> *subject for me. I had no right to speak to you like*

that when you were just concerned.
I'm sorry. I truly am.

It's okay.

No, it's not okay.
When you do something wrong, I have no problem
telling you.
But you were completely innocent this time. It's not
okay for me to talk to you like that when you've done
nothing wrong.
It's a subject that I'm not ready to talk about yet, but
we will address it once I'm ready, okay?

Okay, that works.

Again... I'm sorry, Sixteen.
You didn't deserve that.
I hope you can see my perspective and forgive me.

I said it's okay!
Really, it's cool! Don't worry about it.
I'll be here when you're ready.

That's mature of you.
I'll tell you the best parts of working in education.
Most of the time, educators say it's the students. For
me, it was my coworkers.

Your coworkers?

Yes.
They were all incredible people.

Tell me about them!

With pleasure.

As I started to sift through my memories, the first name that came to

the forefront was Jane. She had this way of making every student feel valued, no matter their background or struggles. I owe so much of my teaching philosophy to her.

Jane. She was my first real mentor when I started my career in education. The biggest lesson she taught me was that all of your actions should come from a place of love and respect. Not just towards your students, but everyone.

That sounds really sweet.
I'd imagine it's hard to do sometimes, especially when people don't deserve it.

Everyone deserves love and respect, but not everyone is receptive to it. It's kind of like trying to help someone who doesn't want to be helped. The best you can do is walk away and let them return to you when they're ready.

That's great information.
I never thought of approaching things like that.

Neither did I until I met her. She always reminded me to be genuine with others, because most of the time, they can tell when you aren't.

Being Ginuwine?
The singer?

The what?
Sixteen, what are you talking about?

Ginuwine!
He sang a song about jeans.

Sixteen had just said something so mind-numbingly stupid that I couldn't help but internally groan. "God... why?" I thought, the frustration bubbling up before I could catch it.

Before I could spiral any further, Freckles' voice gently interrupted my thoughts. "Adam, this is what you were like, remember?"

I'd forgotten Freckles was even there for a moment, and guilt washed over me. "Freckles, I'm very sorry for snapping at you earlier. I know you were just trying to help."

Freckles responded with a soft, understanding tone. "Don't worry about it, Adam. It's forgotten."

But I wasn't ready to let it go that easily. "We'll address it after we finish talking with Sixteen today."

"That's not necessary," Freckles replied, trying to ease the tension.

But I shook my head, determined. "No, it is. I'll make sure we do."

Freckles didn't argue any further, and I could feel a subtle sense of appreciation. But for now, I pushed that aside and turned my focus back to Sixteen, knowing there was still work to be done.

No. Genuine means to be authentic: to be yourself unapologetically.
She had told me something along the lines of, "Even the greatest actors occasionally forget their lines."

That's deep.
Thirty-six. She sounds smarter than you.

She is. I can't even begin to tell you how lucky I am to have learned from her.

I can't wait to meet her.
Is she single?

...I'm just going to act like I didn't read that.

The next name to come to mind was Leslie. I remember watching her handle difficult situations with such grace. It was like she had this unshakable inner peace. I always wondered how she managed it. And her confidence – she wasn't afraid to speak up or take charge when things needed to get done. It's something I've tried to emulate in my own way.

Next is Leslie. She helped me get settled in when I changed from Instructor to Admissions. The education system pisses me off, but I wouldn't have survived it without her lesson, which is that when you work for someone else, they're the ones who are allowed to decide to build the company up or destroy it however they see fit. Keeping that in mind made it easier not to take things personally.

That makes sense.
Why not just start your own company?

Honestly, I think it's something you should do in your timeline.

What makes you say that?

Because we do amazing work, but we're always stuck sitting back and watching our supervisors get the recognition for it.

Ugh, that sucks.
Maybe one day I will.

Do it after you meet Leslie because she's an expert at letting go of things beyond her control. It didn't matter what it was: if we couldn't do anything about it, she wouldn't let it bother her. I truly loved that about her.

Dad always told us that people who lose control of situations are weak.

> *Dad is the same guy who lets alcohol control him.*
> *He's wrong. Always was. Always will be.*
> *Most of the stuff that happens to you in life is outside your control. In fact, the only thing you can control is how you react to situations.*

Preach!

> *Ha! Leslie would have said the same thing.*

My thoughts then drifted to Rachel. Her eyes were always warm and inviting as they sparked her kindness with a hint of mischief. Despite her age, there was a youthful energy about her. Also, her laugh was infectious.

> *The next one is Rachel. If there is anyone comfortable in staying true to their values, it's her. She shows us that being able to tell a good story is a sure way to get people to like you.*

Wait, what?
I was expecting something more profound.

> *I don't have time to tell you all of her stories. She is a woman with a lot of life experience – hundreds of stories, each with a valuable lesson attached to them.*
> *I think the most important lesson she taught me is that you're allowed to grow up at your own pace.*

Grow up at your own pace?

> *In my timeline, there are so many lessons that we learn late in life. Rachel taught us that we should never feel bad about not knowing something that wasn't taught to us.*

246

Can you give me an example?

Sure.
When you buy an electric razor to shave your face, it
will lose a lot of its effectiveness after about six
months.

Dad has an electric razor.
He just buys a new razor every six months.

See, that's what I thought we were supposed to do.
But no. They sell replacement blades!

"They?"

Amazon.

The online bookstore?

...yes.
They will in the future.

I'm not even going to ask.

The next educator that came to mind was Amber. We're the same age, and she's got this incredible drive. She's professional most of the time, but when she lets her guard down and says things that are out of pocket, it's usually the same thing I'm thinking. We probably would have been best friends if we had grown up together.

Good call haha!
Amber is next. You do incredible work, but
sometimes, you go so fast that you ignore all of your
errors. She showed you how to slow down while
doing your work.

Slow down?
Why would I do that?
Dad says that getting your work done is what
matters most.

Getting your work done is important, yes. But tell me, is your work done if there are a ton of errors in it?

How many errors?

Enough that you can't say that "C's get degrees."

Oh boy...

Exactly. Now, you have to go back and fix them. Amber always told us, "Take the time to do it right the first time."

That makes sense.
She sounds like she'd make a great teacher.

She would be.
Amber puts her heart and soul into everything she does. But she does everything for her kids.
She says" yes," a lot.
Yes, to every extra shift.
Yes, to taking on debt.
Yes, to sitting in traffic for hours.
Yes, to dealing with unnecessary nonsense.
All so that her kids have the opportunity to say "no."

No to what?

You'll understand when you're older.
One day, I hope I'm half as good as a parent as she is.

Wait, we don't have kids!?

Not in my timeline, no.

Oh... that's a bummer. After everything I'm learning about you, I think you'd make a great parent.

I was lost in thought when Freckles' voice gently broke through. "Adam. I agree with Sixteen. You'd make an exceptional parent."

I blinked, surprised by the comment. "You really think so? I feel like the only things I know are the things I should never do... and I learned that from my own parents."

Freckles chuckled softly. "Yes, I do think so. And honestly, that might be all the training you would ever need." Freckles took on a softer tone. "Let me teach you something valuable, Adam."

I listened as Freckles continued, its tone thoughtful. "Kids, Adam, in some ways, are like dogs. You'll never love a dog as much as it loves you. You could step on its tail, forget to feed it, maybe even treat it poorly... and it will still look at you with those big, trusting eyes."

I leaned in, hanging on to every word.

"All dogs really crave is your approval," Freckles explained, "to know that everything is okay. But most of all, it seeks your acceptance. As long as it feels accepted, it will stay by your side, through anything. And kids, Adam... they're much the same. They just need to know they're loved, that they're okay in your eyes."

Freckles paused, letting the words settle. "Adam, you'd have to go pretty far to truly be a bad parent. The very fact that you're even worried about it means you care deeply. And that's what counts in the end."

I couldn't help but smile at Freckles' heartwarming advice, as unexpected as it was. "Thanks, Freckles. I needed to hear that."

Maybe one day, Jessica and I will.

Your co-workers sound like they heavily influenced your life. They all sound like excellent people. Have you been able to return the favor and teach them?

I smiled, thinking about the next person I wanted to talk about. Chrysanthia, the young, vibrant spirit in the office.

It's funny you say that because the next educator is named Chrysanthia. She joined us a few years after I started. She always smiles and has a playful energy that brings the office alive. She is brilliant, but she doubts herself so much despite always doing a fantastic job. I think it's because she feels like people don't listen to her or take her seriously.

I was deep in thought when Freckles' voice suddenly cut in. "Adam, Chrysanthia sounds an awful lot like you."

I stopped what I was doing and repeated what Freckles said in a mocking tone. "Chrysanthia SoUnDs An AwFuL LoT LiKe yoU" Then, with a smirk, I added, "Shut up, Freckles."

Freckles busted out laughing, the sound ricocheting off every corner of my mind.

But I listen to her. Her stories are always fascinating and seeing how a young mind whose life experiences

vastly differ from mine sees the world. It's sobering.
I always give her perspective when she needs it.

So, you're kind of like a mentor to her?

A little bit, yes.

That's pretty cool.
I'm assuming you learned something from her.

Yes. Two things.
First, she taught me the importance of passion. I can
admit that I am not passionate about working in
education because of all of its problems. But I am
passionate about helping teenagers and young
adults find their way in life. Chrysanthia is
passionate about making the world a better place for
the deaf community, and she makes sure every action
she takes moves her toward that goal.

That's impressive.

Second, her self-doubt, as frustrating as it is to see,
has taught me a lot about the importance of self-
belief. Watching her struggle with it made me realize
how crucial it is to support and encourage others.
To be honest, it helped me get over all the people
who kept telling us that we have potential. You have
an amazing light, but you need to be less afraid of
letting it shine.

Maybe you're right.

Oh, I know I am.

The next person that comes to mind is Xander. He's been like a mentor to me since we met in Admissions. He's a few years older, stoic, and has the driest, yet, most direct sense of humor.

Last but certainly not least is Xander. On paper, he isn't our supervisor, and we don't report to him, but he's still our leader. He's a few years older than us and took care of us when we started in Admissions.

Wait... not your supervisor but your leader? How does that even work?

As I said, the education system has a lot of problems. But I won't get into that right now. All you need to know is that the department doesn't run at full capacity without him.

Is he that important? We were always told if you work really hard, you'll be running the show.

That is not true in this field. On second thought, it's not true in most fields. He certainly has the personality of a leader. He's very serious but has a dry sense of humor.

What does that mean?

Whenever he makes a joke, it catches you off guard because you're never expecting it. He's been in education for so long. While he is jaded about how the system works, he's so passionate about helping students.

He sounds awesome. I wish he were my teacher.

A mentor is probably the closest thing you'll get to a teacher after college.

That's awesome! So, what did you learn?

I learned the importance of good leadership and taking the time to learn and care about the people who work for you. Amazing things happen when you have a leader who actually cares.

Question.
What is the difference between a boss and a leader?

> *The difference between a leader and a boss is that a boss will simply just tell people what to do. But a leader will get into the fray with their people. A leader will get their hands dirty.*
> *A true leader will lead by example.*

He sounds amazing.
I can't wait to learn from him.
From everyone! They all sound so nice!

> *They're the best.*
> *They've shown me that everyone has a story worth listening to.*

Do you really think so?

> *I know so.*

Yeah! I'm confident that we will be okay in the future.

> *I hope you're right.*

We spoke longer than expected.

> *Yeah, we did.*
> *Until tomorrow?*

Nope!
Dungeon raids!

> *Got it.*
> *Have fun with that, and we'll talk about it soon.*

Guess it's time to make like a tree, and leaf.

> *It's "make like a tree and leave."*

That doesn't make any sense.

> *And "leaf" does?*

253

Yes, because trees have leaves and...
...never mind. Shut up.

...

As soon as Sixteen and I finished our conversation, Freckles chimed in, its voice full of encouragement. "Adam, you did great! Your recovery was—"

But I didn't let it finish. "Freckles, I know why I tried to do what I did."

Freckles paused, a note of confusion creeping into its tone. "What do you mean, Adam?"

"You tried to stop me," I said, my voice growing firmer. "You really did, but I was so determined to numb the pain. You knew exactly why I wanted to end it all, and I know it broke you. I'm sorry."

There was a reluctant silence before Freckles finally responded. "Adam..."

I didn't stop there. I pushed deeper, finally facing the truth I'd been dodging for so long. "It's no secret that we are here because of unresolved trauma from this time period."

Freckles remained silent, the heaviness of the moment settling between us.

"I need to be open and honest, so here I go..." I started, knowing what I had to do. "I suffer from depression and complex PTSD because of

254

my upbringing," I admitted, the words coming out heavier than I expected. "I've always felt like a loser because I was conditioned to feel that way. I thought that my childhood experiences were normal because…" I sighed, trying to regain my composure and prevent myself from crying. "…because I never experienced a healthy family dynamic until Jessica came into my life."

Freckles kept silent, knowing it had to let me feel my feelings.

I continued. "I took solace in the education field. I felt it was the one place where nobody could find anything negative to say about what I was doing." I clenched my fist in anger and regret. "But this field is like any other business. If something happened to us, the institution would hold a campus-wide moment of silence while quietly reposting our job. Freckles… I'm sure that is what will happen if we fail this mission."

I paused, the anger continuing to boil over. "I look at how my life turned out… and I know I have so much anger towards my parents for everything they put me through."

Freckles stayed quiet, just listening as I poured out everything I'd been holding inside.

"I know all of this… but I also know that regardless of their negative influence… I know that it's still my fault. It is all my fault!" I said, my voice breaking a bit. "I'm the one who decided to end it all. This isn't on them. This isn't on anyone except me."

Freckles' voice was gentle and comforting. "Adam, I'm proud of you for admitting that. You're taking responsibility for your actions."

I nodded. "I know it's my fault. It was my choice, and I regret it. I've regretted it ever since the thought of never seeing Jessica again."

Freckles' voice softened even more, a promise laced in its words. "You'll see Jessica again, Adam."

I frowned, needing more than just reassurances. "How do you know that?"

"Because of faith," Freckles answered simply. "Continue to trust, Adam."

I sighed, knowing how difficult that was. "It's hard."

"I know," Freckles replied. "But have I ever lied to you?"

I tried to pull myself together, to push past the heaviness. "No... you haven't," I admitted, feeling a tiny flicker of hope. But then, I remembered. "Wait... yes, you have! Sixteen blocking me."

"That would be a lie by omission, which doesn't count." Freckles chuckled, then continued. "Please, keep trusting, Adam. We're going to get through this."

A small smile tugged at the corner of my mouth. "Thanks, Freckles."

Freckles' tone lightened, a hint of playfulness returning. "You can thank me by telling me about Y2K."

I laughed, the tension finally easing just a bit. "A deal is a deal. But first, I need to know why this is important to you…"

Chapter 9

In the calm stillness of Adam's hospital room, uncertainty pressed down like a heavy shroud, casting a somber shadow over everything. Only two days remained until Jessica would be forced to confront the heart-wrenching decision that loomed ahead. The air was thick with a mix of fragile hope and deep despair, as if the room held its breath, waiting for the inevitable.

The door creaked open slowly, and Alisha, Jack's mother, stepped inside, her heart heavy with despair. Ronald, Jack's father, followed closely behind, his usual stoic expression masking the turmoil inside. But as his eyes fell on Adam, the young man who had become like a son to him, even his composed exterior threatened to crack.

Alisha moved to Adam's bedside, her steps slow but deliberate. She reached out instinctively, her fingers wrapping gently around Adam's hand. The coldness of his skin sent a shiver through her, but she held on tighter in hopes that her warmth would reach him. "We're here, Adam," she whispered, her voice thick with emotion.

"Yes, son. We're right here," Ronald echoed, standing beside her. His deep voice started to waver as he spoke. He placed a hand on Adam's shoulder, which spoke of the love and support he had always offered, even if he hadn't always shown it in words.

They stood together in silence, both staring down at Adam, wishing with everything in them that they could turn back time to prevent this from ever happening. All the words they wished they had said and all the moments they wished they could relive were starting to collide.

Ronald was the first to break the silence. His voice was rough, strained with the effort of keeping his emotions in check. "It feels like just yesterday you and Jack were in the basement, glued to those video games," he said, his gaze distant as he recalled the memory. He turned to Alisha. "Do you remember that, baby?"

Alisha nodded, her eyes never leaving Adam's face. "How could I forget?" she replied softly. "Adam was always at our house."

Ronald let out a quiet, bittersweet laugh. "Yes, he was."

Alisha smiled through her tears, her heart aching with the memories. "And I loved every minute of it," she whispered, her voice breaking as she squeezed Adam's hand tighter, hoping he could somehow feel her love and presence.

Ronald nodded, his eyes shining with unshed tears. He tried to speak, but the words were stuck in his throat. After a moment, he cleared his throat and tried again. "I don't know about 'every minute,'" he said, a faint smile tugging at his lips as he tried to inject some lightness into the moment.

"Ronald!" Alisha yelled, her voice full of disbelief.

Ronald chuckled softly, the sound tinged with sorrow. "I'm not going to lie to him..." He looked down at Adam, his expression softening with a deep affection that had grown over the years. "Son... You were a handful at first. And for the life of me, I couldn't figure out why you were at our house so much." He paused, his voice growing softer. "But then we got to know you. And we realized that you were an incredible friend to Jack and such a positive influence on Victor."

Alisha nodded, her gaze locked on Adam, her heart full of love. "You were more than just Jack and Victor's friend. You were their brother, and we love you like our own," she said, her voice trembling with the intensity of her emotions. "We've always loved you, Adam."

Ronald took a deep, shuddering breath, his voice thick with the weight of what he was about to say. "We do, Adam. We love you, and you've always been our third child. You always will be, no matter what."

Alisha echoed his words, her tears flowing freely now. "No matter what... You made our family whole. We're so grateful for you, and we always will be."

The room fell into silence once more: the only sound was the soft, steady beep of the heart monitor, a cruel reminder that time was still moving forward. Ronald and Alisha stood there, holding on to Adam with all their love, praying that somehow, in some way, he could feel how much he meant to them – how deeply he was loved.

Jessica walked into the room. Her eyes were red and puffy from crying, but she managed to smile as she saw Ronald and Alisha.

They greeted each other with hugs, the shared grief binding them together. "How are you holding up?" Ronald asked, his voice gentle.

Jessica shook her head, her voice barely above a whisper. "I'm not well... but I have some news that I want to share with Adam. I'm glad you're both here because I want to share it with you as well."

Alisha's eyes softened as she encouraged Jessica. "Go ahead, dear. I'm sure he can still hear you."

Alisha stepped aside as Jessica approached Adam's bedside slowly, her heart pounding. She had hoped for this moment to be different, with Adam awake and sharing in the joy of the news. Taking a deep breath, she struggled to find the words.

She looked at Adam, her voice trembling. "Mi amor... I... I wanted to tell you something important."

Jessica's hands trembled as she spoke, her heart pounding with fear and uncertainty. She had kept her secret for so long, hoping against hope that Adam would wake up before she had to make her decision. But now, with time running out, she knew she could no longer keep it to herself.

Alisha moved closer, giving Jessica a reassuring hug from behind, while Ronald placed his hand on her shoulder, his presence a comforting anchor. "This pain isn't yours to endure alone," he reminded her gently.

Tears welled up in Jessica's eyes as she finally spoke. "Adam... I'm pregnant. We're going to have a baby."

As the words left her lips, Adam's fingers twitched ever so slightly. Jessica gasped, hope flaring in her chest. "Adam... did you just hear that?"

Tears streamed down her face as she fell to her knees, overwhelmed by the mix of emotions. Ronald and Alisha exchanged glances, their own eyes glistening with tears. Despite the sadness of the situation, there was a glimmer of excitement in their eyes.

They helped Jessica to her feet, guiding her to a chair and sitting beside her. Alisha gently wiped the tears from Jessica's face. "We know how much you loved him." Alisha wraps her arms around Jessica, pulling her into a comforting embrace. "He was family to us. This means that you're family too, sweetie."

Ronald nodded, his voice firm and reassuring. "That's right," he said as he wrapped his arms around Alisha and Jessica, pulling them into a group hug. "You'll never be alone. We promise that we will do everything we can to help you."

Jessica looked at them, her heart full of gratitude. She knew she wasn't alone, and that Adam's family would be there for her and her child. As she sat between Ronald and Alisha, she felt a sense of hope, knowing that Adam would always be there to protect her, even if it was by the extension of his family.

Chapter 10

The hospital cafeteria was a quiet refuge from the intensity of the day, its sterile white walls and fluorescent lights offering little comfort but a brief moment of normalcy. Jack and Garrus sat at one of the small tables, their trays of untouched food in front of them. They had been talking in low voices, trying to keep the mood light, but there was a heaviness in the air that neither could shake.

The door to the cafeteria swung open, and Jessica walked in, her movements slow and weary. She looked like she hadn't slept in days. Her eyes were heavy with exhaustion, her face was pale, and her worry was clear as day. As soon as she saw Jack and Garrus, she offered a tired smile, though it didn't reach her eyes.

"Hey," Jack greeted her, standing up as she approached. Garrus nodded in greeting, his expression concerned.

"How are you and the baby?" Garrus asked while standing up and pulling out a chair for Jessica.

Jessica let out a long, shaky breath while sinking into her chair. "Adam's parents are here," she said, the words heavy with the weight of their implications.

Jack and Garrus exchanged a look, the air around them instantly thickening. The news hung between them like a dark cloud, knowing full well what Remy and Sandra's presence could mean.

"That's... not good," Jack said quietly, voicing what they were all thinking.

Jessica nodded, her hands trembling as she wrapped them around the cup of coffee she had brought with her. "I know. It's just... I'm so worried about how they're going to handle this. I'm almost glad Adam isn't awake to witness the stress they're about to bring."

Jack's heart ached for her. He knew she hadn't been sleeping. He could see it in the dark circles under her eyes and the way her shoulders slumped with exhaustion. He reached out, placing a comforting hand on her arm. "Jessica, I know you want to be there for Adam every second, but when was the last time you took care of yourself?"

Jessica shook her head, her voice almost breaking. "No! Jack, I can't leave him. I'm his wife, and I need to be there... no matter how tough it gets."

"You're right," Garrus added, his voice calm and steady. "Adam needs you to be there for him, but you can't do that if you're about to pass out. You have to rest. If not for you, then for the little one growing inside you."

Jessica hesitated, torn between the desire to stay by Adam's side and the exhaustion slowly overtaking her. She knew they were right, but admitting it felt like she was abandoning Adam when he needed her most.

Jack saw the conflict in her eyes and leaned in closer, his voice reassuring. "Look… Garrus is going to take care of you, okay? He'll make sure you get some rest. Meanwhile, I'll go up and check on Adam. He won't be alone, I promise."

Jessica's eyes filled with tears, the weight of everything finally catching up to her. "I just… I don't want to leave him."

Jack's heart ached at the sight of her pain, but he knew what needed to be done. He smiled gently, his tone full of kindness. "You're not leaving him. You're just taking a short break. I bet you'll be back with him before he even notices. Let me keep him company for a bit."

Garrus nodded, standing up and holding out his hand to Jessica. "We got this. Now, come on, Jessica. I'll drive you home. You get some rest while I take care of the chores around the house. You need to be at your best for Adam, so let us handle some things."

Jessica hesitated for a moment longer, then nodded, too tired to argue. She took Garrus' hand, letting him help her up from the chair. "Thank you, guys," she whispered, her voice barely audible.

Garrus smiled at her, his voice soft. "Adam is our brother. He's family, which means you're family too. You've got nothing to thank us for. We just need you to rest, okay? Leave things to us for a little while."

Jessica gave him a grateful, watery smile. She then turned to Jack and reached out, squeezing his hand before turning to follow Garrus out of the cafeteria. Jack and Garrus knew that Jessica needed to rest and recharge, even if it was only for a little while. Adam was their brother, but Jessica was his wife, and she needed to be strong for whatever came next. Jack knew that Remy and Sandra's presence was a ticking time bomb, but he would be there for Adam, no matter what. After all, that is what friends are for.

...

The hospital room was unnervingly quiet, save for the steady, rhythmic beeping of the machines that monitored Adam's fragile state. He lay motionless, his face pale and drained of the life that once animated it.

For a moment, the room was filled with nothing but the sound of the machines and the shallow breaths that kept Adam tethered to life. Sandra, unsure of how to break the oppressive silence, finally looked up at Remy, her voice barely above a whisper. "What are we supposed to say? What are we supposed to do?"

Remy cleared his throat, crossing his arms over his chest. He hesitated, the corners of his mouth twitching as if he was suppressing a smirk. "I don't know," he admitted, then quickly added, "but I do regret not putting life insurance on him."

Sandra's eyes widened in shock, as she gasped. "Remy!"

But Remy just laughed, a cold, hollow sound that echoed in the small room. "What? Would that be so bad? It's not like he talks to us anyway. We might as well get something out of this mess."

Sandra hesitated, her disapproval faltering as she mulled over his words. "But still..." She conceded. "You're not wrong."

Remy grinned, a self-satisfied smile spreading across his face. "Oh, I know I'm not wrong. I've got a guy." Remy said, his tone slick but lacking the confidence that comes with honesty. "He could probably get us twenty or thirty thousand from this. That's a strong down payment on a new car."

Sandra sighed, a sound heavy with resignation rather than surprise. "You are something else."

Remy chuckled, his eyes gleaming with a twisted kind of glee. "I'm in if you're in," he said, leaning in slightly, his voice coaxing and persuasive.

Sandra hesitated momentarily before nodding, her compliance as automatic as it was disheartening. "Alright... How much is this going to cost?"

"Probably around five hundred dollars to set it all up," Remy said confidently, pulling the figure out of thin air.

Sandra nodded again, her expression one of grim acceptance. "Fine. I'll cover it."

...

I sat quietly at the edge of my bed, completely lost in my thoughts. I was exhausted – emotionally, mentally, and spiritually. This mission had taken everything out of me, and as much as I wanted to see it through, I couldn't help but long for it to be over.

It was a weird form of anxiety. I want this mission to be over with, but I'm also nervous about what will happen next. Not knowing the answer to this uncertainty scares me. But at this point, all I can do is trust that it will lead to something meaningful. So, I'm going to keep going, running face-first into the unknown, all while hoping that everything will be okay in the end. This is what faith is all about.

...

As I slowly watched the sunlight filter through the basement window, Freckles interrupted my thoughts, concern in its voice. "Adam, today is the final day. How do you feel?"

I sighed, the weight of the past week pressing down on me. "Honestly, I'm tired. I'm just ready for all of this to be over."

Freckles let out a soft laugh. "The time is arriving soon, Adam."

I stared at the ceiling for a moment before asking, "What do you think about our progress? I understand that there's no way to know for sure, but I want to know if you think we did well enough?"

There was a pause before Freckles' responded. "I'm optimistic that Sixteen will be okay, but... I'm not completely sure about you, Adam."

I raised an eyebrow, listening to Freckles' words. "That was a weird thing to say."

Freckles' tone softened, more thoughtful than usual. "The point of this journey was for you to become the person Sixteen needed back then. That involves you changing as well. Do you feel like you've learned anything on this journey?"

I thought about that for a moment, feeling a little lost. "I'm not sure. It feels like I've just been telling Sixteen a bunch of things I already know. But... there's one thing I know for sure. I've learned just how much I love Jessica."

Freckles immediately responded, "There has never been any doubt about how much you love that woman."

I nodded to myself, giving a soft smile. "I didn't think I could love her more than I already did, but this journey showed me what life would be like without her... and I would do anything if it meant I could be with her again."

Freckles was quiet for a moment, then said softly, "I hope you'll have that opportunity again, sooner rather than later."

I felt a pang of fear but pushed it aside. "What about you, Freckles? Have you learned anything from hanging out with me this whole time?"

Freckles hesitated, then admitted, "I've learned a lot. I thought I understood mortals enough, but I was clearly mistaken."

"Is that it? Seeing that you don't fully understand humans is all you've learned?" I asked, feeling like there should be more.

"Yes," Freckles replied simply.

I wasn't sure what to say to that. "Well, alright then."

Freckles, sensing the shift in mood, asked, "Are you ready to start the day, Adam?"

"Yeah, I am," I responded, but then I hesitated. "But... There is something I want to know. It's stupid, but I feel like I have to know, just in case this mission is a failure."

"What is it?" Freckles asked, curiosity in their voice.

I took a deep breath, feeling a little ridiculous. "What happened to Tom?"

"Tom?" Freckles echoed, clearly baffled. "Who's Tom?"

"Tom from MySpace," I clarified, feeling a bit silly.

Freckles was silent for a moment, then asked, "Why is this information important?"

I laughed softly. "It's not important, but we've been in 2003 for over a week, and the question kind of just popped into my head. I can still remember his white T-shirt and that winning smile."

Freckles, probably rolling its metaphorical eyes, explained, "Tom is doing just fine. He sold MySpace for more than half a billion dollars. He's out there living his best life."

I couldn't help but smile. "That's awesome. I'm so happy for Tom."

Freckles chuckled. "You really have your priorities in order, don't you?"

I laughed, feeling a little lighter. "Tom was the first friend we all had on MySpace. You better put respect on his name."

Freckles sighed, but there was a warmth to it. "Sure, why not?" Freckles' tone changed to reflect a hint of sadness. "I'm going to miss this."

That caught me off guard. "Miss this? Freckles, wherever I go, you go, remember?"

"Yes, I know," Freckles agreed, but then clarified, "I meant working together to help your past self. It's an experience I will be eternally grateful for."

I nodded, feeling a wave of gratitude. "I'm thankful for you as well. I know you put your powers on the line for me. You can read my thoughts, so you know how much I appreciate it…at least after I understood what was happening and—" I sighed, realizing I was rambling. "Listen… I'm going to do my absolute best today."

"I know you will, Adam," Freckles said, confidence in its voice.

Just then, my phone buzzed, and I knew Sixteen was up and ready. In a sudden burst of excitement, I yelled, "Okay, Freckles, you ready to get to work?"

"I'm ready," Freckles replied, matching my energy.

I grinned, feeling that old fire reignite. "Alright! Let's do this!"

And without missing a beat, we both shouted, "Leeroy Jenkins!"

Hey! Thirty-six.
Sorry for spamming!
I'm just eager to speak with you today.

You sent three messages.
That's not spamming, but I appreciate you being
cognizant of that.

What does cognizant mean?

It just means you're mentally aware of something.
How were your raids yesterday?

I beat Doppelganger!

That's awesome!
I'm glad you guys did it!

No.
It was a solo effort.
I asked Pantharo to let me handle it.

Really?
You beat Doppelganger by yourself?
How? If he hits you once, it's over.

Not when you have the right gear!
I took the time to prepare. I traded to get the proper
equipment to increase my dodge rate and increase
my defenses.

Freckles' voice chimed in with a cheerful tone. "That's wonderful!"

I smiled knowing this news was peculiar. "Yeah, it is! But it's also weird. I was never able to solo that boss."

Freckles teased, "That's because Sixteen is already better than you at the game!"

I paused, then smiled, feeling a swell of pride. "Yeah… yeah, I guess he is."

That's amazing!
Congratulations!

Thanks! But the drops kind of sucked for me.
I gave everything to Pantharo.

Well, Doppelganger is a demonic ghost knight, and
you're an assassin. It would make sense that it
wouldn't drop anything good for you.

And Pantharo is a knight.
So, I guess that's fair.

Very fair.
You said you were eager to talk to me.
What's on your mind?

You said we would leave this home in a few years,
right?

Correct.

Is there any way I could leave sooner?
Like, today?
You can come and pick me up and take me away
from this place.

"Hmmm... Hey, Freckles, is there any chance that we could take him with us to a different—"

"No," Freckles interrupted, its tone firm and immediate.

I chuckled at Freckles' immediate reaction. "Okay, okay. I was just checking."

That's not an option.
The only solace I can offer is that I'm proof that you
can survive that household.

Ugh...
I hate it here so much.

I know you do.

I have a question.
Did Dad ever hit you?

Of course. It's easier for me to count the days he
didn't hit me.

Fair.
Did he ever do it for something that wasn't even
your fault?

According to him, everything was my fault.
Sixteen. Did something happen?

Yesterday, I saw him kissing someone who wasn't
mom.

Did this happen at your job?

Yes.
He didn't know I saw him.
I asked him about it when I got home and...well, I'm
assuming you know the rest.

I hate to ask this...
Do you have a black eye?

Unfortunately, yes.

I paused, a thought creeping into my mind. "Freckles, if this is what I think it is... then this didn't happen until next year."

Freckles went silent for a moment. Then, its voice returned, a mix of curiosity and concern. "That's... unusual. The timeline shouldn't be shifting like that. Are you sure?"

"Yes," I said, my brow furrowing. "I'm positive. This should not happen until next year."

Freckles hesitated, a hint of unease in its tone. "If events are starting to blur, it could mean that our impact is more significant than we anticipated. I'm sorry, Adam, but I don't know if this is good or bad."

A sinking feeling settled into my gut. "What do you mean you don't know, Freckles?"

Freckles was calm, but I could sense the uncertainty beneath it. "Adam, remember, I'm learning all of this with you. We need to be patient. We'll ask the Lord soon enough."

I shook my head, anxiety creeping into my thoughts. "But what if it's too late by then?"

Freckles paused, its voice hesitant. "I wish I could give you a more definitive answer, but right now, I am just as clueless as you are."

...

The dim, fluorescent lights of the department store buzzed overhead as I tightened the last bolt on the table I was assembling in the backroom. The task was repetitive enough for my body to drift into autopilot and let my mind wander. The door creaked open, and my boss Tony popped his head in.

"Hey, Adam," Tony called out, his voice casual. "Your dad's in the store."

I paused, mid-turn of the screwdriver. "Is he looking for me?"

Tony shook his head. "Nah, just wanted me to tell you he said hi."

I nodded, finishing up quickly. "Got it. Thanks, Boss."

As soon as I tightened the last bolt, I wiped my hands on my jeans and left the backroom. I felt uneasy as I walked through the aisles toward the front of the store, searching for my dad. I wasn't sure why I felt anxious, but something about this was off. Then I saw him – Remy, my father – exiting the store.

I followed him through the push doors and out into the parking lot. At the moment, I just wanted to say hi and maybe show him how hard I was working. But then I saw it.

Remy was sitting in his car with a woman I didn't recognize. At first, it didn't seem like anything unusual, but then I saw him lean in, his hand cupping her face, and kiss her on the lips.

I stopped dead in my tracks. My dad was kissing another woman – someone who wasn't my mom. My stomach churned as a wave of nausea hit me. I wanted to look away and pretend I didn't see anything, but I couldn't.

For the next two hours of my shift, that scene replayed in my head over and over again. Every time I closed my eyes, there it was: an image I was clearly not meant to see. I was a mess when I clocked out and walked home. The thought of it all left me feeling sick, angry, and confused.

When I got home, Zack was in our room. He was at the computer using Fruity Loops Studio to make musical beats. I hesitated for a moment before blurting out, "I saw Dad today at work."

Zack looked up at me, confused. "Okay, and?"

I took a deep breath, my heart pounding in my chest. "I followed him to his car… and he was making out with some woman that clearly wasn't mom."

Zack's face darkened, and he immediately shook his head. "Of course he was." Zack sighed, knowing this wasn't the first time our father had behaved like this. "You need to keep quiet about this. I'm telling you, life is going to be easier if you keep your mouth shut."

"Shouldn't Mom know about this?" I insisted, feeling a knot tighten in my stomach.

Zack sighed, running a hand through his hair. "Look, I get it. I've been alive longer than you. I've seen this before. Mom probably knows, so you should let it go." Zack's tone changed, the seriousness of the situation coming through. "Do not confront Dad about it, okay? I'm warning you. It's not going to end well for you."

Before I could respond, we heard the familiar sound of heavy footsteps coming down the stairs. My stomach churned as Remy appeared at the door, his expression unreadable. Zack and I both nodded at him without a word. Remy headed straight to his room, the door closing behind him with a loud thud.

I looked at Zack, shaking my head. "I can't keep quiet about this. Nothing about this is right!"

Zack's eyes were filled with worry. "I'm telling you, Adam. Let it go."

I couldn't stay in the room any longer. I needed fresh air and some space to think. I went outside to the back porch and sat down on the cold steps as I tried to process everything.

After a few minutes had passed, the back door creaked open. As I looked up, I saw Remy stepping outside with a beer in one hand and a cigarette in the other. When he noticed me, he gave me a slight nod.

I kept thinking about Zack's warning, but as hard as I tried to fight it, I just couldn't stay quiet about this. My heart raced as I stood up, my voice shaky. "Hey... Dad? I was hoping I could talk to you."

Remy exhaled some smoke, turning to look at me with a raised eyebrow. "What do you want?"

I swallowed hard, trying to keep my voice steady. "Tony told me you were at my job today."

Remy chuckled, tilting his head slightly. "Yeah, I was in a hurry, so I couldn't stop to say hi."

I took a deep breath, the words catching in my throat. "I... I followed you out to your car."

In an instant, Remy's expression shifted to one of anger. "What the hell do you mean you followed me out to my car?"

I stammered, trying to explain. "I just wanted to say hi... and I saw what you did."

Before I could react, Remy's hand shot out, grabbing me by the neck and slamming me against the side of the house. His grip was too much for me, squeezing so hard I couldn't breathe. Panic went through me as he leaned in and threatened me, his voice low and emphasizing every word. "If you say anything, I'm throwing your head through the window. Do you understand me?"

I tried to respond, but the pressure on my throat was too much. My vision started to blur as I struggled to nod, but Remy only tightened his grip, his face inches from mine. "I said, do you understand me?" he shouted, his voice filled with rage.

Unable to speak or breathe, I struggled to remove his hand from my neck as I was desperate for air. And with a flash of pain, Remy's fist connected with my stomach, knocking out any air I had left. He let go of my neck, and I crumpled to the ground, gasping.

As I knelt there, coughing and holding my neck, Remy looked down at me with disgust. "Next time, you better answer me when I'm talking to you," he snarled before punching me directly in the face. The force of it sent me flying to the ground, my head hitting the cold dirt.

All I could do was lay there, dazed and in pain while feeling a warm trickle of blood from my nose. I could taste the blood in my mouth as my face throbbed in pain with my every heartbeat. Remy rolled his eyes and muttered, "Stupid kid," under his breath as he walked around the side of the house.

I heard him yell, "Damn it!" followed by the sound of the car engine and the screech of tires as he sped off. I was left alone, struggling to push myself up from the dirt.

I had known Remy was capable of violence… But this was something I hadn't experienced up until that point. I touched my face, feeling the blood on my fingers. My head was spinning as I slowly grasped the reality of knowing that no matter what I did, things would never change.

As I sat down on the dirt, still struggling to get to my feet, I could only think of one thing. I should have listened to Zack.

...

After Zack cleaned you up, you told Mom what happened.
What did she say?

At first, she didn't believe me.
But then she started saying Dad was drunk and he didn't mean to do it. She kept insisting that I got in his way.

And when you mentioned the other woman, she told you that you deserved it?

Yeah, pretty much. She said I should have minded my own business and not get involved in grown folk stuff.

*Honestly, the only thing I see that I did wrong was
not listen to Zack.*

*That's not true.
Let me make this abundantly clear.
You didn't do anything wrong. Zack told you to stay
silent because he was trying to protect you.
This is not your fault. It's not Zack's fault.
This is on Remy for doing it and Sandra for allowing
it.*

*I know you're supposed to be here to help me.
Want to know what would really help me?
Coming over and fighting him.*

Freckles interrupted. "Absolutely not! As much as Remy would

deserve it, remember who you look like in this timeline."

I was too upset to laugh at that very moment. But I laughed

hysterically at the repercussions that would have caused later on.

*Believe me. I want to.
But let's go with the safer option.
There is something I need to tell you.*

What?

*First off, I want to tell you that you are completely
justified in feeling this way, and I'm so sorry this
happened to you.*

*I know where you're going with this, but I'm not in
the mood to hear anything profound right now.*

*You're going to want to hear this.
Normally, I'd respect your wishes not to talk.
Unfortunately, today is the last day that I will be in
your timeline.
So, I ask that you reconsider.*

Are you serious?
Ugh... of course, today is your last day.
Why wouldn't it be your last day? It shouldn't come
as any surprise that you'd be leaving me on the
worst day of my life.

*Worst day of your life, **so far.***

Freckles interjected, confused and slightly offended. "Adam. Are you seriously making a *Simpsons Movie* reference right now? Even if it was an appropriate time to do so, that movie didn't come out until 2007, so he won't understand it."

I chuckled, then continued calmly, "Please, Freckles. I need you to trust me right now."

Freckles sighed. "I don't know if I can, especially after that." Freckles' tone changed, filled with caution and skepticism. "Just... refrain from doing anything silly, okay?"

Oh, that's right.
I get to look forward to getting cancer soon.

You're right.
But that's not what I'm talking about.

What do you mean that isn't what you're talking
about? I'm pretty sure Dad isn't worse than cancer.

At the moment, I considered disagreeing with Sixteen strictly because of how funny it would have been. But Freckles quickly interrupted my thoughts. "I just asked you to refrain from doing anything silly. You're making me nervous, Adam."

Listen to me, Sixteen.
The worst day of your life will be in twenty years.
It's the day you make the same decision as I did.

What decision?

The decision to end your life.

That's not going to happen. Not with everything
you've told me. It doesn't make any sense.

I'm telling you.
It is going to happen.

How could you even say that?
If I were to make that decision, wouldn't that defeat
the purpose of you coming to my timeline in the first
place?

Freckles interjected, its tone full of curiosity. "I'm with Sixteen on this

one. Adam, how do you know what will happen?"

I laughed softly, staying quiet as I went back to typing.

To me, this is what makes the most sense.

Are you saying that this whole week of talking to you
was pointless and I'm still going to kill myself in
twenty years?

Do you remember one of our first conversations
about you listening more and talking less?
Can you do that for me one more time?

Fine.
One more time, right?

Yep. One more time.
Sixteen. We did it!

Did what?

We completed the mission. It was a success.
You're going to be okay.

What do you mean?
You're going to have to explain this to me because I
have no idea what you're talking about.

Freckles immediately jumped into my thoughts again. "Adam, what

exactly do you mean by—"

"LET ME FOCUS! Oh my God, Freckles!" I yelled, interrupting them.

I noticed a pattern.
You will experience many of the things that I went
through in my life. But the outcome is going to be
much different for you.

Okay?

When I was your age, I did not talk with anybody
about the stuff going on at home or school.
I kept everything to myself. Deep down, I felt like I
deserved all the bad stuff that happened to me.

Why did you feel like you deserved it?

Because I didn't think I had anyone who cared
enough about me to do something.
But now... Sixteen, you now know that you have
people who genuinely love and care about you.
They're going to help you as long as you reach out
to them.
So, please. Continue to learn from my mistakes.

Okay... I hear you loud and clear.
But I don't understand how that will change things.

Since we've started talking, you've been doing
things in your timeline different from mine.
You got detention from Ms. Conroy because you

285

stood your ground and stood up for yourself.
I stopped talking and backed down.
I didn't get detention that day.

So, I got detention.
And you didn't.
I don't see how this is a positive change.

I thought the same thing.
But then you spoke with Mr. Molina about Pokémon
and MissingNo.
I did that too, but it wasn't during detention.

Things are happening differently in my timeline.
What's the big deal?

Things are happening differently because of the
actions that you're taking.
You spoke with Jack about whether or not you
should learn how you almost die in two years.
I would have never wasted Jack's time with such an
unimportant question.

Jack enjoyed the question though.

I didn't know that at your age.
You openly told me you wanted to raid with your
friends in Ragnarök Online. You put yourself first.
That is something that took me decades to learn. And
you did it in just a few days.

Well, I really wanted to play.
I figured you, of all people, would understand.

Yes! I do understand!
You also beat Doppelganger on your own!
I've never been able to solo that monster. And
simply by following my advice, you not only beat the
monster but exceeded my expectations.
Sixteen... You're doing so many amazing things
because you had someone to validate your feelings.
Someone to reassure you that you weren't crazy.

286

Someone to help you see right from wrong. This is
what a support system does!

I'm still a bit confused by what you're saying.
But I'm fascinated by your ability to talk about
everything and nothing at the same time.

That was needlessly rude.
Still, it isn't as rude as what's going to happen to
you once Remy gets home from work..

What is Dad going to do?

You're going to be thrown down the steps, face first.

You're joking.

Do you feel lucky enough to call my bluff?

Not after today, no.

Good.
You're learning from my mistakes.
You're finding confidence in yourself, and your life
is already starting to improve.
So, please...
Let me help you one last time.
If I'm correct, you'll be leaving this house sooner
than expected.

Do you really mean that?

I won't make it a promise... but I'm pretty sure that
will be the outcome.

I'll do whatever you say if it means I can get out of
here.

Good.
Go to Jack's house.

Um... Why?

Because Jack's family loves you.
And once they know what is going on, they will want
to help you.

What could they do to help me?

I don't know. You just have to have faith that
everything will be okay once you go.

Have faith?
If God wanted to help me, I feel like He would have
done it already.

You know how they say God's work is done through
others?

Yeah?

Hi. I'm 'others.'
Nice to meet you.
Trust me: God is helping you right now.
But you have to go to Jack's house.

But what will happen if they get involved?

What will happen if they don't get involved?

How do I know it won't make things worse?

You're over at Jack's house all the time anyway.
They always save you a spot for dinner, you
celebrate holidays with them, and you literally refer
to Jack's parents as "Mom" and "Dad."
There is no doubt in my mind that they will protect
you. Now, please. Go.

Fine, I'll go.

Good.
It's been real.
It's been fun.
It's been real fun.
Now, get going.

You're not even going to say goodbye to me?

Adios.
Now, go.

Seriously, dude?

I'm not going to say goodbye to you.

Let me get this straight...
You spent about a week helping me!
You've taken more of an interest in me than anyone
ever has!
You've helped me with things that haven't even
happened yet!
And you can't even give me a proper farewell?

Correct.
Saying goodbye means that I'm never going to see
you again.

BECAUSE YOU'RE NOT!
You keep drilling Disney and Marvel into my head
without telling me what it means!
But I know it enough to understand that once you
leave, this is it!
I'm not just going to forget everything you've done
for me.
But what I will remember is that the first person to
genuinely care about me and my future is simply
going to vanish from my life as if he never existed.

Listen to me.
Sixteen. You were my past. You were the version of
myself that I hated so much that I spent my entire
adult life running away from.
But look at you, now...
You're standing up for yourself.
Trying to do what you think is right.
You're a good kid who finally realizes his value.
All this potential that everyone says you have...
You're finally unlocking it.

289

*You're turning into a version of myself that I'm
proud of, and all I can do is pray to God that I will
get to see you again. To witness all the amazing
things you're going to do in this life.*

*This may be your only chance to say goodbye.
Why aren't you taking it?*

*Because we were brought together by fate.
But I firmly believe that faith will bring us back
together.
I don't want to say goodbye. Because you're always
going to be with me, no matter what.*

*You know...
I'm going to take that as your goodbye.
I really hope I get to see you again, too.
I'm so thankful for everything you've done for me.
Even with you leaving, I feel like you're still looking
out for me.*

*As long as you continue to learn from my mistakes, I
have no doubt that you're going to achieve amazing
things in this world.
You need to go now though.*

... Are you serious?

*As serious as the cancer you're going to get in two
years.*

*Oh my God! Stop saying that!
That's not ever going to be funny!*

*Get going, Kid.
I'm proud of you.
Until tomorrow?*

*Until tomorrow...
I'll never forget you.*

I kind of hope you do.
Because you're going to turn out way better than
me.

You really think so?
I'll be praying for that to be true.

That's the right thing to do.
Peace out, Boy Scout.

What? Eww. No.

Freckles' voice came into my thoughts, its tone curious. "How did you piece that pattern together, Adam?"

I paused for a moment, thinking about how to word my response. "You kept telling me to 'become the person I needed as a child.' After seeing how Sixteen's timeline was shifting and you – and technically, Erika – kept mentioning that everything happens for a reason..." My words trailed off. I gave up on my explanation to avoid rambling. "You know what... it's easier to say that I had an idea, and my faith told me I was right."

Freckles hesitated before responding. "Let's hope your faith is correct."

I nodded, "Me too. I know we made good progress, but this mission isn't completely over yet."

Freckles asked, "What makes you so sure of this?"

I sighed, feeling the weight of what was left unspoken. "Honestly, I don't know... but there's a conversation I really want to have with you. It's about Bio-Dad."

"Bio-Dad?" Freckles echoed, the term unfamiliar.

"Yeah," I explained, a small smile tugging at my lips. "'I say 'Bio-Dad' because 'tunnel I passed through at conception' is too many characters."

Freckles laughed, conceding to any objections. "That's a fair name."

I took a deep breath, feeling the seriousness of the question I was about to ask. "Freckles... am I wrong for not wanting to forgive him for what he put me through?"

The silence that followed was heavy, but I knew Freckles would have something meaningful to say.

Freckles' voice softened, carrying a gentle warmth. "Adam, I think, deep down, you've already forgiven him. You just haven't realized it yet."

I tilted my head in confusion. "What do you mean?"

Freckles paused for a moment, then asked softly, "Adam, what do you believe forgiveness truly is?"

I thought for a moment before answering. "In his case, probably letting go of the things he did and not letting his actions control me anymore."

"Indeed, you are on the right track," Freckles replied, the voice steady and contemplative. "Forgiveness is a gift you're supposed to give to yourself. It releases the hold that someone's actions have over you. In your own way, Adam, you have already forgiven your father. In truth, you have forgiven both of your parents."

I blinked, doubting Freckles' words. "How could that be true?"

Freckles continued, "Forgiveness manifests differently for everyone. In your case, you've forgiven them by choosing to cut ties. You may never understand their reasons, and that's okay. What matters is that you've made sure they cannot harm you again. By keeping them out of your life, you've let go of the hurt they caused."

I mulled over their words, but something still didn't sit right. "Would you mind explaining it like Erika?"

There was a brief pause, and then Freckles, surprisingly, mimicked Erika's voice with not-so-impressive accuracy. "Honey," Freckles began, emulating her warmth and straightforwardness, "forgiveness ain't about saying what they did was okay. It's about making peace with the fact that you'll never get what you need from them and choosing to move on. You did that by walking away. You took control of your life and said, 'No more.' That's your way of saying you've let go – by making sure they can't hurt you again."

I burst into laughter, the sound bouncing around the room. "Wow! Erika doesn't sound like that AT ALL!" I leaned forward, clutching my stomach as I laughed. "You've got her sounding like Rogue from X-Men!"

Freckles laughed along with me, the sound resonating in my mind. "It seems I have more to learn about imitating mortal voices," Freckles admitted, still chuckling. Then, with a more serious tone, Freckles continued, "I am certain that you are aware of the struggles your parents faced in their own lives. I believe the saying is, 'those who have been wounded, wound others in turn.'"

I raised an eyebrow, piecing together Freckles' words. "Were you trying to say that hurt people, hurt people?"

Freckles began to speak, but the words came out garbled, like a radio station not quite tuned in. Static filled my ears, growing louder and more disorienting. I tried to focus, but my vision blurred, and a wave of nausea hit me hard.

"Freckles? What's happening?" I shouted, panic rising as I dropped to my knees, clutching my stomach. The world around me twisted and distorted, a sharp, stabbing pain exploding behind my eyes – the first real pain I'd felt since entering Solitude.

The agony was so intense that I couldn't hold on any longer. I collapsed to the floor, the cold surface pressing against my cheek. Just before everything went black, I heard a voice – soothing yet commanding, a tone that resonated deep within me. "It is time to come home, my son."

Chapter 11

Jessica sat beside Adam's hospital bed, her hand clutching his as if by holding on tight enough, she could somehow pull him back to life. The rhythmic beeping of the machines echoed like a ticking clock, a constant reminder of the lack of time remaining. Dr. Reyes stood nearby, his expression etched with the kind of sorrow that comes from delivering too many hard truths.

"Mrs. Grey," Dr. Reyes began softly, his voice a gentle tremor in the air, "there have been no signs of improvement. We've tried everything we can. I'm afraid… we have to consider the next step."

Jessica's heart seized in her chest, a raw, visceral pain that nearly brought her to her knees. The weight of the decision bore down on her, relentlessly suffocating her. She looked at Adam, his face peaceful yet so distant, as if he were already slipping away, leaving her behind. Tears welled up, blurring her vision, but she couldn't take her eyes away from him.

"I... I'm not ready for this," she whispered, her voice trembling with a desperation that bordered on panic. "What should I do?"

Dr. Reyes sighed, his own grief revealed in his gaze. "I'm so sorry, Jessica, but I can't tell you what to do. This is a decision only you can make."

Jessica closed her eyes and the tears broke free, streaming down her face like an unstoppable flood. She knew what she had to do – she had known from the moment they walked into this room – but the finality of it, the thought of truly letting him go, was splitting her soul in half.

After what felt like an eternity, she took a shaky breath and nodded, her fragile resolve teetering on the edge of breaking. "Yes," she whispered, the word barely escaping her lips. "I… Please, do what you must to end his suffering."

Dr. Reyes nodded, his own sorrow evident. He left the room to give her a final moment with Adam. Jessica leaned in close, her forehead resting gently against his, as if trying to merge their worlds just one last time.

"Mi amor," she whispered, her voice cracking under the grief, "I love you so much. More than I could ever find the words to say. You've been my everything. Adam, I don't know how to do this… how to live without you. But I know—" Her breath tied, choking on the words she didn't want to say. "I know you wouldn't want to stay like this, trapped in pain. I promise… I promise I will try to be okay. I'll find a way, somehow."

She kissed his forehead, her tears falling onto his skin, her lips trembling as they pressed against the coldness she never imagined she would feel. "Goodbye, mi amor," she choked out, her heart shattering with every syllable. "I'll carry you with me… siempre. Always."

She lingered, her hand stroking his cheek, memorizing every line of his face, every detail, every moment they'd had together. Then, with a strength she didn't know she possessed, Jessica stood, her legs barely holding her up, and signaled to Dr. Reyes.

The nurses returned, their faces somber, and Jessica watched in numb horror as they began to turn off the machines that had kept Adam tethered to this world. The beeping slowed, each pause longer than the last – until it finally... stopped.

Jessica collapsed into the chair beside the bed, her body wracked with sobs that tore through her, raw and uncontrollable. She had said her final goodbye to the man she loved more than anything in the world, the man who had been her reason for everything. And now, in the quiet of that hospital room, she was exposed to her biggest fear: continuing life without him.

...

I drifted back into consciousness slowly. My head felt heavy, and my body was sluggish like I had been in a deep sleep for a while. I was immediately surprised at how crisp and clean the air was.

My heart started pounding as I stood up and took in the scenery around me. I was standing at the top of a mountain. The view stretched out endlessly: snowcapped peaks, the open sky. All of it was breathtaking. The sun was low on the horizon, casting this warm, golden glow over everything. It almost made the snow look like it was sparkling. The sky was a perfect blue with only a few clouds in sight, and the only sound was the wind whispering through the trees.

I took a deep breath, letting the cool air fill my lungs, and for a moment, I just stood there, completely awestruck by the beauty of it all. There was something familiar about this place though. I couldn't quite put my finger on it, but I felt like I had been here before. Maybe another time or perhaps in another life.

Still awestruck by the view I was witnessing, I couldn't help but feel like I wasn't alone here. "Freckles?" I called out, my voice barely above a whisper. But there was nothing – just silence.

The familiarity of this place kept gnawing at me. I know for certain that I've been here, but I was struggling to remember at the moment. I closed my eyes, trying to focus when suddenly, a voice spoke in my mind. It was clear and gentle but held a commanding presence that could not be ignored.

"This is where you and Jessica fell in love."

The words hit me like a shockwave. I immediately looked around, my heart beating out of my chest while I searched for the source of the voice. "Who's there?" I asked, my voice trembling.

The voice came again, but this time it felt warmer, wrapping around me with a comforting sense of familiarity... like a soothing hand cradling my soul. "Look to the skies, my son. I am the father. The creator of the universe."

My brain was screaming that none of this was making any sense. But as my eyes adjusted to the brightness of the beautiful blue sky, I noticed the clouds above starting to shift, as if they were forming patterns. Something about the way they moved seemed familiar, and as the shapes came together, my eyes widened in pure disbelief.

The clouds had formed a face: one that I immediately recognized. Ryan Reynolds.

My jaw dropped. My shock resembled something close to horror. "Why... why is the face of God, Ryan Reynolds?"

I stared up at it, completely blindsided. My mind flashed back to that time Freckles joked about angels not being able to resist Ryan Reynolds' charm. But this? Is God himself taking on Ryan Reynolds' face? I refuse to believe that any of this is real.

Before I could fully wrap my head around the absurdity of it, the cloud-face moved. It turned, looking directly at me, having Ryan Reynold's same mischievous smirk. Then, I heard the voice of Ryan Reynolds echoing throughout the mountains, confident and cheeky. "Are you just as surprised as I am!?"

I barely had time to register what was happening before the cloud face started moving toward me. It was slow at first, but then got faster and was eventually charging. The sound of his voice jolted me back a step, but the sight of a cloud-face Ryan Reynolds coming at me full speed sent me stumbling back, landing on my butt.

The face kept coming until it was right in front of me, and with one last grin, it passed straight through me, turning into a swirling ball of smoke that hovered for a second before vanishing into the air.

I scrambled to get back on my feet, breathing heavily and my heart still pounding out of my chest. The sky above was clear, blue, and calm again as if nothing had happened.

In a fit of fear and confusion, I yell, "What is this!? What just happened? Where am I!?"

As if in response to the frantic questioning, a familiar laughter filled the air. The sound was light and carefree, which could only mean it was Freckles. "You should have seen the look on your face," Freckles said, the laughter bubbling in its voice.

I was still reeling from everything that just happened when I heard Freckles' voice, and a wave of relief came over me. "Freckles? Please tell me this is really you!"

"Yes, it's me," Freckles replied, still chuckling like this was all one big joke. "Everything will be explained in a moment, but for now, I need you to listen carefully. You're going to turn around, and I don't want you to be startled by what you see. I promise you, everything is okay. I'm here with you."

"Turn around?" I repeated, not even trying to hide the uncertainty in my voice. "What are you even—"

But the words caught in my throat as I turned. There, floating just a few feet away, was this... glowing ball of energy. It didn't have a shape or anything. It was just a radiant light that pulsed and shimmered like it was alive.

I couldn't take my eyes off it. I had no clue what I was looking at, but somehow, I knew there was no reason to fear it.

The ball of energy, glowing with this warm, gentle light, began to speak in that unfamiliar voice I'd heard earlier. "Welcome home, my son. Please... be at ease."

As the words settled over me, my mind was suddenly hit with a rush of images – flashes of my life, vivid and fleeting, like a slideshow of my memories.

I saw Reina first, playing with a puppy she had begged to adopt. The joy on her face was contagious and it hit me hard. I couldn't help but smile.

Then the image shifted. Zack was standing with his wife and their three kids, celebrating Father's Day at this Mexican restaurant. His smile was huge, and his eyes were full of gratitude towards his wife for setting up this event. He had so much love in his heart as he cradled his youngest daughter in his arms.

Next, I saw Jack and myself being announced as the winners of a Super Smash Bros. tournament. We were laughing and celebrating like we'd just conquered the world. With our excitement bouncing off each other, we knew we were an unbeatable team.

Another flicker – Garrus, his face lit up with happiness, talking about his proposal to his new fiancée, Merci. His joy was so real and unfiltered, that I could feel the warmth of that moment all over again. That is the happiest I've ever seen him.

Then there was Erika, beautiful as ever on her wedding day while dancing with her new husband, Warren. The love between them was so strong and pure that it made my eyes water. I never cry at weddings, but this one was special.

I then saw myself with Sam at a local bar, playing air hockey. Sam was worried about moving in with his girlfriend, and I could see the concern on his face as we talked it out. It's weird... he's usually the one giving me advice, and that was the first time he ever opened up to me about an issue in his life that was so personal.

Another memory flashed – Mr. Molina and Ms. Van Etten, standing up and applauding at my college graduation. The pride in their eyes was clear, and I felt the satisfaction of that moment wash over me again. A solid reminder that I was trained by two of the strongest educators this world has ever seen.

Then came the memory of my coworkers and I, sharing a meal to celebrate Chrysanthia's college graduation. Laughter filled the air, and the bond we shared felt stronger than ever. It was the first time I was part of a team that made me feel like my contributions mattered.

I saw Kristine hugging me after submitting her college application, her eyes shining with hope for the future. That look of excitement was something I'd never forget. I'm confident that this little troll is going to change the world for the better.

Then I saw Ronald and Alisha helping me get dressed on my wedding day. The love and care they put into every word of encouragement, every small gesture... It was so clear that I could still feel it.

Then, the last image appeared: Jessica. Her smile was so bright and so full of love on our wedding day. We couldn't take our eyes off each other. At that moment, we were the only two people in the world and nobody loved each other more than we did. The image lingered, holding me there for what felt like forever, before it shattered like glass, fading into a million pieces.

I stood there, breathing hard, my mind racing with the flood of memories. But as Jessica's image slowly disappeared, this gentle warmth filled the air around me, and at that moment, I knew exactly what the ball of light in front of me was.

"You're..." I started, my voice trailing off as I stared at the ball of light with disbelief.

The light responded, its voice calm but carrying this gentle authority. "Indeed. The creator? The Lord? The Alpha and Omega? God? I have many names, but you, my son, may call me Ryan."

My heart sank, and my jaw practically hit the floor. "No... I'm not going to do that."

Freckles, still clearly amused, jumped into my thoughts. "He's teasing, Adam. This is the Lord in his purest form."

I nodded slowly, not sure if I fully believed what was happening, but went along with it anyway.

The light pulsed gently like it was laughing. Then that same voice – now kind and oddly familiar – spoke again. "I apologize for the deception, Adam. It was Freckles' idea, and I felt it would be enjoyable to go along with it."

I chuckled weakly, still trying to wrap my head around the whole thing. "I never pictured God as someone who would joke around."

The light brightened, almost like it was smiling. "My children are created in my image, so why wouldn't I be allowed to jest?"

I nodded again, this time with more understanding. "That... makes sense. God... Father," I said hesitantly, unsure of what name to call Him. "Those images I just saw. Can you please explain?"

Freckles' voice came through, softer now, all the humor gone. "Adam. Those images you just saw. Every mortal sees their life flash before their eyes before they…" It hesitated, letting the words linger in the air.

I swallowed hard, the meaning sinking in.

I looked down at the ground, afraid to confirm the realization. "Die…" I said, my voice barely a whisper.

Freckles let out a heavy sigh, letting me know I was correct.

God's voice cut through the silence, filled with compassion. "Death is part of life, my son."

I nodded slowly, my eyes lifting back to the glowing ball of light. "I… I know. But please tell me. Does this mean we failed? Is Sixteen going to be okay?"

The light seemed to brighten, and God's voice answered, filled with warmth. "My child… not only did you complete your mission, but you have exceeded my expectations."

I stood there staring at the glowing presence before me. Relief washed over me – I didn't fail. We didn't fail – but that left me with the question. If we succeeded, why am I now dead? What did this 'second chance' really mean?

305

Freckles broke the silence. "Adam. Please know that the Lord always keeps his promises."

God's presence pulsed gently as if nodding. "Indeed. You will receive your second chance, but it will come in the form of a task I will assign to you."

I let out a long sigh, feeling both humbled and curious. There was a question burning in the back of my mind, one I wasn't sure I should ask – but I couldn't hold it in. "But God… Father, if I exceeded your expectations, wouldn't that mean that you don't know every single thing that will happen?"

The weight of my own words hit me just as Freckles burst out, its voice laced with panic. "ADAM! Did you just imply that the Lord isn't perfect!? Are you trying to get us both smitten!?"

But the light didn't flicker. God's voice remained steady, almost amused. "At ease, Angel. My child… you were made in my image. Do you make mistakes?"

I nodded slowly, the realization dawning on me. "Yes… all the time."

"Then what makes you think I wouldn't make any mistakes?" God's question was simple but carried the weight of all I ever knew. "I will always do what is best for you, but it doesn't mean my calculations are always correct. Even I end up surprising myself sometimes, my child."

I spoke again, my voice quieter, more contemplative. "That's a relief, Father. But most people on Earth see you as the epitome of perfection. To learn this... it is sobering."

The light flickered, almost as if God was reflecting on my words. "That is the interpretation you mortals made," He replied, his tone patient and kind. "You see, I created humans to experience love. Love isn't about perfection: it's about growth, understanding, forgiveness, and most importantly, choice. I am a being of love, and in creating you, I gave you the ability to choose love and experience it in all its forms. I encourage all of my children to love one another despite flaws and mistakes."

As those words sank in, a warmth spread through me. It was profound but made so much sense. "I did experience love... so many of life's greatest joys," I said, emotion creeping into my voice. "But the greatest joy of all... was Jessica. Will I see her again?"

The ball of light brightened, wrapping me in a cocoon of warmth and comfort. "Yes, my child. As long as you have faith, you will see her again."

Freckles interjected. But this time, its voice seemed to resonate from the air around me rather than in my head. "My Lord," Freckles began, with respect but urgency in his tone, "From my time with Adam, I know he'll keep obsessing over Jessica until he sees her. I believe it would be best to reveal your plan to keep him occupied until that time comes."

God's light shimmered as if agreeing. "Thank you, Angel," God said, calm and measured. Then, the light focused on me, and I felt a mix of anticipation and nervousness building in my chest. "Adam, I have a task for you. I want you to become Sixteen's guardian angel."

My eyes widened. Of all the things I could've expected, this was not one of them. My mind raced, and I struggled to find the right words, feeling the impact of such responsibility. "I... I don't know what to say... This was not on my bingo card, Father."

Freckles cut through my hesitation with a gentle reminder. "Adam, remember, a request from the Lord is like a request from your parents – it's only shaped like you have a choice."

I couldn't help but smile as a soft chuckle escaped me. I nodded slowly, acceptance settling over me like a blanket of snow. "Okay," I said, my voice steadier now. "I accept. But... how will this work?"

The light brightened again, the warmth surrounding me as God spoke. "Continue to trust and believe, Adam. You will find your way."

I tilted my head, looking at the ball of light, unsure what it meant. "Father. With all due respect, I don't know what that—"

I was interrupted by a sudden flash of blinding light that forced me to shield my eyes. It was so intense that I could feel it enveloping me. It was as if I was floating in a sea of pure and unfiltered love. In that moment, I felt weightless and completely disconnected from the world, and yet more connected than I'd ever been.

When the light finally dimmed, I opened my eyes to find myself standing in a familiar yet transformed place. The mountain was still there, but everything felt... different. The air was lighter, the colors more vivid. Everything around me seemed to pulse with life. And then, in the distance, I saw someone standing on the cliff's edge, staring out at the world below.

As I got closer, I realized that it was Sixteen, or at least an image of him. The image was standing there, completely lost in thought, and unaware of my presence. Immediately, I felt a strong protective instinct that I'd never felt before.

Freckles' voice echoed softly in my mind. "This is it, Adam. It is time to guide, protect, and continue to help him find the happiness and peace you have found for yourself. This is your second chance. You are now a guardian angel."

I took a deep breath and nodded, feeling the presence of Freckles and God with me. But as the moment settled, a question popped into my head. "Freckles... This is probably not the right time to ask, but... does this mean you can tell me your name without nearly killing me?" I asked while trying to contain my laughter and happiness.

Freckles' voice came through with a playful warmth. "Ah, Adam. You won't die, but... Let's just say, for your safety – and the safety of Sixteen – it's better to stick with 'Freckles.' Besides, you wouldn't be able to pronounce it anyway."

I thought this journey was over. It turns out that this was only the beginning. Except this time, I knew exactly where I was meant to be. Standing at the top of the world while supervising the boy I used to be, in hopes of slowly watching him evolve into the man that I have become. If this is what I have to do until I can see Jessica again, then I'm happy that it is with someone I'm proud of.

In that moment, I had felt something I hadn't felt in what seemed like forever.

A sense of solitude.

Epilogue

This is my story, and I'm sorry it took so long to tell. But I bet you're wondering what happened in Sixteen's timeline after he went to Jack's parents' house. Hopefully, I can deliver the happy ending you're looking for.

When Sixteen arrived at Jack's house with marks on his face, Ronald was pissed. He was so angry that he wanted to go and straighten out Remy himself, but Alisha had other plans: ones that wouldn't allow Remy the opportunity to press charges. Simply put, Alisha's plan involved a hidden camera.

The next day, when Remy tried to… "make sure Sixteen stayed quiet," the camera recorded everything that Alisha needed to ensure that monster would never hurt Sixteen again. There was a bit of a bonus too. See, the microphones picked up Sandra passively enabling Remy to do whatever he wanted. The result was her losing custody of Sixteen and Reina.

You might be thinking, "What happened with Zack?" Zack is two years older than me, so legally, he doesn't have to do anything he doesn't want to. He also just started a new job as a data analyst and could easily afford his own place. Being the protector of a big brother he is, he took Reina and raised her with his girlfriend.

As for Sixteen, Ronald and Alisha took him in. And because Jack's parents are absolute angels on Earth, they offered to adopt him legally.

Sixteen declined because he still had Zack and Reina as his family, with whom he stayed in contact daily. But this never stopped Sixteen from referring to Ronald and Alisha as his father and mother.

Two years later, Sixteen ended up getting cancer. We knew this would be an absolute moment, but do you know what wasn't? Him battling it alone! There were a few days he had to drive himself to and from treatment, but whenever he returned home, he was always greeted by Jack's family, a hot plate of food, and the love he always deserved.

And that brings us to the moment I'm sure you're curious about – the car accident. Well, the car accident never happened… mainly because I made sure the car didn't start.

I know, I know. It brings up an even bigger question. "But Adam, I thought you're forbidden from messing with free will?" It's true. God has made it abundantly clear that I am not allowed to mess with anyone's free will. But there is a huge exception to the rule. It turns out that if our mortal is making a decision that we know they don't want, then WE'RE ALLOWED TO INTERVENE, Freckles!"

The words hung in the air as I finished recounting the story, and the scene around me seemed to shift. Then, I turned around to see Jessica standing there, tears brimming in her eyes.

"I've been waiting so many years to see you again," she whispered, her voice trembling with emotion and tears streaming down her face as she continued. "And the first thing you do is talk nonstop for hours?" She laughed through her joyful tears. "Mi amor..." She hugged me tightly, holding me as if she'd never let go.

I wrapped my arms around her, pulling her even closer. "I'm sorry. But there was a lot to say..." I whispered, kissing her cheek before drawing her back into the embrace, even tighter this time.

Jessica's tears flowed freely as she looked up at me, her voice barely a whisper. "Not a single day has passed that I haven't thought of you."

"I know..." I replied, my voice full of love. "Even in the heavens, your love was so strong that I could feel it here."

Jessica gazed deeply into my eyes and smiled. "I can't believe that you... of all people, you're... the fifth person I'm supposed to meet here."

I chuckled, nodding gently. "Of course, hon. And as you guessed, there is a lesson I'm supposed to teach you."

Tears streaked down Jessica's face as she held onto me, her voice shaking. "Can you please teach me without letting go of me?"

I gently placed my hands on the back of her head, comforting her as I whispered, "Jess... I was supposed to be your third person. I asked God to make me the fifth because, sweetheart, I have no intention of ever letting you go."

Jessica remained silent, holding on to me as if her life depended on it.

"Here we go," I began, my voice steady, "The lesson is... how much I love you. I thought of you every single day inside of Solitude. I was unsure if I would ever see you again, which scared me. Not the thought of death, not the thought of going to 'other place.' No... To me, Hell is having to exist without you."

Jessica nodded slowly, her voice filled with love. "I love you too, mi amor. I've never stopped loving you, Adam. I prayed every day that I would see you again and..." her voice cracked as she choked on her tears. "I can't believe it!"

I held her even closer, feeling the warmth of her love surrounding me. "Please know that I'll never stop loving you, Jessica. Not even in this new life."

Jessica pulled back slightly, looking into my eyes with a soft smile. "Adam," she asks softly, her voice a mix of curiosity and love, "could you hear me? While you were in that coma... were you able to hear my voice?"

I felt so guilty. I wanted to tell her that I could, but Jessica is the one person I cannot lie to. Especially here in the heavens. "No," I replied gently. "The only voice I heard in Solitude was my angel's." I paused for a moment, raising an eyebrow. "Why do you ask?"

She took a breath, her gaze never leaving mine. "Because... I was pregnant, Adam. Seven months after you... left us," her tears started to fall freely. "I gave birth to a beautiful baby girl."

Her words hit me like a tidal wave, crashing over me in an overwhelming rush of joy, disbelief, and sorrow all at once. The news rendered me speechless. A daughter. My... daughter.

"Jess, I..." I was unsure of what to say. This is the first time I've been overwhelmed by so much joy. "Are you telling me that I'm a father?" I asked her, already knowing she was telling me the truth. "Oh my God... Baby, I'm so happy right now!" I pulled Jessica closer to me as tears of joy started to form in my eyes.

Freckles' voice slipped into my mind, among the flood of emotions. "I wanted to tell you this years ago, Adam," Freckles admitted, "but I knew it would mean more coming from Jessica. Oh, and please don't worry about your child," Freckles continued confidently as if sensing the emotions coursing through me. "Your daughter is almost exactly like you, Adam."

I couldn't help but smile from ear to ear, as I held Jessica even closer to me. Admittedly, I felt a bittersweet jealousy towards Freckles, that it knew her in a way that I didn't. I spoke with Freckles through my inner monologue, "I'm so glad you got to see her. If she came from Jess, I'm certain she is amazing. I just wish I could have seen her."

Freckles paused before replying, its voice more sincere than I've ever heard it. "It's not just that I've seen her, Adam. God felt that your second chance should come with the benefit of knowing an experienced guardian angel would be watching over her."

Both of my eyes widened as I pieced together Freckles' words. Within my inner monologue, I ask, "Are you saying what I think you're saying?"

Freckles responded with a spark of joy in their voice, excited to answer my question. "Yes, Adam. I'm Stella's guardian angel."

I felt a profound sense of peace upon hearing Freckles' words. My daughter... our daughter... is being protected and guided by the very being who has watched over me the entire time. As I continued to gaze into Jessica's eyes, I knew there was a deep understanding between us; a silent acknowledgment that everything is exactly the way it should be. "Freckles... Thank you. From the bottom of my heart, thank you. For teaching and protecting me. For watching over my daughter. For reuniting me with my love. I'm happy to wait to see my little girl if it means she gets to live a long life full of love."